# THE ROCK AND THE KANGAROOS

## BY
## JIM O. ROGERS

**ZONE PRESS**
Denton, Texas

# THE ROCK AND THE KANGAROOS

SECOND EDITION

All Rights Reserved © 2004 by Jim O. Rogers
Zone Press
an imprint of Rogers Publishing and Consulting, Inc.

For information address:
2272 Hollyhill
Denton, Texas 76205

Author's Contact Information:
jim@zonepress.com

Any resemblance to actual people and events is purely coincidental.
This is a work of fiction.

Printed in the United States of America
ISBN:0-9727488-6-5

# Dedication

This book is dedicated to the Teachers and Coaches who make a difference by **"Giving it Back."**

# Foreword

I grew up in the fifties in a small town in Oklahoma, totally consumed with playing sports, primarily basketball. I ultimately played four years of college basketball in Sherman, Texas at Austin College. I was fortunate enough to be involved with remarkable people and many great stories related to high school and small college sports. As time went on, after graduation from college, I coached at the high school level, met other old "jocks" and heard their stories. In about 1985 I started "playing" with the idea of compiling all of these stories and their characters into one group of guys on one team, in a setting from 1959 through 1964. Nothing was written until 1992 when I wrote the first chapter of *The Rock and Kangaroos*.

On my fifty-second birthday, my daughter Paige gave me, John Irving's, *A Prayer for Owen Meany*. Paige wrote the following on the inside cover of the book:

*3/15/93*
*Happy 52nd*

*To my father,*

> *I hate to be obnoxious in giving away books and expecting people to read them. However, this book made me think of you with many visions of what your*

*generation experienced as children.*

*I don't care if you read this 20 years from now; just read it at some point. A story such as this one is great to share with some you love so dearly.*

*I love you,*

*Paige*

Paige was trying to encourage my efforts with *The Rock and the Kangaroos*, but after reading "Owen Meany," even though I loved it, I decided that I could not compare to John Irving's talent and I put "The Rock" aside.

As the years passed, I kept thinking about *The Rock and the Kangaroos* and began to rationalize that I had to tell this story regardless of "Owen Meany." In fact, John Irving's book and Paige's letter ultimately inspired my story.

In the fall of 2000, *The Rock and the Kangaroos* was started once more and I was consumed with it. As I finished a scene, I would read it to my wife Sonja and she would tell me "it's good" or "wonderful." At one point, I asked her if "the world" would like it? She told me, "forget the world and just write it for you." This was the best advice I ever had and is exactly what I did. I am not presumptuous enough to believe this work is comparable to John Irving's but I do believe *The Rock and the Kangaroos* is a heart felt coming of age story that "the world" will enjoy.

# Acknowledgement

The old cowboy song **"Goodbye Ole Paint"** (Author unknown) is a theme that runs through *The Rock and the Kangaroos*. For me, "Cheyenne" is home, "Montana" is a place of high adventure and the "hoolian" is the adventure.

# Prologue

*The Rock and The Kangaroos*

"Jim Green, you're the most hardheaded, stubborn man ever born," my wife said to me from the porch. "Those dandelions are growing back faster than you're pulling them; you're going to be exhausted and tonight's your big night. You're going to be too sick to go. Have you forgotten who the party's for?"

I stopped weeding and silently set off toward the house, *I know your right Pat but I'm going to enjoy my pout just a little longer.*

She followed and the scolding continued as I kicked off my boots on the patio and walked into the kitchen to eat my sugar-free, fat-free, taste-free lunch of tuna and lettuce.

"Why are you so angry with me? Why are you angry with Chris and Anna? Why are you angry with Dr. Ingram?" Pat asked, as she sat down to eat tuna and lettuce with me.

"I'm angry because I have to quit -- quit the only thing I'm good at and the only thing I know how to do."

"But why are you mad at us?" Pat questioned.

"Because you, Chris, Anna and Dr. Ingram told me I had to quit."

"Jim, you're diabetic and you're a high school basketball coach. And coaching high school sports is about as high pressure as it gets. The kids and I love you and Dr. Ingram has told us if you eat properly, take your medicine and find a less demanding occupation, we might be able to keep you around a few more years."

"I know." I finally admitted, "Anyone that would eat this damn tuna and lettuce with me when they could have a cheeseburger, has to be the best person in the world. You know I'm not mad at you. I'm just mad at God and taking it out on you."

She looked at me with a perturbed grin.

"I mean I just can't figure God out."

"You never cease to amaze me, Jim. Most of us have given up on trying to do that a long time ago."

"It's not that. It's just that I always sort of believed God puts each person on earth to accomplish at least one significant thing and I don't think I have done my significant thing and now he's 'putting me out to pasture'."

"What!" she said, dropping a forkful of tuna, "You have coached and taught for thirty-eight years and you've been honored as 'Coach of the Year' seven times; you've won five state championships; you were selected as the best teacher in Oklahoma and you don't think you've done anything significant?"

"Somehow I just don't think God gives a rip about how many basketball games I've won or lost. I'm talking about one single monumental event that makes an important difference in the world. Like the teacher that sparked Jonas Salk's interest in science ultimately was responsible for a cure for polio."

"So now you're feeling sorry for yourself because you didn't find the cure for polio?" She put her fork down and leaned forward with both hands on the table.

"That was just an example, Pat…and I'm not feeling sorry for myself."

"What about the time you gave that referee mouth to mouth in the middle of a game? That was pretty significant…you saved the man's life."

"I only did it because I was the only person there that knew CPR and besides I don't even think God likes refs."

"You're a crazy man, but because I love you, you are going to retire tonight and enjoy your party. Come to think of it, if you haven't done anything significant in God's eyes, maybe he will let you live until you do, which could be sixty more years." Pat laughed as she stood to clear the table.

"Good point." I said, as I also got up, smiled and kissed her on the cheek.

As I got out of the shower and looked forward to "cooling it" for a while, I heard the phone ring. In a moment Pat said," It's Aaron Savage for you." The instant she said "Aaron Savage," I was scared to death. I wasn't frightened because it was Aaron; he is one of my favorite people. However, when Pat said his name, it occurred to me that Aaron might be my significant contribution and if he was, God might decide my days are numbered.

Aaron was in one of my algebra classes about twelve years ago and was probably the brightest kid I had ever taught. He got into some serious drug, vandalism and behavior problems with school and the law. Just prior to him being shipped off to reform school, I convinced the authorities to let me try to turn him around.

The second semester of his freshman year, his class schedule was the same as mine: two classes of algebra, two classes of art and basketball. He was great in algebra, okay in art, but not even a consideration as a basketball player. I made him the manager. Whatever I did with this kid worked.

In fact, he is now Dr. Savage, calling to thank me for coming to his graduation from med school last weekend and to let me know he's coming to my party tonight.

"Do you know how proud I am of you?" I asked.

"Was there ever a doubt, Coach?" Aaron kidded.

He told me he was going to say a few words at my party tonight and continued as he kidded about telling some things I didn't want told during his remarks.

Before I told him good-bye, I said, "Aaron, I want you to know they've already discovered a cure for polio."

"What are you talking about, Coach?"

"It's a long story but remind me to tell you about it sometime."

My new career starts tonight with the retirement party at the gym. I am more apprehensive than during any of the state finals I coached. I don't like the fuss. I am looking forward with great anticipation to seeing many old friends and former students. Over one hundred guys I coached, plus my old coaching "buddies" from around the state and the faculty from Ferguson are going to be there.

The group I am most excited about seeing are the guys I played ball with at Baker College and our coach, Ralph Jenkins. He is seventy-eight years old and he called last night from Tulsa to tell me he would be at the party and for me to expect him to spend the night because he is "going to have a few beers and not driving home at midnight."

During my whole career I've carried in my heart the friends I made at Baker. Jerry "All-American" Miller, who played both football and basketball and was twice named All-American as a quarterback, will be there. Dudley "Suitcase" Prater, an attorney in Houston, Ken "Slugger" Chapman, the retired city manager of Douglas, Texas, Ronnie Peters, a retired Navy officer and Billy Joe Jackson, the greatest basketball player in the history of Baker College are all coming.

Billy Joe played ten years in the NBA and then spent the rest of his career coaching at the professional and college levels. He always tried to get me to take a college job, but I knew it wasn't my niche. I never aspired to be anything more than a high school teacher.

Even though everyone called me Coach Green, I considered myself a teacher. A good coach is a good teacher. I coached high school basketball for thirty-eight years, but I also taught two classes of algebra and two classes of art for thirty-eight years. I was a high school teacher first, but I loved coaching.

Pat had spent the last few weeks compiling information about my career. My art classes then put together a Power Point presentation they planned to show tonight. I hadn't seen the video and they initially intended for it to be a surprise, but none of them were very good at keeping a secret.

As I sat in my recliner, watching golf and thinking about the old friends I would see this evening, Pat came in with the list of accolades she had compiled for the video. "You'll have to wait until tonight to see the clips but I thought you'd like to read the list now," She said.

I had no idea how many games I had coached, or how many we had won or lost. However, I did know that she was there for everyone of them and she had kept scrapbooks of articles neatly clipped from the *Tulsa Tribune* and *Ferguson Journal*.

Our son, Jeff, now thirty-five years old, was one of the best players I have ever coached. He went on and played four years at Oklahoma City University and is now a high school coach in Cleveland, Oklahoma. One of the high points in our family's lives came in 1996 when Jeff and I coached against each other in the state finals. It was my seventh time in the championship game, Jeff's first. It was very emotional for both of us, but I can't imagine what Pat went through. Jeff and I were professional and we worked harder at trying to beat each other than any game we had ever been involved in.

When he won, it was the first time I didn't feel the pain of defeat as I had in my other two championship loses. Pat never admitted it, but after spending thirty-three years as Ferguson High School's number one supporter, when we played against her son,

I think she had to root for him.

I felt reluctant, to read the list of my accomplishments. "Jim, if you're concerned about everyone making such a big deal over you tonight, this is the reason," she said, as she handed me the list. "It's just one page, but it says a whole lot."

<u>*Coach Jim Green*</u><br>
*Lettered 3 years Basketball at Ferguson High School - 1957-1959*<br>
*All Conference 1958 and 1959*<br>
*Lettered 2 years Track at Ferguson High School – 1958-1959*<br>
*Conference Champion – High Jump - 1959*<br>
*Lettered 4 years Basketball at Baker College - 1960-1963*<br>
*MVP – 1961*<br>
*All National Tournament – 1962*<br>
*Lettered 1 year Track at Baker College – 1962*<br>
*District Champion - 1962*<br>
*38 basketball seasons as Ferguson High School Basketball Coach*<br>
*Won 812 games*<br>
*Lost 154 games*<br>
*29 Conference Championships*<br>
*11 Regional Championships*<br>
*5 State Championships – 1969 – 1975 – 1983 – 1988 - 1998*<br>
*Voted Oklahoma's High School Coach of the Year 7 times*<br>
*26 players made All State*<br>
*34 players received college basketball scholarships*<br>
*Oklahoma Education Association Teacher of the Year – 1992*

"What do you think?" Pat asked.

"If it hadn't been for 'your son' I would have won another state championship in '96." I jokingly said.

"And if hadn't been for my son, you wouldn't have won the '83 state championship," She quickly pointed out.

"I guess you're right, but you didn't put my 77 yard punt

in that football game in there."

"Knowing you, I'm not real sure how accurate some of those old jock stories are and I only put things I could document as your accomplishments."

Again, I started thinking about those days in the Fifties and Sixties at Baker College. The time Ronnie Peters cut his head on the rim and the time Rock told "Whiskey" to stick the basketball up his ass. The time Rock and I buried the kangaroo and the night we built a fire in the snowstorm. Then I started to cry and Pat did too. I knew why I was crying and she was just crying because I was.

"Why are we crying?" she asked.

"Just thinking about the good old days," I said.

The remainder of the afternoon, the glory days at Baker College lay heavy on my heart -- they were good times, growing up times, triumphant times and times tinged with sadness. The day The Rock and I left Ferguson in August 1959 for our freshman year at Baker College came to my mind as if it had happened yesterday. As far as I am concerned, all those days at Baker happened yesterday, because they are part of me like the marrow in my bone. Who I am today, started the moment we left Ferguson.

# Chapter One

*"Goodbye Ole Paint, I'm leaving Cheyenne,*
*I'm goin' to Montana to throw the hoolian."*

"That'll Be The Day" played on the radio as The Rock and I drove out of Ferguson, Oklahoma August 27, 1959. The day steamed like the radiator of our '52 Ford, which the boys down at the Texaco had laid five to one odds wouldn't make Seminole. The Rock and I had faith, there was no doubt in our minds we would be in Texas by mid-afternoon.

We were both nervous as we traveled south on Highway 99, but even though we had known each other since we were six and could read each other like a farmer could read the sky, we didn't want to talk about how scared we were. We were totally confident about the environment we were leaving and totally unsure about what we were entering.

There was nothing in a ten-mile radius of Ferguson, Oklahoma, The Rock and I couldn't handle. We knew every hill, valley and creek. We knew what was open, what was closed and who was there after midnight. We had keys to the high school, could get free cokes and hamburgers at The Cream and Dog and could pick the lock on the gym in the First Christian Church basement. We could shoot pool and snooker with the "big boys" at The Deluxe Bar and we had enough sense not to get caught going in the front door. We knew the location of every old oil lease, the best ones for parking with our girlfriends and the best ones for "drip" gasoline. In the oil field during the winter, natural gas on the wellhead would condense and make gasoline. If you got to the "drip" before the "pumper" ran it out on the ground, gasoline was free.

Through all of this we played on the same grade school and high school teams and now headed toward our ultimate dream -- joining the Baker College Kangaroos in Douglas, Texas, for four more years of glorious adventures and basketball.

As we departed the only world we had ever known, we carried a couple of beat up suitcases stuffed with all the clothes we owned. We also packed all our hopes and dreams, our innocence and the little measure of confidence we'd gained in Ferguson.

The Rock was 5' 8" tall, 155 pounds, wide shoulders, narrow hips, long arms, huge hands, blond curly hair, ice blue eyes, pigeon toes and the biggest heart of any man I'd ever met then or since. He had a presence about him that straddled the border between humility and arrogance and he was a master at knowing which way to lean. He never took himself too seriously and would not allow anyone else that luxury. Above all, he was a damn good basketball player.

The total population of our small world was no more than five thousand and we knew and liked most of them. We were born there and knew very little beyond it. As we rolled down 99 with that hot summer air blowing in our faces, we had no idea what the future held.

The Rock and I made fun of others who left home for the first time. They would leave, struggle for a couple of weeks and return for a visit, expecting everyone to be glad to see them. Most never realized they were gone. We were now exactly like them. Barely two hours into our drive we were already talking about the good old days and had a longing to turn around and go back. However, both of us had far too much pride to show our faces in Ferguson before Thanksgiving.

The Ford was the "eighth wonder of the world" and typical of our many adventures. It had been wrecked three or four times and by the time we bought it for $50, it didn't even have a body. The Rock and I got it running and eventually got a body from a junkyard for $15. With a few other parts, we merged it into a hell of a machine with a total of $87.57 invested. Other than numerous flats, its endearing tendency was to vapor lock. I never knew for sure what vapor lock meant but Rock figured out we could temporarily fix it by putting half of a grapefruit on the fuel pump.

Growing up in Ferguson, we had more adventures than Tom Sawyer and Huck Finn. It was The Rock's intellect, wit and creativity that made our friendship special. We pulled each other behind the Ford on water skis when snow packed the roads. We walked a pipeline like a tight rope across the Cimarron River during a spring flood. We built everything from tree houses to the '52 Ford.

When we were only ten, we found an old gasoline motor

from a Maytag washing machine. During the Thirties and Forties in Oklahoma, not every home had electricity so washing machines had gasoline rather than electric motors. By the early Fifties these old motors were mostly in junk piles. The Maytag motor was a fairly simple 2-cycle engine and with very little effort we got it running. After a few days, The Rock decided we needed to put the engine to use. "Do you want to build a go-cart?" he asked me.

"We can't build a go-cart," I said.

But with an old wagon, some pulleys, a fan belt and several days of hard work, we built a not-so great, but operational motor vehicle. The Rock became disinterested in the cart in a pretty short time and came up with the idea to use the Maytag engine to power an oil-drilling rig.

Believe it or not, he designed one and we built it. We used some old two by fours, a sharpened six-foot steel bar, some cable, pulleys from the go-cart and the Maytag motor. We could only drill about thirty feet deep and of course, we never struck oil. We did, however, drill little water wells all over town.


By the time we were driving down 99 to Baker College, those experiences were in the past and I had no idea what wonderful gifts The Rock had given me.

The Ford beat the odds at the Texaco, even though we had to put a fresh grapefruit on the fuel pump in Konawa. We stopped for lunch in Tishomingo at a barbecue joint in a river rock building on the corner of 99 and Highway 78. This place would become our regular stop in our travels from Ferguson to Texas. That first day at Smokey's we agreed that the chopped beef and curly-cue fries were the best meal we had ever eaten.

Continuing our drive, we reminisced about our childhood adventures, lied to each other about all the girls we had our way with and talked about the good times we had in the Church gym. We spent more time in that gym, growing up, than any other place. The Church, built on the side of a hill with the gym in the basement, had a ground entrance. I don't think it was built to be a gymnasium but at some time backboards and baskets were hung on each end and the floor was marked off. As far as I knew, no one ever played in the gym but The Rock and me.

Sometimes the Church organist would practice upstairs and we would pass, shoot and dribble to her music. We fantasized the state championship game -- one point behind, three seconds on the clock, I pass Rock the ball, he shoots from thirty feet, swish, the crowd goes crazy. Same scenario, he passes the ball to me, I shoot, swish, the crowd goes crazy. If we missed the shot we called foul and went through the drama of shooting free throws.

We practiced and played out virtually every possible situation in a basketball game and even some situations that were not possible. Once he bet me he could hit six out of ten free throws blindfolded. I called his bet, blindfolded him, put him on the free throw line and gave him the ball.

He shot and then asked, "Did I hit it, Big Jim?"

"No," I answered.

"You lying son of a bitch."

"You quit cussing in the Church."

"You stop lying in the Church."

I gave up and admitted he hit it. I gave him the ball. "Here shoot again."

He shot and said, "Did I hit it, Big Jim?"

"No."

"You lying son of a bitch."

"Quit cussing in the Church"

"You quit lying in the Church."

After that experience The Rock always referred to me as "the religious nut."

As we drove and after a few minutes of silence, The Rock said, "Big Jim, since you're a 'religious nut', is it all right to cuss and lie everywhere but the Church?"

"I suppose so," I replied.

He grinned and said, "You lying son of a bitch."


We both came from one-parent homes, back when one-parent homes weren't fashionable. My mother died when I was in the fifth grade. My dad, Tom Green, was a pumper for Getty Oil Company. It was a job that took relatively little effort on his part. It made a living for us and he was able to work alone. After Mom died, Dad worked, went to my ball games, grieved for Mom, drank more than he needed to and watched the "Gillett Friday Night Fights" on TV. He drank at home and never got mean or violent. Rock and I watched the fights with him and were amazed by his boxing knowledge. He paid Rock's Mom $10 a week to cook breakfast and lunch for me. He didn't talk much and we got along. Home life was okay, but it wasn't some kind of "Father Knows Best" world for the two of us.

Dad taught The Rock and me to play basketball and took us to all the high school games as little kids. He played ball for

Ferguson High School during the Thirties and loved to hear the "old timers" debate whether I was as good as my "old man."

Rock's dad was in the Navy and was killed at Pearl Harbor in 1941 when Rock was six months old. Even though he never saw his son, he left Rock with a hell of a name -- Rockford William Riley. Rock's mother, Ethel, was "a salt of the earth…best person you ever met" kind of woman. She took in ironing to feed the two of them and after my mom died she became a mother to me too.

Looking back on it, The Rock and I had real good excuses for a lot of self-pity, but we were too excited about life to know we were entitled to it. We had more friends than anyone in town, we loved the little kids and were good to the old people. I think most everyone liked us. I think they liked us because we had hope. In those small oil field towns in the Fifties that were trying to dry up and blow away, hope was hard to find. I don't know for sure what we were hoping for, but The Rock and I had a heavy enough dose of it to carry us far away from that dusty little town.

Our high school principal, Mr. Burnett, always gave Rock and me special attention. He worked with us in the spring of 1959 helping us make decisions on college. We wanted to go to college together and were offered basketball scholarships to several junior colleges and some small four-year state schools. Somehow none of them seemed quite right.

Just prior to our high school graduation, Mr. Burnett called us to his office and told us of an old friend, Coach Ralph Jenkins, who was the basketball coach at Baker College in Douglas, Texas. Neither of us had ever heard of Baker College, but there were a lot of places we had never heard of. Mr. Burnett told us it was a very good college. He thought we could get accepted and he would give Coach Jenkins a call if we wanted him to. The idea of going to Texas was exciting, so we asked Mr. Burnett to make the call.

At the time The Rock and I thought we were going to Baker College on basketball scholarships. That's what we told our friends and family. But Baker College had stopped giving athletic scholarships in the late Forties. It was a Presbyterian College and rated as one of the best small liberal arts colleges in the country. I wasn't real sure what liberal arts or even Presbyterian meant, but The Rock probably knew and I figured he would tell me later. Coach Jenkins's motivation for recruiting us centered on his team and he liked our basketball ability. However, we were accepted and financed for other reasons.

The coaches at Baker College, because they couldn't offer athletic scholarships, would seek out and recruit athletes with good high school grades who were poor. The grades would get the athletes accepted and the poverty level would determine grant and aid packages. The Rock and I, even though we were ignorant about the ways of the world, were not stupid and we had pretty good high school grades. In fact, Rock graduated number one in our high school class.

Our poverty level was Coach Jenkins's dream. I qualified for a full tuition grant and The Rock got an academic scholarship. We both were given campus jobs to pay for our room and board.

As we crossed the Red River Bridge into Texas, Rock broke into a chorus of "Goodbye Ole Paint." Rock always sang "Goodbye Ole Paint" when he was excited. I had been expecting his monotone rendition of the old classic for the past three hours.

We learned the song in grade school from Mrs. Akins, an itinerant music teacher that came to our classroom once a month.

It was the only song I ever heard Rock sing. After he sang the opening verse, I would make up a verse and then we would sing the chorus together. When we finished, as always he said, "Big Jim, what's a hoolian?"

As always, I replied, "I don't know."

We laughed, relaxed a little and rolled the final twenty miles to our destiny.

*"Goodbye Ole Paint, I'm leaving Cheyenne.*
*I'm going to Montana, to throw the Hoolian.*

*Tom Green had a bottle and he had a son.*
*The son went to college; he filled the bottle with rum.*

*Ethel Riley had some ironing and she had a son.*
*The son went to college; and the ironing was done.*

*Ride around little doggies, ride around them slow,*
*For the Fiery and Snuffy are raring to go."*

# Chapter Two

As we parked our dusty, beat up Ford in front of Austin Hall, we saw other guys in late model cars and trailers, with their parents helping them move into the dorm. We never thought of bringing our parents and we sure didn't need a trailer because everything the two of us owned fit in the trunk of the Ford.

In fact, we carried all of our belongings in when we went to get our room key. We could feel the stares of the other boys on our backs as we made our entrance. I don't know if they were amazed we got there in that old car, of if we were dressed strange for their tastes. We didn't think we were dressed all that bad. We wore white T-shirts, Levis, white socks and loafers. That was pretty much the way we had dressed all our lives.

"Pop" Hill greeted us. He was an old man with a wrinkled face, gray hair and a kind smile. He introduced himself and told us he was the Dorm Director. Then he said, "I'll bet you're the boys from Ferguson."

I smirked with pride thinking he had seen our pictures on the sports page. In reality he recognized us because we were the two biggest hayseeds on campus. He showed us to our room on the first floor next to the exit leading to the parking lot. Eventually our room became the stopping off place for our gang as they left or returned to the dorm.

It took only a day or two for us to determine there were only two groups of students on campus: a small group of poor athletes and a large group of affluent non-athletes.

Checking out our bleak little room that first day in Austin Hall, it didn't take us long to move in. With two twin beds against one wall, closets against another wall, two chests and built in desks next to the window, our options were limited. We stuffed our meager belongings into the closets, chests and desk and finished up quickly. A couple of guys from down the hall came by and introduced themselves. Larry Sikes and Wallace Threadgill were from Dallas and The Rock and I should have been impressed when they said they graduated from Highland Park High School.

When we told them we were from Ferguson, Oklahoma, Wallace's reaction was "Where in the hell is that?" As we eyed each other from head to toe, it was obvious either The Rock and me or Larry and Wallace didn't know how to dress. Our clothes were dictated partly by James Dean in *Rebel Without a Cause* but mostly by economics. 501 Levies cost $3.95 a pair, white T-shirts were six for $5 and we stole our socks from the Ferguson High School athletic department.

They wore button down madras shirts, starched khakis, argyle socks and black and brown saddle oxfords.

When college kids meet for the first time, after the question, "Where are you from?" the next is, "What does your dad do?" or as Larry asked, "What does your father do Jim?"

When I answered, "He's a pumper,"

Wallace immediately asked, "What the hell is a pumper?"

"It's a guy that takes care of oil wells."

"Oh," Wallace said, as if he was impressed.

"What about you, Rock?"

"My dad's dead."

Wallace shuffled his feet, trying to hide the fact that he must have felt like a dumb ass.

"It's okay," The Rock said. "What does your dad do?"

"My dad is an attorney and Larry's dad is a doctor." Wallace replied in an apologetic tone.

"Where did you guys get that car?"

"We built it from an old wreck," Rock said, "Do you guys have a car?"

"Yeah, we have cars but they were graduation presents. There's no way we could build a car."

"How did you guys ever get interested in Baker College?" Larry questioned.

"The basketball coach recruited us," I said.

"Do we have a basketball team?" he said.

"I hope to hell we do," I replied as everyone laughed.

When they complained about how bad the rooms were, we agreed with them, even though it was the best we ever had. We soon realized we were from two different worlds. The Rock and I were thinking, *are we here to become like them?* and they were probably thinking the same thing about us. I wondered if we would fit in but realized Larry and Wallace were just as scared as us. We decided they were okay guys, even though from that moment on we called them "silver spooners."

When we checked in, Pop gave us a list of functions we had to attend for orientation and enrollment. It was now 4:00 PM and the schedule was pretty full for the next three days, starting with supper in the cafeteria at five o'clock.

The only students eating in the cafeteria at that first meal were the freshmen and the football team. Most of the freshmen looked like Larry and Wallace and The Rock and I felt a little self-conscious about our T-shirts and Levis. Standing in line with our plates, we couldn't decide where to sit. A guy in front of Rock tried to strike up a conversation, "Wallace told us that you guys built that old car you're driving."

Rock told him we did. We were beginning to think the whole freshman class already knew who we were because of the Ford and this made us feel a little more self-conscious.

There were groups scattered all over the dining room. We were relieved when we spotted a guy we played ball against in high school named Jerry Miller. He sat at a table with some guys who appeared to be football players. Jerry and most of the football players kind of dressed like us and this relaxed us a little bit. As we approached him, Jerry recognized us as he stood and said, "What the hell are The Rock and Big Jim doing at Baker College?"

The Rock responded with, "The question is -- What the hell is Jerry Miller doing at Baker College?"

"I'm just here to play a little football, a little basketball and maybe even get a little education. You guys sit down." Jerry said as he introduced us to the other football players.

"How long have you been here?" I ask.

"Ten days and working my butt off. When did you all get here?"

"About three hours ago." Rock answered.

"Have you met anyone?"

"Just you football guys and two "silver sponners" named Larry and Wallace." I replied and started eating my cheeseburger.

" 'Silver spooners' -- I love it. There's a lot more of them than there are us. Are you guys going to play basketball?" Jerry asked?

"We're thinking about it." Rock laughed.

Jerry then leaned over to the football guys and said, "Rock and Big Jim have named the rich kids 'silver spooners'. That kind of says it all doesn't it? Wait till you all see these guys play basketball. They kicked our ass every time we played them in high school."

Hooking up with Jerry made us feel a little more excited about Baker College and we both knew we had made a great friend.

As we went through the orientation process, The Rock and I met other students. In developing friendships we discovered the "silver spooners" were intrigued by us and were hungry to hear about our "primitive cultures." They begged for stories about drip gasoline and The Deluxe Bar.

We later found a pool hall in downtown Douglas and taught a group of them to shoot snooker. Their poolroom deportment wasn't much better than our cafeteria manners and they nearly got all of our asses whipped.

I am sure we didn't realize it at the time and I'm not even sure the college realized it, but to accomplish the goals of a liberal arts education, some cultural diversity was necessary in the academic environment. Granted, the only diversity that existed was between poor whites and affluent whites and no other ethnic group was represented on campus. Looking back, I think we were as beneficial to the affluent as they were to us. In a sense we were critical to each other's education.

The "silver spooners" grew up in a protected environment and were fascinated that The Rock and I had experiences like building the old Ford. They didn't even know how to change a flat on an automobile. Our stories about camping out by ourselves on a creek bank when we were twelve, or going to some illegal roadhouse when we were sixteen were beyond their comprehension. Most of the adventures we had as kids were ideas that cost nothing but were far more creative than anything they had done. We had been allowed an uninhibited exploration of our environment growing up and they had experienced a protected and structured situation.

I think we were more aware of the fact they existed than they were aware of our existence. Their stories didn't go much beyond spiking the punch at the debutante ball or some mindless high school prank. I don't know how valuable our experiences were as they related to knowing and understanding the world, but they were a hell of a lot more interesting than the silver spooners' experiences.

We gained from them a sense of how to treat and respect each other. Even though some of them were snobs, most were not and all of them were polite and well mannered. The Rock and I didn't have a clue about which fork to use at dinner, or to put our napkin in our lap, or to stand when a lady came to the table. The most important experience the "silver spooners" gave us, however, was a feeling that it was okay to be curious and knowledgeable about the world we lived in.

Except for the teachers we had in the public schools in Ferguson, The Rock and I didn't really know anyone who had attended college. We had no idea how a college worked. As we scheduled our classes, we were thrilled that we only had to go to class about fifteen or twenty hours a week, as opposed to thirty hours a week in high school. The Rock understood, however, that in order to be successful you needed to spend thirty or forty hours a week studying outside of class. I'm not sure I ever understood that.

We had to spend a full hour, one on one, with our advisor during orientation in what was called our "advisors conference." My advisor was Dr. Robert Williams, who was head of the economics department. I never talked to anyone in my life that was more intimidating.

I assumed the primary purpose of college was to train students to make a living. Dr. Williams was quick to let me know that this may be the primary purpose of some colleges and universities, but it was not the primary purpose of Baker College.

He said, "The Baker College goals don't focus on making a living, but rather on how to live. This is an environment of total immersion in arts, sciences and humanities with no intentions of training single dimension individuals. If you graduate from Baker College, you will be well rounded and well educated, with the capacity to analyze the world and humanity in a perceptive and non-dogmatic manner. This will happen despite efforts on your part to prevent it."

Even though the college was affiliated with the Presbyterian Church, required chapel attendance and required religion courses, Dr. Williams also told me, "There is no indoctrination related to the Presbyterian faith. Questions related to all religious dogmas are encouraged and each individual is expected to find for himself meaning as it pertains to God, time, space and the universe."

We didn't have to declare a college major during our "advisor conference" but were encouraged to indicate our areas of academic interest. I chose art and business using the rationale that business administration was the only degree offered that didn't require a foreign language and I could already draw pretty well, so art should be easy. Dr. Williams agreed with my choices but I didn't share my rationale with him. I don't think he realized how far over my head he was, but before the conference was over, I was at least smart enough to keep my mouth shut. It would be several years before anything he said made any sense to me.

The Rock knew all of his life he wanted to be a science teacher and basketball coach, so he began a course of study in physical education and biology. I told him he was crazy because Baker College was the best pre-med school in the state and all of those "pre-medders" would be majoring in biology. The Rock, however, wasn't the kind of guy to be intimidated by a few "pre-medders."

As we enrolled for our classes, we were also assigned our campus jobs. I was the janitor for the music building and Rock was assigned to the campus maintenance crew. The music building was an old Army barracks that had been moved on campus and had open flame gas heaters. I had to clean the building and light the stoves about 6:30 each morning. They never complained about the job I did cleaning, but if it was cold and I didn't light the fires, those music guys were on my ass. Rock worked in the afternoons doing general maintenance, mostly mowing grass. It was through Rock's job that our college careers almost ended.

# Chapter Three

Katy the Kangaroo served as the Baker College mascot. Fraternity pledges were assigned to transport her to the football games and run up and down the track on the home side, either chasing or being chased by Katy. The responsibility to take care of Katy the rest of the time fell to Rock's maintenance crew.

One night, shortly after the beginning of school, some wild dogs attacked Katy in her pen and killed her. The maintenance crew had the grim task of disposing of Katy's body. The Rock found me in the music building the morning they discovered the dead kangaroo. After telling me details, he said, "It would be a hell of an idea to give Katy a formal burial and wake."

He found an apparently vacant field on the outskirts of Douglas and without permission from the landowner, designated it as Katy's final resting place.

"Big Jim since you're the religious nut, you can help make this a Christian burial. Go to that funeral home down town and get one of those wooden boxes coffins are shipped in and put Katy in it."

"Yeah," I said.. "And we'll drape that old red and gold

Baker College blanket you found over her casket. And put her in the Chapel."

"That might not be a good idea Big Jim. Maybe we should let her lay in state in the maintenance shop."

The idea took on a herd mentality with the other students. In a matter of hours, virtually every fraternity, sorority, club and team on campus wanted to be a part of our service. They wrote speeches, songs, poems and brought a lot of beer to the burial site Saturday night. About two hundred of us performed several irreverent rituals, like me editing the twenty-third Psalm to include, "Surly goodness and mercy shall follow us all the days of our lives and we shall dwell in the land of the kangaroos forever."

As we lowered the kangaroo into the ground everyone sang the school song. Then The Rock sang "Ole Paint." The other students then made more speeches, sang more songs, read more poems, drank more beer and tore up fences, crops and roads.

Realizing we were probably in trouble, The Rock and I left early and began to make plans on how we were going to get out of this mess. It was obvious the police were going to come and with two hundred students there, our names would probably be mentioned. The only thing we thought might save us was we weren't involved in the beer drinking.

It apparently didn't take very long to investigate Katy's Christian burial because by Monday morning The Rock and I were summoned to the College President's office. Most students go through four or five years of college and never get summoned to the President's office. The Rock and I managed to get there in six weeks. We received ample advice from our fellow students on how to handle our meeting with the president. Mostly, everyone was just trying to cover their asses. One guy did tell us they had a dog buried in the end zone at Texas A&M and the administration supported it.

President Thomas D. Odem was a Presbyterian minister who had been sent to Baker College by the Church some twenty years ago to close the school. After arriving, he decided Baker College was worth saving and he saved it. He had a reputation of superior intellect and integrity and ran the college in a fair but somewhat autocratic manner. Ordinarily he would have turned our case over to the Student Senate. However, over two thirds of the Student Senate had also been involved in Katy's burial. Also at issue was the police report that indicated the students had been drinking and the college had very strict policies against drinking. It was not the college's policies against drinking we feared the most; it was Coach Jenkins's policies. We made peace with him on Sunday prior to our meeting with Dr. Odem. We went by his house on Sunday afternoon and explained our dilemma, assuring him we were not involved in the beer drinking. He told us to just tell the truth and let Dr. Odem know we were sorry for any problem we caused.

Dr. Odem's office was pretty intimidating for two kids from Ferguson, Oklahoma. There was a big oak desk, walls lined with bookshelves and impressive looking books, two side chairs and the man sitting behind the desk, even though in reality he was an average size man, looked to be ten feet tall. He asked Rock and me to sit down. In a very stern manner, he said, "Tell me what happened east of town Saturday night."

"We were trying to have a Christian burial for Katy." This was not a good idea and he wasn't impressed with the damn dog at Texas A&M either.

"You gentlemen are already guilty of sacrilege and you need to start from the beginning and tell me everything that transpired, from the death of the kangaroo to the present."

I wasn't sure what sacrilege meant, but I knew it was not a good thing to be guilty of. Totally out of options, Rock and I, heeding Coaches Jenkins's advice, went through about thirty minutes of telling the truth.

Dr. Odem then said, "I am not happy; the police are not happy; and the farmer, whose property you destroyed, is certainly not happy. I realize other students were involved and I believe you were not involved in the drinking. However, I expect you to take your misguided creativity and leadership abilities and put them to work making peace with the farmer and paying for the damages he has suffered. And furthermore, if you don't successfully accomplish this, you will be expelled from Baker College. Lastly, I never want to see you in this office again."

Neither of us said anything as we walked out of the administration building. We both wondered how we could ever get through four years without getting in trouble again. On the way back to our room, Rock broke the silence, "Ole Thomas D's pretty much a hard ass.... huh."

We laughed for a moment and then focused on the business

of making the farmer happy.

The other students came to our rescue but not because of our creativity or leadership. It was because The Rock and I took the heat for something that involved a lot more folks than us. They put money together to buy materials and we all went out and repaired the farmer's damages. The farmer, after a short time, came out and helped us. I think he began to enjoy the whole thing. He even put a big rock on the spot where we buried the kangaroo with "HERE'S TO KATY" painted on it. I always thought it was kind of clever of the farmer to paint a toast rather than an epitaph on Katy's marker. At Rock's request, he also called Dr. Odem and assured him we had taken care of our obligations. I suppose Dr. Odem was satisfied because we didn't get expelled.

*Big Jim and The Rock, the inseparable two.*
*Nearly ended their college, 'ore a damn kangaroo.*

*Ride around little doggies, ride around them slow,*
*For the Fiery and Snuffy are raring to go.*

We did get into one other disciplinary problem the first semester, but it related to "cutting chapel." The Dean of the Chapel handled it and it never got to Dr. Odem. For the most part chapel was like a church service with prayers, congregational hymns and a sermon by the Dean or an invited guest. There were only 1000 students at Baker College but when "The Powers That Be" tried to account for their attendance in required chapel on Tuesday and Thursday of each week, it seemed to us it would be an administrative nightmare.

When we went in the chapel for the services, we were given a program with a tear off sign in slip on the back page. We would rip it off, put our name on it and turn it in as we were leaving the service. Sometimes you could get another student to sign in for you, or you could sign in and sneak out if there was a drop box instead of a real person collecting slips. Most everyone got caught cutting chapel at least once during their college careers. If you got caught, you were put on chapel probation, which meant if you got caught again, you could be expelled. I never knew of anyone who actually got kicked out of school for cutting chapel and The Rock and I assumed there was no way anyone was going to match those sign in slips with the total enrollment twice a week. So we didn't go to chapel for a couple of weeks. We were wrong in our assumptions and were placed on chapel probation. For the remainder of our careers, we were faithful chapel participants.

Coach Jenkins was probably having second thoughts about recruiting The Rock and me after the kangaroo deal, but I think, kind of like the farmer, he enjoyed it a little bit. However, he was not happy about the chapel probation and let us know of his displeasure, in a pretty convincing manner.

# Chapter Four

We started basketball practice the week after our meeting with Dr. Odem and for the first time since we left Ferguson, The Rock and I were in an environment we totally understood. Ten players came out for the freshmen team and about twenty upperclassmen came out for the varsity. Back then; in Division I ball, freshmen could not play on the varsity. We were in Division II, however, and freshmen could play on the varsity. Coach Jenkins used this as a selling point when he recruited us and The Rock and I were anticipating playing with the varsity. In spite of this, Coach Jenkins made it clear the first day of practice that all the freshmen would be staying together on the freshmen team and would play a separate schedule. We were a little disappointed in this news but didn't complain, even to each other.

As the workouts began, we discovered there were several good freshmen out and we were going to have a pretty good team.

We had been hanging out with Jerry Miller since orientation. He helped us clean up the kangaroo mess and had been a constant companion. He was a small forward type kid and we already knew he could play from our high school competition. He was nearly as "country" as The Rock and me and could shoot the eyes out of the basket, which compensated some for his totally inadequate foot speed. A quarterback for the Kangaroos, Jerry started the last three games that season and could thread a needle with the football. He was a great athlete, very confident and loved life as much as anyone I ever met.

Ken Chapman, was about 6' 2", a hell of an athlete and the quickest hands you've ever seen. His basketball skills weren't all that great because he was the victim of a high school coach who either didn't give a damn or was just plain dumb. This was typical of lots of kids that came from small Texas football schools. He grew up in Howe, Texas, which was only fifteen miles south of Douglas. Ken was a Presbyterian, knew a lot about Baker College and was smart. I've never seen a player as unselfish and team centered as Ken. His mom cooked for us every Sunday and the drive to Howe for her home cooking was the highlight of our week.

"Suitcase" Prater was a clumsy 6'8" kid from Houston and his given name was Dudley. We played our first game at Perin Air Force Base, which was in Douglas. In preparing to travel across town for the game, the coach asked if there were any questions. Prater responded, "Do we need to take a suitcase?"

From that day forward he was "Suitcase" Prater. He wasn't the greatest player in the world but if he were, at 6'8", he wouldn't be playing for Baker College. "Suitcase" was the kind of "out to lunch, good ole boy" everyone loved and as time went on would break all Baker College rebounding records.

Ronnie Peters was a 5'6" quick point guard from Abernathy, Texas, but like Ken he suffered from no one ever caring enough to get his skill level where it needed to be to play college basketball. He was a good back up at the point guard, but, for the most part, played only when the game was well in hand. In spite of this, he had a great attitude, was the team's best fan and ended up as the "butt" of most of our jokes and pranks.

Chris Wright was the only "silver spooner" on the team. He was good enough to play anywhere but was Presbyterian and his dad, prior to becoming a real estate giant in Dallas, had played for Baker College. It was Chris's legacy to be a Baker College Kangaroo and it didn't take us long to drag him down to our level, which was necessary for him to fulfill his destiny. Chris loved basketball and loved to play the game. I think he was envious of the stories we told and eager to get involved in some of our "hell of an ideas." He was one of the ringleaders when we buried the kangaroo.

The Rock was the most complete player on the team. He passed the ball -- left-handed, right handed, between his legs, behind his back, up the court, down the court, to the side and in the middle. He dribbled. Our delay game demanded we get the ball to Rock and stay out of his way while he dribbled the clock out. His defense was his strength; he was the best I ever saw. He could shoot, but because his role was to get the ball to the other players, he mostly made great passes. He led the team like Bart Starr led the Packers.

I could do two things on the basketball court. I could shoot and I could jump. I was the only guy on the team that could "slam dunk" the ball. Even though "Suitcase" was 6'8", he couldn't get six inches off the floor. Because Rock knew my every move and I knew his, The Rock got the ball to me more than any player ever deserved. If you get the ball a lot, shoot a lot and have any kind of luck at all, you will score a bunch of points. I wasn't necessarily the best player, but I was given ample opportunities to score. As it had been in high school, thanks to The Rock, I was the team's leading scorer.

The freshmen team had a schedule of eighteen games, but since most small colleges didn't have freshmen teams the schedule was pretty creative. During the Forties, Fifties and Sixties it was not unusual for large corporations and military bases to have pretty high-level basketball teams. In fact, there was a time in the early Fifties when Philips Petroleum probably had the best team in the world including all the major colleges and the NBA. They were located in Bartlesville, Oklahoma and had a following that included the entire state with crowds of eight to ten thousand as they played a schedule against major colleges and world teams. The Armed Forces had teams on most military bases in an effort to build moral and provide entertainment for the troops. Some of these teams played at a pretty high-level and had a large fan following, mostly from their respective bases and communities. Some of the military teams and the industrial teams played state and national tournaments and the best teams played at the international level in AAU ball.

Our freshman schedule included several of these teams plus a few other small college freshmen teams and junior college teams.

At one point we even played a high school team. A 4-A high school team in Dallas had won the state championship in 1959 and had all of their starters back for the 1960 season. The sports writers in Dallas reported they thought this high school team could compete with the small college teams. Of course, no small college team would play them and it would have been a violation of the high school rules if they had. Coach Jenkins did, however, agree to let the Baker College freshman team play a practice game behind closed doors against them. Coach knew how to shut those Dallas sports writers up. He invited them to the game with the understanding they would report nothing. At half time we had that super high school team down 53 to 17; they went home and we didn't even play the second half.

Our first game at Perin Air Force Base was an education for all of us. Most of those Air Force guys had played some high school and college ball. They were not bad players and were twenty-five to thirty years old. There's a hell of lot of physical difference between thirty-year-old guys that were in the Korean War and a bunch of eighteen-year-old kids just out of high school. The game was getting out of hand by the second half when I broke to our end as one of their guys put a shot up from about thirty feet. Suitcase got the rebound and hit me with a long pass on the breakaway. Just as I left the floor to go up for the lay in, this Air Force monster hit me from behind and we crashed into the wall at the end of the gym. He got up and called me "a damn snowbird" at about the time The Rock hit him from behind calling him "you dumb son-of bitch." There was some pushing and shoving from both teams, but, fortunately for us, Coach Jenkins convinced everyone, "this is not the best thing for college-military relations."

The Rock kind of pressed on, however, as he asked the big guy who hit me, "Do you guys have a rule against snow-birding down here in Texas?" Snow birding was simply when a player broke away alone for an uncontested basket.

The big guy wouldn't let it go, " We have a rule against smart assed college kids trying to show us up."

At that point the officials and Coach Jenkins got us all together and told us the next time anyone did something dumb, the game was over. I was kind of hurting from my crash into the wall, but wouldn't dare let on I was feeling any pain. I stayed in the game and thanks to good coaching and The Rock hitting six free throws down the stretch, we won the game and left in good sprits. We shook hands with the Air Force guys and they kidded us about getting tough enough to play real basketball.

# Chapter Five

By the time basketball season started, mid-semester grades were being posted. The Rock was taking biology, algebra, religion, English and German. I was taking Western Civilization, algebra, English, religion, which were all required courses, and art. The Rock had three A's and two B's at mid-semester and this was pretty much how his grades went all through college. I had three C's, one D and one B (my art decision was a good one) and even though they got slightly better, this was pretty much how my grades went through college. Rock's grades were very good and I was proud of him. With my 2.0 grade point average, however, I was on track with all my academic goals. These goals consisted of not losing my financial aid package and remaining eligible to play ball.

The Rock loved to read and studying for him was a pure pleasure. As for me, I never read anything that was not required and failed to read some things that were. I did attend most of my classes, took notes and tried to satisfy the professors. After all, I did have academic goals.

Nearly every night, after we went to bed, just prior to going to sleep, The Rock would say, "Big Jim, did you know that?" Then he'd proceed to tell some obscure fact he learned in his frequent trips to the library. I got through my freshman year without ever going to the library and he constantly harassed me about it. He knew I believed if there was something in the library I needed to know, he would find it and tell me.

The freshmen basketball season was going great. We were 5 and 0 at the Thanksgiving break, playing the likes of Perin Air Force Base, Cooke County Junior College, Murray Junior College and two small college freshmen teams. I was averaging over 20 points per game and Rock and I were having the time of our lives. Even though no one else cared, since a good crowd for a freshmen game would be fifteen or sixteen people, it was nice the cheerleaders always showed up.

We weren't much on the social scene at Baker College. I think the rich girls intimidated us and most of the girls were rich. We both had girl friends in high school. I had several and The Rock had a couple. Rock spent most of his time studying and never got too serious about the ladies. I fell in love with half the girls I went out with. Neither of us, however, even considered asking a girl out at Baker College. We used the excuse of not having any money, but our real reason was our fear of being turned down. Despite our apparent self-confidence, we didn't have the guts to ask a Baker College girl out. We did go to the SUB (Student Union Building) to listen to the jukebox and watch other people dance. It wasn't like we couldn't dance. We could dance better than most of the people out there. We were just afraid to ask anyone to dance with us.

There was a girl from Oklahoma City whom we both liked. Carol Wilson was as good looking as any girl we had ever seen, a cheerleader who could do flips and cart wheels and was as smart as Rock. She kind of flirted with us but had shown more interest in Rock than me. I kept trying to get him to ask her out, but he would shrug and say, "Big Jim, I don't have the time or money to get interested in some Oklahoma City cheerleader."

I started referring to Carol as "The Cheerleader" and as others picked up on it, like "Suitcase," her given name was essentially forgotten.

When we went home that first Thanksgiving, it would be the last Thanksgiving we would spend at home. A couple of days before we left for home, The Cheerleader asked Rock if it would be out of the way to take her to Oklahoma City. "No problem," Rock told her. "It's right on the way."

The truth was, it was about a hundred miles out of the way and by the time we went through Oklahoma City traffic, it extended our trip home by about two and a half hours. We enjoyed our trip, but I told The Rock it was a pretty good sacrifice for a girl he wasn't interested in.

We had kept our promise to ourselves of not coming home until Thanksgiving and we felt good about it. Rock's mother, Ethel, baked a turkey with all the trimmings and Dad and I shared dinner with them. I think all of us kind of felt like family when we sat around the table in Ethel's tiny kitchen. As she went to the stove and spooned up a bowl of gravy, she said, "Tom and I were talking the other day about how proud we are of you boys."

I was glad she included Dad in the compliment, but knew if he was proud, he probably didn't do any more than agree with her when they talked.

"Do they feed you good at Baker College?" Ethel continued.

"It's okay." I said, "but not as good as this."

"We're going to try to come to the game when you guys play in Tulsa in January," Dad said as he helped himself to more gravy.

"That's a varsity game," Rock said.

"And so far we haven't played in any varsity games," I said.

"You will," Ethel quickly added.

"Maybe you all could come to a freshmen game in Douglas," I offered as I began to eye the pumpkin pie on the counter.

"We're a little afraid to try that trip in my old pickup," Dad said.

"We will just have to make the varsity then," Rock chimed in. "You guys have to see us play this year."

*Rock is setting pretty lofty goals for us; but this is such a nice day, I'm not going to argue with him.*

Over the weekend we saw old friends and tried to top each other's stories of college life. After I embellished it some, however, no one could top our Christian burial of Katy story. We noticed our old friends were pretty much the same as they had been in high school. There wasn't anything wrong with this but The Rock and I were feeling our prospects were different than theirs. Most of them were either commuting to Oklahoma State or living in an apartment at one of the colleges close by and coming home every weekend. They were continuing to do the same things they did in high school with the same people and it was obvious to both of us that their awareness of the different priorities in life had not changed at all. In fact, none of them really had any new stories in our bullshit sessions.

We went to see Mr. Burnett to let him know we were doing all right and were making our grades and playing pretty good ball. Again he told us, "Not many kids from Ferguson ever get this kind of opportunity. You boys are fortunate to be going to such a good school." We really didn't understand the significance of what he was telling us, but after our encounters with our other classmates, I think we were beginning to see we were on a different path.

We worked out with the high school team on Saturday and enjoyed beating up on them like that bunch of Air Force guys beat up on us. By the time Sunday rolled around, we were ready to head back to Douglas.

On the way back we noticed an area on 99 about fifteen miles south of Ferguson where a farmer had cleared a bunch of land and had this row of huge brush piles along the highway. We talked about it and wondered why he hadn't burned them. We decided it was so dry last summer he was afraid of starting a fire he might not be able to put out.

In the three weeks between Thanksgiving and Christmas we won three more freshmen games and took our finals. We felt pretty good about our first semester of college and looked forward to the Christmas vacation.

The trip home for Christmas started out in a fairly routine manner. We left Douglas about 5:00 PM and at 6:30 we stopped in Tishomingo for some barbecue. That night I won sixty games on the pinball machine so we didn't leave Smokey's until 8:30 when they closed. We were doing fine until about fifty miles from home when the wind began whipping out of the east. The temperature dropped about twenty degrees and since the Ford didn't have a heater, we started shivering. About ten miles south of Stroud, big snowflakes hit our windshield and became steadily heavier. At Stroud, we stopped at an all night gas station, just twenty miles from home. We filled the Ford up because the gasoline was nineteen cents a gallon, which was a hell of a deal. We bought some candy bars and cokes and the man behind the counter said, "If you boys are going to Ferguson, you better get on the road because if this storm doesn't let up, I look for them to close 99 in a little while."

As we started on the final twenty miles of our journey, the snow became so thick we could only make fifteen miles per hour. Visibility was cut to a few feet through the blowing snow and our teeth were chattering and our fingers felt like icicles. We told Ethel and Dad we were coming home tomorrow, so if we became stranded, no one was going to miss us.

I was driving and Rock was thinking while going through

the glove box.

"What the hell are you looking for?" I asked.

"I'm not looking I found them," he said, "matches."

"What are we going to do, set the back seat on fire to try to keep warm?"

"We're not going to make it another three miles and it may be a week before anyone comes along here and finds us," he said. "Do you remember those brush piles that farmer had along the highway when we went back Thanksgiving?"

I told him I remembered.

"If they're still there, we should be passing them in a couple of minutes. They're on your side, so as soon as you see them, pull up as close as you can get to the first one."

As soon as I saw one of the brush piles, I pulled over into about thirty feet of the huge mound of snow-covered wood. "Do you mind telling me what the hell we're doing?"

"Here's the deal, Big Jim. We're going to be out here at least all night and if we don't do a little planning and a little work, we could freeze to death. Now the car gives us a wind break for your side and we're going to go out there and set that brush pile on fire."

"You're crazy as hell if you think we can set that brush pile on fire in this snow and in this wind with those matches."

"You just watch me." He then got a bunch of old rags from the back seat and tied them to the end of a coat hanger. While I cleared the snow off a spot on the brush pile, he stuffed the rags into the gas tank with the coat hanger until they were saturated and then draped them on the spot I had cleared.

"This is kind of like that Jack London story." He carefully struck one match close to the soaked rags and we had a hell of a fire.

We got back inside the Ford and I left my door open. It wasn't long until we could feel the warmth from our huge bonfire. We then got so hot we had to close the door. The fire melted all the snow around the car. When we were freezing to death, I regretted not having anything warmer than my Ferguson High School letter jacket. Now I was peeling it off.

I asked The Rock, as he shed his letter jacket, "What was that about Jack London?"

"You know, *To Build A Fire*, that short story we read in high school, where that guy was out in this snow storm, with only a few matches and was trying to build a fire," he said.

"I must have missed that day," I said, "What happened to the guy?"

Rock looked at me, smiled and said, "The son of a bitch froze to death."

We didn't sleep any, but we were warmer and even though the smoke from the fire was seeping through the cracks in the windows and burning our eyes, our attitude became less fatalistic. As we ate the candy bars we bought in Stroud and talked, we both realized we'd had a pretty close call and our conversation took on a pretty heavy tone.

"After all we went through to get to college, it would have been hell for us to freeze to death between Stroud and Ferguson when we were 18 years old." The Rock said.

"Yeah," I agreed, "Before we ever played in a varsity

game or dated any of those rich girls."

"Big Jim, don't you think there is a little more to life than basketball and dating rich girls? We've been given a 'hell of a ride' so far and to die without having a chance to give it back would be the worst thing that could happen."

"What do you mean we've been given a hell of a ride? Your dad died, my mom died and we've been dirt poor our whole lives."

The Rock then tried to make me understand what he was all about.

"You know, Big Jim, neither one of us have ever complained for one minute about our lot in life. There have never been two guys in this world who have been given more or enjoyed life as much as you and me. We have brains, talent and opportunities. We have an obligation to ourselves to take advantage of everything life gives us and then we have a duty to give it all back. I'm going to get every 'drop' of education I can from Baker College. I'm going to become an officer in the Navy. I'm going to be the best damn teacher and coach in the world and I'm going to spend my life 'giving it back'. What are you going to do?"

"I'm probably not going to study as much as you. I would like to give it back but I don't have a clue about how to do it. To tell the truth Rock, basketball and girls are about all I think about, but I'm still glad we didn't freeze to death."

We talked all night as we opened and shut the door, raising the temperature to hot as hell and lowering it to freezing our butts off. Our conversation concentrated on the future with Rock having a lot of answers and me having a lot of questions.

Rock thought the big fire might be a good enough signal for someone to come rescue us. But about 6:30 the next morning when we heard a road grader coming from the north, we knew it was the county clearing the road. When the grader got to us, the driver told us he had cleared the road all the way from Ferguson. He pulled the Ford back onto the highway with the grader and asked us how that brush pile caught on fire?

"I guess lightning hit it," Rock said, "and we were sure glad it did."

By the time we got to Ferguson, the sun was shining and it was a winter wonderland. We both found some part-time work over Christmas and made a little extra money. We worked out with the high school guys and when we got in the bullshit sessions with our old friends, we thought we would again top all stories with our snowstorm adventure. However, several of them got caught in the same snowstorm. At least they had their own versions.

# Chapter Six

Returning for the second semester, our classes remained the same and our grades for the semester were the same as they were at mid-semester. I made my 2.0, was eligible and kept my grant and aid. Basketball, however, took a different twist. Even though the freshmen team was winning, the varsity struggled. Seven seniors dominated the varsity and it seemed they were just going through the motions. They had really lost interest in playing.

On a Saturday morning after the second semester started, we found a note on our door. "Green and Riley...Suit up with the varsity tonight.... Coach Jenkins."

We immediately began to wonder what was going on. Is this someone pulling a smart-ass prank? Do we play in the freshmen game first? Would the other freshmen also suit up with the varsity? And should we ask them?

We decided to play it cool and not say a word to anyone. We just showed up to play the freshmen game and waited for Coach to make a move. When we got to the locker room and started to get undressed, Coach Jenkins came in and asked if we got his note. At this point we knew it wasn't a prank. We acknowledged the note and asked if we were to play in the freshmen game.

"Yes," he said, "and when it's over, come back to the locker room, drink a coke and put on fresh gear. Then come on the floor and just stand around during warm up." He then laughed and said, "I assume you will already be warmed up."

We were playing Harden University that Saturday night and the freshmen game was tough. We managed to win it by six, but neither The Rock nor I came off the floor the whole forty minutes. When we went to the dressing room after the game, Coach Jenkins held the varsity, which usually took the floor as soon as our game was over, and had both teams sit down.

Coach then pitched varsity uniforms to The Rock and me and said, "Riley and Green are going to continue to play on the freshmen team but we're going to see if they can help us some."

The freshmen guys were proud and immediately started encouraging us. The varsity guys, understandably, were apprehensive. Coach then said, "Let's go get 'em" and the varsity took the floor.

The Rock and I drank our cokes, put on our varsity suits, warm up jackets and pants. We picked up a game program that was on the bench. For the first time, we saw our names listed on the varsity rooster:

| | | | |
|---|---|---|---|
| 22 ROCKFORD RILEY | 5'8" | FROSH. GUARD | FERGUSON, OKLA. |
| 24 JIM GREEN | 6'3" | FROSH. FWD | FERGUSON, OKLA. |

We then went onto the floor and stood around. We watched the other varsity players warm up and when the horn sounded we took our place on the bench wondering if we would get to play. *If we play, it will be late in the second half and only if the game gets out of hand.*

The Harden team jumped out to an 8 to 2 lead in the first few minutes of the game. Coach Jenkins looked down the bench and shouted, "Green,"

I didn't move thinking maybe there was another guy on the team named Green.

"Green," he said again, "get down here and get 'em off."

I got the warm ups off and was kneeling in front of the coach in a matter of no more than two seconds.

"Get in at that strong forward and when we drag the ball across the middle... you get us a bucket."

The first time I went down the floor the drag came my way and I nailed a twenty-foot jumper on the first shot I ever took as a college player. When we came down the floor again, Coach called for the same play, but the senior point guard, Johnny Walker, didn't want a freshman to get out of hand and he went the other way. Coach called time out and the next time down the floor, The Rock was the point guard.

The Rock started "feeding" me and I hit everything I put up. With about five minutes to go in the game, we had them down by 12. I went to the boards and this 6' 10" center from Harden, we called Moose, came off with a rebound and caught me in the eye with his elbow. As I went to the floor, he said, "Welcome to college basketball Green."

He was called for a foul and as I was getting up I heard Rock say to Moose, "He's just a freshman."

"Yeah I know."

"But you knew his name...think about it, Moose," Rock

said, as he walked away.

The Rock and I had our greatest game ever. We won and the once apprehensive seniors, rallied behind us and were just as proud as the freshmen guys had been earlier. I have often thought this was the greatest day of my life.

Over half the student body came to the varsity home games and coupled with the townspeople and a few faculty members, we had a crowd of about 1000 on that January night in 1960, when we made our varsity début. After suffering through several tough loses, they were hungry for something to cheer about. As the game progressed, they became more and more enthusiastic and when we won, all of them came onto the floor slapping us on the back, shaking our hands and hugging us. This was about the closet thing to heaven I'd ever known.

When we got back to the dressing room, Rock said, "Big Jim...The Cheerleader asked me to come over to the dance at the SUB with her."

"That's great," I said, "You damn sure need to go."

"Yeah, I know," The Rock responded. "She asked you to come too ... She said she had someone she wanted you to meet."

"A girl?" I said.

"I hope to hell it's a girl," he quipped. "Get your damn pants on and let's go."

When we went back through the gym lobby, The Cheerleader was waiting and with her was Christine Blankenship. I knew Christine because she was about the sexist girl in Texas and every guy on campus would have given his right arm to go out with her. She was a sophomore and I thought she was engaged to some guy named John who was in med-school. At least that was the story. The Cheerleader introduced us and like a total idiot, I said "But I thought..."

Christine cut me off. "John and I broke up over Christmas."

"I'm real sorry, but that just tickles the shit out of me."

The Rock wanted to kill me but fortunately The Cheerleader and Christine found some humor in it and we all laughed as we headed for the dance.

The Cheerleader held Rock's hand as we walked from the gym to the SUB. It looked like they were about to ride off into the sunset. Christine and I walked behind them and she told me how much she enjoyed the game. I was pumped and even though, I had just finished two basketball games, I could have played two more. We weren't at the hand holding stage, however. *That damn Rock has been seeing The Cheerleader before tonight and bull shitting me about not being interested in her.*

"Pretty Woman" played on the jukebox as we walked in the SUB. A few people were dancing and several came over and said "good game" or "way to go, Big Jim." Christine said she was turned on by these compliments and by the black eye Moose had given me. With this uninhibited burst of honesty by Christine, another half pound of adrenaline pumped through my body.

This business of winning the game and getting the girl was exceeding all my expectations. We danced and laughed but never talked about anything of substance -- as if I knew anything of substance.

About eleven I noticed The Rock and The Cheerleader had disappeared. This meant he had taken the Ford and Christine and I were on foot. Back then the Baker College girls had a curfew at midnight so I walked Christine back to her dorm. After a somewhat passionate kiss good night and an agreement to see each other again, I went back to the room and waited for The Rock. I knew he would be there soon because The Cheerleader had to beat the curfew too.

I turned off the lights and was in bed pretending to be asleep when The Rock tried to sneak in about 12:15. He undressed quietly in the dark and slipped into bed, wanting to escape my interrogation about his love life. I waited a minute or two, then said, "What did Coach say when he put you in for Johnny?"

"I knew damn well you weren't asleep," The Rock said. "After you nailed that first jumper, Coach got up and motioned for Johnny to get you the ball again. When Johnny went the other way, he told me to 'get in there for that son of a bitch'. God, you had a hot hand tonight. What did you get about 20?" Rock continued talking, trying not to give me a chance to ask about his love life. I listened for about a minute while he rattled on about the game.

"No, I got about 22. What did you get, LAID?"

He quickly replied, "Hell no, Big Jim, The Cheerleader and me are just good friends."

"You lying son of a bitch."

# Chapter Seven

Baker College life that second semester took on a completely new meaning for The Rock and me. We started on the varsity basketball team and still played all the freshman games. We received new and positive attention from our fellow students and both of us had girlfriends. The Rock and The Cheerleader were together a lot. She became so much a part of our friendship; it was like she had always been there. It seemed from the beginning she and The Rock were meant for each other. The Rock, who always had plans, had just filled in a couple of the blanks in his future. He would graduate from college, join the Navy, serve his country, get a job coaching and teaching in some high school, find a wonderful woman, have two or three kids and "give it back" to the world for his good fortune. He talked about his plan constantly and would chastise me for not having any plan of my own beyond the next basketball game.

The Cheerleader was premature in his plan but she was his "wonderful woman" and there was no doubt in my mind, she would be the only woman ever for Rock -- the most important ingredient in his "perfect plan."

The Cheerleader was about five feet four inches tall, with long blond hair, ice blue eyes (just like Rock's) and the most incredible body of any woman I'd ever seen. She was a great athlete and could shoot free throws better The Rock and me. I have never met anyone as socially confident; she was always relaxed and in total control. She picked The Rock and was perfect for him but there were many times I secretly wished she had picked me.

We got to know her because we were all from Oklahoma and the Okies on campus had an informal bond with each other. We gave the Texans a little bit of hell, they gave us a whole lot of hell and there were a lot more of them. Sometimes all the Okies sat together in the cafeteria and this is where we met The Cheerleader.

Her parents were teachers in Oklahoma City and she was one of the few girls on campus that was not a silver spooner. She was Presbyterian and had been valedictorian of her high school class. She was on a full academic scholarship at Baker College and she and The Rock were cut from the same mold. I felt privileged just to be able to hang out with the two of them.

Christine, on the other hand, was a silver spooner and even though she probably didn't have quite as good a body as The Cheerleader, she was sexier. She had long legs, a perfect waist and bust, dark hair and a wardrobe that accentuated every inch of her. She and The Cheerleader were good friends and when I met her that night after the ball game, I thought I had conquered the world. Christine had a great sense of humor that made her fun. She loved to hang out with The Rock, The Cheerleader and me. She constantly encouraged our many stories and couldn't believe some of the things we told her about growing up in Ferguson. She was a good student, majoring in psychology with no intentions of ever having a job or professional career. She was compassionate and… passionate. Two qualities a guy had to admire. We had absolutely nothing in common, but I think that is what attracted us to each other.

Christine was my girlfriend, at least for a while. I liked her cynical wit and I loved her physical presence. Deep down I knew the two of us would probably never work but I was enjoying the moment. And, as The Rock said, "Big Jim, your plans don't go much beyond next Saturday night."

The Rock, The Cheerleader, Christine and I went out together some and always had a good time, but The Rock and I usually had a good time, regardless of who we were with. The basketball games were the ultimate for a couple of junkies like The Rock and me. We were playing four or five games a week, winning most of them and had two beautiful girls waiting for us after every game.

After Rock's promise to Ethel and Dad at Thanksgiving, it was fortunate we were on the varsity in late January when the Kangaroos played the University of Tulsa in Tulsa. The gamblers' line had us as a thirty-one-point underdog as we traveled to Oklahoma to challenge the Golden Hurricane. Tulsa was a division one school and only played us to "pad" their schedule. Dad, Ethel and half the population of Ferguson showed up for the game.

Rock and I talked to Dad and Ethel during warm-up as all

our Ferguson friends gathered round acting as if we were some kind of celebrities. Coach Jenkins appointed us co-captains for the game and we were busting with pride as we met the Tulsa captains at mid-court prior to the game. Coach Jenkins was a master at making you feel good about yourself. It didn't make any difference who was captain for a game. It was just a symbolic jester, but it made a difference that night to those people from Ferguson and they were proud of The Rock and Big Jim.

At tip-off, Tulsa batted the ball to their end and scored on a big slam-dunk. The Rock immediately decided we were not going to get humiliated in front of our family and hometown friends. He took control of that game and fed me for jumper after jumper and I hit nearly every one of them as we took the Golden Hurricane to double overtime before losing 91 to 89.

At the final buzzer, even though we lost, all the Ferguson people poured onto the floor, which made The Rock and me feel as if we'd won the National Championship. That was the only game Dad saw me play in college but it was a night I would cherish forever.

The Rock and The Cheerleader spent most nights studying in the library and even though it was beyond my comprehension, they seemed to enjoy it. While they were in the library, Christine and I spent time exploring the passions of our youth and I also spent a lot of time bullshitting with the guys in the dorm.

Rock always said, even though I had no plans for the future, I would make it through life on my bullshit. I could embellish a story better than anyone and when The Rock came up with a "hell of an idea," I could take it to the next level. I had that kangaroo burial out to a point of pure folklore and the story was only six months old. The Rock thought I had taken it about as far as it needed to go, however and he was getting annoyed with my exaggerations.

One night, just as we were about to go to sleep, he said, "Big Jim, did you know that Katy wasn't a kangaroo?"

"No, I didn't know that," I said. "What the shit was she, a mermaid?"

"No, she was a wallaby...Wallabies are cousins to the kangaroos but are smaller and slower."

"What are you trying to tell me?" I asked,

" I just want to see what kind of bullshit you can make of this," The Rock replied.

"Well, kiss my ass," I said. "We nearly got kicked out of school over a damn wallaby." At that point The Rock lost it and we laughed for about an hour.

Our sense of humor was probably warped, but we could totally surprise each other with some of the most off-the-wall, funniest things ever said. I should say, we thought they were funny, but again we were warped.

When basketball season was over the first year, Rock worked a couple of weeks at a gas station in Douglas. When he finished the work, the owner paid him with a fifty-dollar bill. It was the first fifty-dollar bill either of us had ever seen. As we occasionally would go out for a burger or movie, The Rock would offer to pay and then pull out the fifty-dollar bill. Back then, no one had change for large bills, so I would have to pick up the tab. After this happened five or six times, I told Rock the next time he pulled that fifty out, I was going to whip his ass.

When we were going home to Ferguson for the Easter break, we stopped for gas at a little country store about ten miles north of Durant. When we walked in the front door, there was a huge table covered with bananas sitting in the middle of the room.

"How much you getting on your bananas?" The Rock asked the old man behind the counter.

"Six for a dollar," the old man replied.

I quickly cut my eyes at The Rock and he said, "Give me three hundred of the son of a bitches."

I had to admit The Rock was sharp on his feet to figure out that quickly he could buy three hundred bananas for fifty bucks. From what I knew of his intelligence, coupled with the time he spent in the library, I saw a well-educated guy emerging. The Rock was one of those students who fulfilled the purpose and goals of Baker College. I doubt if the college was aware of this and it certainly wasn't by design, but The Rock was totally engrossed in his classes and hungry for all the knowledge and awareness he could absorb. Even though most of us didn't study that much and were not all that engrossed, we couldn't avoid The Rock's enthusiasm for sharing with us what he was learning. Many times when he did this sharing, it was hard for us to distinguish between facts and his bullshit. But, he always set us straight when we expressed some naïve or ignorant opinion related to a religious, political, or social situation. It was like The College educated The

Rock and he educated the rest of us.

One of the reasons The Rock spent so much time in the library was because our room had become a social center for about half the guys in Austin Hall and it was difficult to get much studying done. Rock had to have some quiet time. The room was a convenient place to socialize and we always had some "hell of an idea" adventure going.

During the first semester Rock helped the maintenance crew clean out the basement of the science building. Among the things they threw away were an old record player, a slot machine (which had been used by some math teacher years before to teach probability and was illegal as hell to own now) and some Hank Williams records. I always wondered why the science department had old Hank Williams records. True to our childhood mechanical abilities, we repaired both the record player and the slot machine. It worked on dimes or pennies but paid off only in pennies. The Rock and I grew up around country music, but, as all high school kids in the late Fifties, we were into rock and roll. When Buddy Holly died on that winter day in 1959, however, it was "the day the music died" and The Rock and I went country.

We started playing those Hank Williams songs and the "silver spooners" thought it was some kind of musical revolution. No wonder we always had a crowd in our room -- we had slots, country music, lots of bullshit and The Rock filling in the gaps in our liberal arts education.

Alex Glover, one of the regulars in our room, was a small, frail guy from a wealthy family in San Antonio. During the second semester he began wearing a tweed coat, tried to grow a beard and started smoking a pipe. He wasn't happy his parents made him attend Baker College and he saw his primary mission as getting kicked out of school. He didn't want to get expelled for some meaningless prank; he wanted to be a victim of some great educational or political injustice. Alex wrote several, what he thought were, inflammatory articles and submitted them to the student newspaper. Soon after our kangaroo debacle, we became friends and he wanted to tell our story to defend our rights.

The paper never printed any of his work and he vented on us over his frustrations about freedom of speech. One night in the midst of one of Alex's tirades, The Rock suggested he publish his own paper. When Alex whined about not having the equipment to publish a paper, I told him there was a mimeograph machine in the music building and I had keys. Alex's excitement became almost uncontrollable.

"I can publish anything I want with my own underground newspaper," he said.

I began to think this was "a hell of an idea." "If we're going to do this, Alex," I said, "You're going to do a sports section in your paper."

Alex had never been to a football or basketball game and he immediately whined, "but I don't want to have to go to all of those games."

"Remember Alex," I said, "I have the keys to the music building and you don't have to go to any games. Just come by here every week and The Rock and I will tell you what to put in the sports section."

Alex agreed and then started trying to think of a name for his paper. The Rock finely suggested *The First Amendment* and Alex loved it. He published the inaugural *The First Amendment* one week later.

Alex ran a few news stories in his paper, but he wrote mostly editorials about his campus and political concerns. He printed about two hundred papers and put them on a table in the SUB. He also put a jar with a slot in the lid beside the papers and charged a dime for each paper. Most everyone paid and since he was stealing his supplies from the music department, all he took in was profit. He filled most of the first four editions of *The First Amendment* with his concerns with apathy in student government.

We finally convinced him to do a story on "Who gives a damn about apathy in student government?" and to lighten up a bit with his editorials.

The Rock, Ronnie Peters, Jerry Miller and I gave him the sports stories. We had a great time embellishing and exaggerating the games and all the players. By the time Alex wrote his article it was pure fiction. Ronnie Peters rarely got in a game, but from what we told Alex, he thought Ronnie was the star player.

During warm-ups for the freshmen games, we always ran a five-man weave at half-court. As we broke off, Rock took the ball to the side as Suitcase bent over about three feet in front of the basket. Ronnie, at a full run, jumped off Suitcase's back as Rock lobbed him the ball and Ronnie slam-dunked it. This little bit of showmanship put Ronnie pretty high in the air. One night, he hit his head on the rim. He had to be taken to the emergency room for stitches and missed the game.

Alex, impressed when we told him how Ronnie cut his head open on the rim, couldn't believe we won the game with Ronnie in the emergency room. According to his information, Ronnie was our best player. Rock suggested he write a story with the headline "Kangaroos Win With Peters Out." We all laughed, but Alex didn't get it.

"Think about it Alex," Ronnie said.

When it finely registered, he thought it was the funniest thing he ever heard. He couldn't get kicked out of school because of his left-wing political beliefs, but maybe he could be expelled for off color humor.

Although the student body loved it and he sold out of papers for the first time; the headline didn't phase the school officials. Much to his surprise, he didn't get kicked out of school. He became the only non-ball player in our very tight group and remained a vital part of our group through college. His paper became the official chronicle of all our bullshit.

There was a Greek system at Baker College composed of five fraternities and four sororities. They were local social organizations chartered by the college and most had a heritage going back to the 1920s. To be involved in the social life of the college, it was critical to be a member of one of the Greek groups. Fraternity and sorority houses were not allowed at Baker College, but the individual floors or wings of the dorms informally isolated the various groups. There were only two fraternities The Rock and I would consider joining. One was the Tri Delts, which were mostly jocks. The other was the Omegas and the cool guys on campus who dated Alphas and Kappas made up the membership of this group. Alphas and Kappas were the good looking girls on campus, but I don't know why The Rock and I were so damned impressed with the Omegas, because we were already dating the two best looking girls in school.

Until we started playing on the varsity, we didn't think we would be given a bid for membership in either group. After that first varsity game, however, both the Tri Delts and Omegas started rushing us hard. Every time we looked up guys from each group were coming by the room and asking us to go out to eat or go to a movie. We went to their open rush parties and this gave them enough of an indication we were interested; they invited us to their closed party. The other guys from the freshman basketball team and Alex also got invitations to the closed parties and we were all feeling pretty special.

The Omega party was at an exclusive lodge on Lake Texoma and they served venison for dinner. It was the first time The Rock and I had eaten deer meat and even though it wasn't worth a damn, we raved about how good it was. They talked to us about the bonds of brotherhood and the status we would achieve by being a part of their group.

They had a keg of beer and some of the guys got pretty drunk. We were still in basketball season and didn't drink. It wasn't because we didn't want to, but we abstained because of our fear of Coach Jenkins.

Christine was a member of the Kappas and they were, of course, rushing The Cheerleader. They were putting pressure on

The Rock and me to pledge Omega. Even though we thought the whole thing was kind of silly, we were caught up in the situation. I guess the Omegas thought it would be a major coop to get the three big freshmen jocks away from the Tri Delts, so they turned on all of their charm for Rock, Jerry Miller and me. They were also rushing Ken Chapman and Chris Wright real hard, but I think they were after Ken and Chris because they were cool guys, not because they were jocks.

The Tri Delts didn't have venison at their party, but they did have rib eyes, which were the first steaks, other than chicken-fries, The Rock and I ever had. We were impressed and felt we would get bids from both groups.

On the Saturday night bids came out, each prospective pledge was to go to his mail box at 7:00 PM and if a bid for membership was offered, it would be there, accompanied by instructions for accepting or rejecting the invitation. When The Rock and I went to our boxes, we had bids from both the Tri Delts and Omegas telling us to accept by signing and sliding the bid under the door of a designated room in the SUB.

All the guys, The Rock, Ken Chapman, Jerry Miller, Chris Wright, Suitcase, Ronnie Peters, Alex and I agreed to pick up our bids and meet in Rock's and my room at 7:15 to decide which way to go.

When we met, The Rock, Ken, Jerry, Chris and I all had Omega bids. The Rock, Suitcase and I had Tri Delt bids. Ronnie and Alex didn't have a bid.

As I looked around the room and saw the pain in Ronnie and Alex's faces, I felt sick. Then The Rock did one of the most outstanding things I ever saw a man do. He took both of his bids, put them together, tore them in half and dropped them on the floor. I followed, doing the same thing. Ken, Jerry, Chris and Suitcase did likewise and Rock said, "Our fraternity is sitting in this room, right now. We don't have a name and we don't have a charter, but we do have a brotherhood. We may add to this group in the future, but it will happen without any rush parties or bids. It will happen just because it happens and be based on nothing more than trust and loyalty." At that moment a bond was formed that was stronger than anything I have ever known.

We later found out Alex didn't get a bid because they thought he was a nerd and Peters didn't because he wore red socks.

The Cheerleader pledged Kappa and that was okay because the sorority system was less pretentious than the fraternity system and seemed to have a mission beyond contempt for nerds and red socks.

When we were in high school, The Rock and I hung out in a place called The Deluxe Bar. It wasn't really a bar, because Oklahoma was dry until 1959 and the only alcohol that could be legally sold was 3.2% beer. They did sell beer and had a grill that served burgers, chili and French-fries. The bar also had pool and snooker tables and the old men played dominoes by the front door. The back half of the building was a gym for aspiring boxers. We worked out some on the weights, speed bag and jump ropes and played a lot of pool and snooker. There were several old farts that were always searching for a fighter to train. Hanging around them, coupled with watching the Friday Night Gillett Fights with Dad, got The Rock and I semi-knowledgeable about boxing. At one point, I helped one of the old farts and we trained Rock. We took him to Tulsa for a lightweight bout, which was not a high-class fight, but was professional because Rock was paid $25. He lost in a 10 round decision. The old fart thought Rock had possibilities, but I figured boxing might jeopardize his basketball career, so it wasn't hard to convince him he should hang it up.

In the spring of 1960, right after basketball season, as we were about to go to sleep one night, Rock said, "Big Jim did you know they're having a regional Golden Gloves tournament here in Douglas in about a month?"

"No," I said, "Are you thinking about entering?"

"I can't enter, Big Jim, because I'm a professional, remember."

"I guess you want me to enter" I replied, not knowing where he was going with this.

Rock then laughed. "No, you can't enter, Big Jim, because you're a chicken, remember."

"Okay, what's the deal, Rock?" I asked.

The Rock then proposed his "hell of an idea." He said we could train Ronnie Peters and Ken Chapman and we could enter them. "They are both damn good athletes and are about as quick as any two guys I know. Ronnie could fight as lightweight and Ken as a light heavy. The competition wouldn't be all that great here in Douglas and they might just win a bout or two. We probably know more about boxing than anyone around here and this will be a hell of a good time," The Rock concluded.

It became my job to sell Ronnie and Ken on the idea and they were both easy sells. Ronnie was anxious to do anything he thought would bring him into favor with The Rock and could see an opportunity to excel in a pretty macho sport. Ken had extremely quick hands and he was smart enough to know he was a natural for boxing. When they agreed, we filled out the applications and started their training. We marked off a ring with athletic tape on the gym floor. There was already enough equipment in the gym to get the job done. As the training progressed, Ronnie looked pretty good and Ken was great. I decided someone needed to spar with them because Ronnie was so much smaller than Ken, sparing with each other wasn't working out. I convinced Rock to be their sparring partner and it worked so well they both got in a lot of good training.

One sparing session, Ken was nearly killing Rock and The Rock quit and ran out of the ring. As he tossed in a towel, he said to Ken, "I've had enough, Slugger."

The first time both Ronnie and Ken entered a real boxing ring they both won their opening matches in the Douglas Boys' Club Annual Golden Gloves. Coach Jenkins and all the guys were there to cheer them on as Ken stepped into the ring for his first fight.

His opponent was a cocky kid from Denison who had nicknamed himself "Big Thunder." He taunted Ken as he climbed into the ring, "Your momma's not here to take care of you college boy."

Ken answered the first bell with two left jabs and a jarring right that sent Big Thunder back to Denison.

Ronnie drew a good fighter for the first bout but out pointed him with his aggressive quickness to win a unanimous decision. They both won their second round fights and fought in the finals Friday night. One more win and they were on their way to the state tournament in Fort Worth. Ronnie fought first in the finals and we were disappointed when he lost a split decision. We, of course, thought he got robbed. We were jubilant when the ref stopped Ken's final fight as he TKO'ed his guy in the second round, won the gold medal and a trip to Fort Worth for a chance for the State Championship.

Ronnie became a part of our training team for Ken as the three of us worked Ken's butt off in preparation for the state title. We all went to Fort Worth with aspirations of Ken winning and going to the national tournament in Chicago. In his opening fight in the state tournament Ken drew a good fighter from Longview but had him out-pointed after the first two rounds. When he came to the corner prior to the final round, he said, "Guys, I think I broke my right on that last punch."

"It's okay," Rock said.

"Just stay away from him this last round, jab with your left and we will out point him."

Ken performed as instructed and did win the decision. X-rays after the fight, however, revealed that Ken's diagnosis was correct and he was disqualified from the tournament. We were all disappointed but proud of Ken's effort and as we returned to Douglas, we started planning for Ronnie and Ken to enter again next year and both of them advancing to Chicago.

The Rock and I loved to give people nicknames and we had been thinking about several for Ronnie and Ken. Anticipating them making it big, we knew they'd need a catchy name for their fight cards. We talked about "Kid Peters" and "Rumbling Ronnie," but with a last name like Peters, how could you improve on it? Ronnie became just "Peters." Rock named Ken the day Ken nearly killed him and he remains "Slugger" to this day. It was probably a blessing Slugger didn't make it to the national tournament in 1960, because the guy who won the light-heavy division in Chicago was a kid from Louisville named Cassius Clay.

The Rock and I had a hell of a freshman year and the opportunities for high adventure were so numerous it's a wonder we survived.

# Chapter Eight

As we prepared to go home to Ferguson for the summer, we both had jobs lined up at the same places we had worked the past three summers. Rock worked for a gasoline plant and I worked for an oil field construction company.

These summer jobs were critical to us because the money we earned was all we had for the next school year. If we wanted clothes, dates, gasoline and toothpaste, it was important for us to make five or six hundred dollars over the summer.

The Rock faithfully executed his plan and I limped along with 2.0 GPA, just enough to be eligible for student aid and basketball our sophomore year. The Cheerleader spent the summer in Oklahoma City and The Rock and she continued their storybook romance. Christine got back with John and broke it off with me for the summer. It hurt my pride, but because I was thinking about a couple of girls back home, I didn't really didn't care.

I let Rock have the Ford for the summer to do his courting in and I drove Dad's old pickup. We both worked about the maximum fifty hours a week. At $1.25 an hour and time and a half over forty hours, we earned about seventy dollars a week. If we didn't piss it off having fun, we expected to save about six hundred dollars for the next school year.

A girl I dated in high school named Judy Patrick was now living with her sister in Tulsa, which is about forty-five miles east of Ferguson. She went to secretarial school for nine months just out of high school and was now working for a Tulsa oilman. She came home the first weekend we were home and I got hooked up with her. Before I knew it, I had this hot and heavy romance going and was driving to Tulsa nearly every night. I went to work at seven and got off at five, went home, showered and headed for Tulsa. I wouldn't get back home till about 1:00 A.M. and swear to myself, as I struggled out of bed at six the next morning, I would not go back to Tulsa that night. As the day passed, however, the closer it got to five o'clock, the better I felt and when that five o'clock whistle blew, I headed home for a shower and back to Tulsa.

Fortunately, after about two weeks of this, she started talking about us getting married and scared the hell out of me. The last thing I needed to do was get married and if I kept making those trips every night I wasn't going to save a nickel over the summer.

Rock was seeing The Cheerleader once in a while but was far more prudent with his gasoline money than me. After I broke it off with Judy, I dated a couple of other "old" girl friends. They were home in Ferguson for the summer and I made sure they didn't start talking about marriage.

For the most part The Rock and I spent our summer evenings trying to stay in shape through pick-up games at the park. Ferguson was a haven for basketball junkies. The school had three gyms and the city had a great outdoor, lighted court where ball players of all shapes and sizes showed up to test their skills. Ever since we could remember, we went to the park on summer evenings, looking for a game.

We would show up at the park about 7:30. There would always be between ten and twenty guys. Most of them would be Ferguson high school players but there were always a couple of seventh and eighth graders who thought they could play along with the older guys. We divided up by letting the youngest guys be the captains and choose the teams and we ended up with two to four teams. The Rock and I were always the first ones chosen and kidded each other about who got picked first. We were never on the same team and the competition was mostly between The Rock and me.

If there were two teams, we just played each other in games to twenty-one. If there were more than two, the winner stayed on the court and rotated opponents. We didn't shoot free throws and each basket counted only one point. We had no officials and rules were on the honor system. If you walked with the ball or stepped on the line, it was up to you to make the call against yourself. As the years passed, I discovered that guys have played pick up games for the past fifty years all over the United States with basically this same set of unwritten rules. This is sport in its purest form and the most fun of any of my basketball experiences.

Dad and I had always watched the Gillett Friday Night

Fights, but in the summer of 1960 we also got into the political conventions. Dad lived through the depression and thought Franklin Roosevelt was the greatest man in the world. We cheered when John Kennedy won the Democratic nomination because Dad thought he was the only man who could beat those damn Republicans.

I missed Rock's constant company, but Dad was really glad I was home. He wanted to sit up late every night watching the fights or the conventions. It gave me time to tell him about every basketball game we played the previous year. He'd been able to come to only one game, the one in Tulsa during February when he brought Ethel, but he had my press photo hanging in his bedroom next to his picture of Mom. Newspaper clippings I sent him were taped on the wall in the living room and it was obvious Dad was proud of me.

When I came home or anytime we hadn't seen each other for a while we would shake hands and exchange words like "How's it going?" or "Good to see you." Even though I knew he still grieved for Mom, he never talked about her. In fact, the only things we ever talked about were ball games, politics and the Gillett fights. In spite of this, I don't think I had any animosity toward him and I didn't feel deprived. Our lack of affectionate behavior toward each other was as much my fault as it was his.

On the first Friday night after Judy "scared me off," he surprised me when he asked, "What happened to your Tulsa girlfriend?"

"She started talking about getting married and I don't think I'm quite ready for that," I said.

He laughed. "Well I'm glad you have a good head on your shoulders. I don't think it would be a very good time for you to get married either."

He continued to talk and continued to surprise me when he said, "I know I'm just an old drunk and probably haven't been a real good dad…but guys like me for some reason…I guess, are scared to tell people we care about…how we feel."

"I know you care about me Dad…It's okay."

"No, it's not okay, Jim. I don't want you to be like that and I want you to know I love you more than anything in this world and you make me so proud, I could bust."

I didn't say anything for a moment as I was overcome with emotion.

"I love you too, Dad and I wouldn't trade you for any dad in the world."

We both laughed as we stood up and hugged for the first time I ever remembered.

That summer was probably the best time Dad and I ever spent together and it helped make the summer of 1960 one to remember.

The Rock and I renewed our relationships with old friends from high school and could see they were growing in positive ways, just as we were. They had some new stories that were great and, of course, we were always full of new stories. We also probably found a comfort zone with them that was at least as secure as our friendships at Baker College.

However, when the summer ended, we were anxious to return to the land of the Kangaroos.

# Chapter Nine

*"They feed 'em in the coulees, they water in the draw,
Their tails are all matted, their backs are all raw."*

The fall of 1960, everything was different. We were more confident and more relaxed than we had been at the same time the previous year. We tried to mingle and encourage the freshmen students, but I was mostly interested in checking out the new girls. I saw Christine the first day we were on campus and we had a cordial but chilly chat. She let me know she and John were again engaged.

I had a few dates that fall but nothing to write home about. The Rock and The Cheerleader's romance remained steady. We had the same dorm room and the crowd continued to cram inside for the slots, Hank Williams and bullshit.

Our campus jobs did change. Rock was assigned to work cataloging books in the library while I was assigned to custodial work in the gym. I no longer had keys to the music building, but now I had the keys to the gym. We moved Alex's operation to Coach Jenkins office, which was done without Coach's knowledge. The Athletic Department's equipment was much better than the music department's and Alex was delighted with the move.

Early in the school year the college invited a distinguished philosopher from London to the campus and he spoke for five consecutive days in chapel services. We were required to attend chapel all five days. Most of us had just gotten off chapel probation and were not eager to be there again so we were stuck with going to all five of the philosopher's lectures.

By the third day, we were annoyed with the whole deal. Not only did we have to go to chapel every day, but also, the guy was keeping us till 12:15. On Wednesday night there was a crowd in our room and everyone complained about chapel. We had a lively discussion concerning how to make a statement expressing our dissatisfaction.

"It's bad enough to have to go to chapel twice a week but five times is ridiculous." Alex said.

Suitcase followed up, "And the guy is keeping us past noon every day. Maybe we need to form a picket in front of the chapel tomorrow."

Even though I complained as much as anyone, I had no intention of making a statement. I was content with enduring two more days and couldn't believe it when The Rock came up with "a hell of an idea."

He said, "I've been looking at the organ pipes in the chapel and was wondering how much they would amplify the sound if an alarm clock was dropped down one of the pipes."

The others became excited. Alarm clocks in 1960 were the wind up kind set to ring a nerve-wracking bell. They decided to drop four or five clocks down the organ pipes, set to ring about one minute apart starting at noon.

Always remembering Dr. Odem's warning that he never wanted to see me in his office again, I told the group I thought this was a bad idea.

"It's not a bad idea, Big Jim, it's a 'hell of an idea' but you're right, we don't need to do it." Rock said.

The rest of the group agreed it was somewhat drastic and disrespectful, so we went on to other bullshit.

On Friday at noon when that first alarm clock went off in the organ pipes, we all nearly shit. The first clock ran down just as the second one started and then a third and then a fourth. We never knew for sure who did it. I knew it wasn't The Rock or me, even though it was The Rock's "hell of an idea." I always suspected these two football players who were in the room when we talked about it. I hesitate to mention their names, because Dr. Odem was so damn mad, I believe if he found out today, he would have their degrees voided.

Jerry Miller was the starting quarterback on the football team and The Cheerleader was cheerleading. Because of the football guys support the previous basketball season, coupled with our special interest in Jerry and The Cheerleader, we really got excited about football season. We had a good team and Jerry kept us posted on inside information, like when they were going to run trick plays and what to watch for on the sideline. The Rock, Chris Wright, Suitcase, Slugger, Peters and I all sat together on the fifty-yard line. Because of The Cheerleader, The Rock made us do every damn one of those yells with them. Not only could The Cheerleader do cartwheels and flips, she was the best dancer I'd ever seen. She could move everything she had in a different direction at the same time, so watching her and doing the yells was a pleasure. We were enthusiastic the entire game and as soon as the game finished, we rushed onto the field to shake the players' hands. We reported our pure bullshit about the first game to Alex and *The First Amendment* continued its fictitious sports coverage.

After the first game, Alex decided to come to the games and do his own reporting. I think he just wanted to hang out with us, but his on the spot reporting turned out to be further from the truth than the bullshit we'd been giving him.

The third football game of the season was at East Central State in Ada, Oklahoma. It was on Thursday night and was broadcast on a local radio station. Rock had volunteered to drive the cheerleaders' van to the game, so the rest of us congregated in our room to listen to the game. The reception on the radio was terrible and at the end of the first quarter, we decided to go to the parking lot and listen to the rest of the game in the Ford, which lacked in a lot of areas, but it had a hell of a radio. Slugger, Peters, Chris Wright, Suitcase, Alex and I piled into the Ford and in a real intimate environment, listened to the most exciting football game we ever heard. Jerry Miller, on that September night in 1960, broke every Division II single game passing record on the books. The score was tied 35 to 35 with two seconds left on the clock. We were on their ten-yard line and just as Jerry threw a pass into the end zone, the radio broke. We stayed up till 2:00 AM to meet the bus, to find out if the pass was complete. It was and we won.

I worked for Coach Jenkins in the gym, cleaning rest rooms and offices. They moved me from the music building to the gym because I hadn't done the best job in the world as a janitor in the music building and they thought Coach could keep a better eye on me.

Norm Shelton, the head football coach, was a huge man and a former NFL player. The players loved him, even though he ran the football team with an iron hand. In addition to his duties as head basketball coach, Coach Jenkins was also Coach Norm's assistant coach. The afternoon after Jerry broke all those records, Coach Jenkins called me in and told me Coach Norm needed an assistant trainer for the football team. He said if I wanted to do that instead of cleaning the rest rooms, I could have the job.

*This is great. I can go to all the games with the team and it will be a soft ass job like Rock's.*

After a moment, I said, "Do I have to wear those white pants?"

He told me it was part of the territory and I reluctantly agreed. After that, The Rock quit calling me "the religious nut" and started calling me "ice-cream britches."

At the homecoming game I noticed Christine with a guy

whom I assumed was John. As the crowd came onto the field after the game, Christine stopped me and introduced John. As I stood there in my "ice-cream britches," I wondered why she did this.

John, immediately said, "So, you're the guy that shot me out of the saddle last year."

"I don't know if that's quite true," I kind of laughed.

"Are you calling me a liar?"

And just prior to me doing something real dumb, Rock came from no where, stepped between us and told John unless he thought he "could whip both the basketball and football teams, it might be best to forget this bullshit."

John took Christine's arm and said, "Let's go."

I could tell she was embarrassed and didn't want to go with him. As they walked toward the gate I thought, *that dumb ass just handed her back to me. Happy days are here again.*

As assistant trainer, my responsibility was doing whatever the trainer told me to do. The trainer was a graduate physical education student named Clyde Menard. Clyde had been the football trainer for the past four years and the college had sent him to a few seminars on sports medicine. He had also picked up enough skills from the coaches to know what he was doing. He taught me to wrap ankles and how to identify all the items in the medicine chest. I helped him wrap ankles before practice and games. I handed him tape, ammonia caps and ice as he tended to injuries.

In addition to taking care of the football team's needs, we also worked as trainers for other college sponsored sports events such as youth gymnastic meets, tennis tournaments and high school track meets. Just prior to Thanksgiving, I worked a high school girl's basketball tournament. The work was easy because the coaches took care of most of the problems and unless there were a lot of neurotic kids, there were very few injuries to tend to.

I enjoyed watching the tournament because I loved any kind of basketball and some of those girls were pretty good looking. There was a girl from Van Alstine who was about 5' 11", a smooth as silk player and drop dead good looking. She got a "charlie horse" in the semifinal game Saturday morning and after the game, her Coach asked me to put her in the whirlpool, rub her leg with balm and wrap it. The thought of rubbing her leg was pretty appealing, but I acted like a professional as I followed her coach's request. She flirted with me and gave me her phone number. Her name was Sandra Mayo, she was a junior at Van Alstine High School and she was sixteen years old. She had a good game in the finals and her team won the championship.

The Rock convinced me it wouldn't be cool to take out a high school girl, so I never called her. The guys started kidding me about her and Coach Jenkins called me in his office one day and chewed my ass out. This was the only time I ever got pissed off at the Coach, but looking back on it, he was right to confront me. He told me the last thing he ever wanted, was for his players to "create bad feelings with the surrounding communities." I told him I didn't do anything.

He told me; "In a deal like this you don't have to do anything to get in a hell of a lot of trouble." He did cool down a bit and acknowledged the girl's coach shouldn't have sent me to the training room alone with her, but told me, "Never let yourself get into a situation like that again."

I was always amazed with how Coach Jenkins never seemed to miss anything and how he addressed every issue that needed his attention. He didn't care how mad it made me, he was going to make sure I understood my actions could cause a great deal of pain and that college guys had no business getting involved with sixteen-year-old girls.

# Chapter Ten

We reported for basketball practice shortly after the homecoming football game. Because we had graduated a bunch of seniors, we were a little short handed. Several of the guys on last years varsity and freshmen teams decided the freshmen starters from '59 were going to get all the playing time on the varsity this year and so they didn't come out. As it turned out except for three new freshmen Coach Jenkins recruited, it was pretty much The Rock, Chris Wright, Slugger, Peters, Suitcase and me. Jerry Miller would join us after football season and it was obvious the three freshmen weren't going to be much help.

I helped Clyde wrap the football guy's ankles at 3:30 and then reported to basketball practice at 4:30. Johnny Walker, the senior point guard who The Rock replaced as a starter the year before, became a graduate assistant coach. While Coach Jenkins helped with the football team, Johnny worked us out. We started calling him, "Whiskey" after we joined the varsity the year before. Come to think of it, that's what was wrong with that bunch of seniors in 1960. They had been playing ball with Johnny Walker for four years and were never creative enough to call him "Whiskey"

I guess "Whiskey" still had a little anger to work out with The Rock. He took it out on him early in the season when he had us working half court on offense. When Whisky worked us out, he tried to be a real "hard ass" and most of us knew a hell of a lot more about basketball than he did. Rock missed a pass to me and then he tried to hit Suitcase in the middle. Suitcase muffed the ball and it went out of bounds. It wasn't a great pass but Suitcase should have caught it. Whiskey picked up the ball, tossed it back to Rock and said "Riley, you need to be thinking a little more about basketball and a little less about that Cheerleader stuff."

"Whiskey, when I have to choose between this basketball and that Cheerleader stuff, you can stick this basketball up your ass." Rock threw the ball to Whiskey and walked off the floor.

None of us said anything when Rock slammed the locker room door and Whiskey was smart enough to know Coach Jenkins needed The Rock more at the point guard than he needed him as assistant coach.

The Rock never said a word about the incident but the rest of us couldn't wait to get out of the gym, so we could laugh our asses off. Coach Jenkins caught me the next day while I was wrapping ankles and asked if there was a problem with The Rock and Whiskey.

"I don't think Rock has a problem and the rest of us thought the deal was sort of funny," I told him.

"Well, I think Whiskey will be okay too," Coach said and then asked, "Did Rock really say, 'when I have to choose between this basketball and that Cheerleader stuff, you can stick this basketball up your ass'? "

"That's pretty much it," I said.

Coach Jenkins laughed, "That is pretty damn funny."

Even though he had pissed me off about the deal with the high school girl, one of Coach Jenkins' greatest strengths as a coach was he didn't make some kind of disciplinary crisis out of everything that happened.

Coach Jenkins demanded our best efforts and could be plenty tough when he needed to. He could laugh and joke with us, however and still retain our respect. Our primary motivation on the court was to please him and gain his approval. He looked out for our welfare in all aspects of our lives and was quick to give us praise and recognition.

The other students, because of the special attention he gave his ball players, accused him of manipulating and exploiting us. They thought since our financial aid was not contingent on playing ball, he pampered us to keep us out for the team. Nothing could have been further from the truth. Coach loved to be a coach more than anyone I've ever known. He loved the workouts, he loved the long road trips, he loved telling us stories and listening to ours, he loved the ball games and all of his players.

When a player had a real good game, with about a minute to go Coach would send in a substitute and as the player jogged off the floor, Coach would meet him and vigorously shake his hand. The crowd responded with a tremendous ovation and the player felt like superman.

During the spring of my freshman year, the art department had an outdoor show on a Saturday. Each art student had four or five works for sale. On the Monday after the show, Dr. Leslie, the head of the Art Department, handed me $12 for two works of mine that sold. One was a drawing of a woman that sold for $7 and the other was of an old man that sold for $5.

I couldn't believe it. Someone had actually bought my art! I asked Dr. Leslie who bought them and he said he didn't know. My self-esteem, however, pitched to its highest level since that first varsity basketball game.

I found out years later Coach Jenkins bought those drawings. I don't think Coach purchased them because he was an art lover or was rich. I think he bought them because he was a hell of a good man.

We stayed in Douglas over the Thanksgiving break and had home games with Rogers University, from Rogers, Arkansas Friday and Saturday. Staying at school over the holidays meant we had to move out of the dorms into a large room above the gym. The room accommodated visiting football and basketball teams and had about thirty sets of bunk beds, arranged barracks style. It was a converted football dressing room with adjacent showers and bathrooms. We were allowed three meals a day at a local cafe, with a $.75 limit on breakfast and $1.25 for each of the other two meals. On the first two nights of the Thanksgiving break we had the barracks to ourselves but the next two nights the Rogers University guys bunked with us.

When a bunch of guys live together with nothing to do but wait for practice, they can get pretty bored. That particular year we got into bowling to relieve our boredom. There was a two-lane bowling alley in the gym with manually operated pin-setting machines. The pinsetter went into the pit and loaded the knocked down pins into a bin and then pulled a lever to reset them. He sat on a small bench, out of sight to the bowlers, directly behind the pit while the bowlers rolled their shots.

None of us had ever bowled before, but Slugger knew how to keep score and as competitive as all of us were, we started getting into some great matches in a couple of days. When the Rogers University guys got there and were bunking with us, we decided to let them bowl with us. Except for one guy, they were pretty much beginners like us. But their one guy bowled about 230 every game. I told him The Rock was a great bowler too and he wanted to challenge Rock to a game. I volunteered to set the pins. Rock was pissed because I got him into this deal, but decided to go along. When The Rock made a shot, I would hold out one of the back pins and just as his ball would strike, I would throw the loose pin into the set. The Rogers' guy marveled at Rock's pin action and dumb-ass Rock began to believe he was good.

Both of them bowled over 200 and I don't remember who won. After we got back to the barracks, I told everyone what I had done and the Rogers guys started laughing and bullshitting with us. We became friends to a point our games Friday and Saturday became more like inter-squad scrimmages than college basketball games.

The Rogers University team wasn't very good and on Friday night we beat them by about twenty points. On Saturday between bowling matches, one of their guys asked Rock to help him with his free throw shooting because Rock hit about nine out of ten the night before. Coach Jenkins walked in the gym while

The Rock was showing the Rogers guy how to shoot. Coach didn't say anything and walked back to his office.

That night, Rogers hit everything they put up and beat us by four. After the game, Coach was not happy. He chastised us about "loafing up and down the court, not having our heads in the game and being a disgrace to Baker College." He then said, "Hell we didn't ask them down here to fraternize with them and teach them how to shoot free throws. You guys played like this was some kind of pick up game in the park. What do you have to say for yourselves?"

No one said anything for a minute. Then Rock, assuming his leadership role, said, "Coach, we didn't play well and we are embarrassed that those guys beat us. As far as the fraternizing and me helping that guy with his free throws, aren't you the one that put us in the barracks together?"

Coach then smiled and said, "That's a good point Riley and it won't happen again. At least you didn't tell me to stick the basketball up my ass."

We played hard in all of our games during the fall semester but lost several tight ball games. Without Jerry Miller, Peters or Slugger had to start and even though they were good players off the bench, neither of them was ready to be a starter. The real bright spot on the team was "Suitcase." He improved every game and was becoming a great rebounder.

Christine didn't say anything to me until after the Thanksgiving break when she stopped me in the cafeteria one day and apologized for John's behavior at the homecoming game. She wore a tight red skirt, a black sweater and was about the sexiest thing I'd ever seen.

"I've broken up with John for good." She said.

"The last time you broke up with him, I was real happy for me. But this time, I'm real happy for you because he is a real jerk."

With a coy smile she said, "You're not a little bit happy for you?"

"I am if I should be," I said.

"You should be," she quickly replied.

"Are you busy tonight?"

Christine came to every basketball game and we began to spend most of our time together. It was just like the spring before. At the football games, however, I don't think she was very impressed with my "ice cream britches."

The football team got a bid to play Southeast Missouri State in the Mid-American Bowl in Springfield Missouri, December 28th. We didn't go home for Christmas because both the football and basketball teams had games over the holidays and The Rock and I had responsibilities with each of them. We did meet Dad and Ethel at Smokey's in Tishomingo on Christmas Day and exchanged gifts with them. Dad and I gave each other bottles of Aqua Velva and we had barbecued ribs for Christmas dinner.

Dad and Ethel seemed to be a little more attentive to each other than I remembered from other times when we were all together. As we started back to Douglas, Rock said, "Big Jim, do you think Mom and your dad might have a thing going?"

I was glad he brought it up because I was thinking the same thing. I knew, however, Ethel was a pretty good catch and Dad had a little "baggage." I would love to have her for a step mom but I didn't know how Rock felt about Dad.

Ethel was in her mid-forties, was a real attractive woman and probably the best person I'd ever met. As far as I knew, she never went out with another man after Rock's dad was killed and had devoted her entire life to Rock and her Church. Dad was fifty years old and was a tall slim guy. I guess women might have thought of him as handsome. He had consumed several barrels of whiskey and smoked a lot of cigarettes, however and it wore on his face. I don't think he ever, actually had a girlfriend after Mom died, but I am reasonably sure he had several flings…mostly with ladies he met at The Deluxe Bar.

Rock adored Ethel and so did I. I loved dad and he loved me more than anything in the world. I was able to look past his transgressions and The Rock and I both knew that had it not been for Dad, neither of us would be playing college basketball.

From the time we were about eight years old until we graduated from high school, Dad worked with us on the fundamentals of the game. This was his only mission in life, other than working in the oil field and he was proud of the two ball players he had developed. Of course, Ethel probably did more to teach us the values of life than Dad, but they both raised us.

It was sort of like Ethel was a parent to both of us and I was pleased when Rock said, "You know, Big Jim, I sure wouldn't mind if Mom and old Tom Green got married. Hell, you might not be a bad brother."

I left Douglas for Missouri with the football team on December 26th and The Rock followed driving the cheerleaders on the 27th. The stadium in Springfield was not all that grand, but, at the time, was the best I'd ever seen. The crowd, which was mostly Missouri people, was by far the largest crowd the football guys had ever played for.

Southeast Missouri had a wide receiver named "Strike" Chandler, who had already been drafted by the 49ers and was supposed to be the best receiver in Division II. Bobby Charles, a quick, young freshman was assigned to cover Strike.

Jerry Miller threw a thirty-yard touchdown pass early in the game and Bobby was doing a hell of job on Strike until he busted an ankle with about four minutes left in the half. Strike got behind Bobby's replacement and scored just before the clock ran out in the first half and we went to the dressing room tied 7 to 7.

Clyde and I were already in the training room working on Bobby's ankle when Coach Norm came in and asked Clyde, "How bad is it?"

"He's done for the year, Coach," Clyde replied.

"I don't know how we're going to beat these guys without a damn defensive back," Coach said under his breath.

I blurted out, "Coach, I have a theory that if a guy is a real good defensive basketball player, he probably could play a pretty good defensive back in football."

"Are you trying to tell me you can cover Strike?" Coach Norm snapped.

"No, sir," I said, "but The Rock can."

"I don't know why I'm standing here listening to some

nineteen year-old round-baller tell me how to coach football." He walked to the door then turned and said "Bobby get your gear off. Green go get The Rock."

When I found Rock, he was lolly-gagging around with The Cheerleader on the sideline. I told him Coach Norm wanted to see him.

"What the hell for?" Rock asked.

"He wants you to play the second half."

"Big Jim, don't you think you've taken your bullshit a little too far?"

"No bullshit, Rock," I quickly replied.

"Well I'm not going to do it," Rock insisted.

"He said if you wanted to keep your scholarship and job, you damn sure better get your ass over there and suit up," I responded.

Rock reluctantly walked with me to the dressing room. He donned Bobby Charles's pads and uniform and I had a good laugh to myself.

Jerry Miller threw two more touchdown passes the second half and Strike never caught another pass. The Kangaroos won the 1960 Mid-American Bowl 21 to 7.

# Chapter Eleven

When we registered for second semester classes after Christmas break, Rock started leaning on me about my career plans. I still pursued my business major and art minor and I didn't have any intentions of doing anything different. The Rock kept telling me I was a poet and should consider writing poems and songs as my life's work. He based most of this on those corny verses I wrote about "Ole Paint." I had written some poetry in high school but it wasn't much better than the "Ole Paint" stuff. He thought, I spontaneously wrote all those verses as he gave me the cue. I never had the heart to tell him I always anticipated his cue about three hours before he gave it and anyone can write a two-line poem in three hours.

In late January of 1961 we were doing pen and ink drawings in art class and I was doing a flamingo standing in some still water surrounded by cattails. I was real pleased with the drawing and was nearly finished when the pen burped as I drew the underside of the bird. A blob of ink ran down in a perfectly straight line and stopped when it touched the ink on the horizontal water line. Dr. Leslie walked by just as this happened and shouted—"Stop."

I quickly said, "I know, I messed up, but the pen burped."

"Sometimes you get lucky," he said, "That's your best work. You couldn't have drawn a better leg for that flamingo if you tried?"

When that damn bird won a blue ribbon in the Douglas Area Art Show, I made one of the few A's of my college career. Rock became convinced I should make career plans to be an artist rather than a poet. I kept telling him I wasn't all that good and that the people who were good, were starving to death as artists. He was persistent and even though he wasn't much of an art critic, I was flattered by his confidence in my artistic talent.

As reinforcement for his support of my endeavors, he came up with "a hell of an idea" during the latter part of basketball season that year. As we took road trips and stayed in cheap motels, he took along two or three of my drawings and replaced the pictures hanging in the motel rooms with my work. He simply took the motel pictures off the wall, disassembled them, placed my stuff over the original picture, reassembled them and hung them back on the wall. He rationalized over the course of the next two basketball seasons; he could put up enough of my work in those motel rooms that I would become a household name. He also framed the one legged flamingo and hung it in our room as our only wall decoration.

The Rock knew that no one ever looked at art in cheap motel rooms and we couldn't take enough road trips to affect the art world. In spite of this, he continued to talk with me about how I could give it back with my art.

"Giving it back" was the central theme in Rock's

philosophy of life. He said to me, "Big Jim, since you're a religious nut, you should understand that when it's time for you to meet your maker, he's going to ask you, 'What did you get down there on earth?' and your going to have to tell him about all the fun you had playing ball, writing songs, drawing pictures and the other great things life gave you. Then he's going to ask you, 'How did you give it back?' And that, Big Jim, is where you better have a damn good answer. You can't declare 'I made a lot money and gave it to the poor', because he's going to ask 'Was this your greatest talent?' and you're going to have to say 'No,' and then he's going to ask you 'Why didn't you give back your best?' And I don't think he's going to accept, 'I was afraid I would starve to death as an artist'."

The Rock's philosophy was hard to argue with, but my confidence in my art wasn't as great as his. I was trying to think about my future but didn't have a clue what it should be. Rock, however, knew what his future was going to be and one day during early February, he came in with a bunch of booklets and pamphlets about the United States Navy. He had always included the Navy in his plans. I suppose it was because his dad had been a Navy man.

In 1961 all young men lived with the reality they were going to be required to do a certain amount of military service. The Rock was the kind of guy who would prefer to pick his military career rather than be drafted by the Army. We were all deferred from the draft as long as we were full time college students. When we graduated, we would need to exercise one of three options: go to graduate school and remain full-time students;

join the military; or get drafted. Plans for me to go to graduate school were pretty much out of the question. I couldn't afford it and unless my grades got significantly better, I doubt if any graduate school would accept me. Rock, on the other hand, was on a track that might get him a fellowship and he certainly could get accepted to any graduate program he applied to. It didn't matter, his plans included the Navy and he had found a program that was perfect.

A Navy recruiter told him he could join the Navy now, stay in school, attend Navy summer camp the next two summers and be sworn in as soon as he graduated. He would then attend Officer's Candidate School for six months and be a commissioned officer for a four-year tour of duty.

"Can you believe this?" he said, "I can prepare myself as an officer, get paid for it and the only thing that changes while I am in college is I work summers for the Navy instead of that gasoline plant in Ferguson."

By his excitement, I knew he had already made up his mind. He didn't push me on it, but suggested I might want to do the same thing. I did give it consideration and it seemed like a pretty good deal since I was going to have to do some kind of military duty anyway. However, I couldn't quite bring myself to make the commitment and deep down I was thinking I could do the National Guard thing after I graduated and have just six months active duty and a few two-week summer camps.

President Kennedy was inaugurated in early January 1961 and his optimism and leadership inspired the whole country and even inspired our basketball. After Jerry Miller joined the team in January, we started to jell into a solid unit. Suitcase continued to get tougher on the boards and all that extra play the first semester made Peters and Slugger better ball players. We played in a district with four other Texas division II colleges. They were Harden University, Wesleyan College, El Paso State University and Kirby College.

Our last eight regular season games would be two games with each of the four district schools, playing four games at home and four on the road. The winner of the district would represent District 9 at the National Tournament in Kansas City March 20th through the 23rd.

We got off to a good start in our run to Kansas City, beating Harden and El Paso State at home and Wesleyan in Abilene. The trip to Midland was a different story. Kirby had also won their first three games. None of the District teams, including us, had winning records going into District. We were seven and eight but had played well the last three or four ball games. We had a little momentum going as we faced Kirby on the road, but they had more. On that February night, with a packed house of screaming fans, they thrashed us 66 to 48. Despite Coach Jenkins' monumental ass chewing and then an effort to motivate us, we were still dejected as we arrived back in Douglas preparing to play Wesleyan the following Saturday night at home.

Wesleyan had been the pre-season pick to win the District but had dropped three out of four the first half of District play. I hadn't been able to buy a bucket against Kirby, but, somehow, I relaxed against the Wesleyan Indians and both Chris Wright and

I had big scoring nights. We won the game handily. This fired us up and we could again see a glimmer of hope in our Kansas City plan. We had to beat El Paso State and Harden and assume Kirby would do the same and then beat Kirby the final regular season game to tie for the District Championship. This would force a one game sudden death play off with the winner going to Kansas City.

We beat Harden in Wichita Falls and that same night the "Basketball Gods" smiled on us. Somehow El Paso State beat Kirby and we were tied for first in the district race. Our Kansas City plan now was to beat El Paso State in El Paso and Kirby at home.

Our biggest problem was we would play El Paso State on Thursday and Kirby on Saturday. It's further from Douglas, Texas to El Paso, Texas, than it is from Douglas, Texas to any place in Nebraska. This road trip would take about twelve hours each way and if we managed to beat El Paso State we were going to be exhausted for the Kirby game.

At halftime the El Paso State Lions had us down by eight and Coach Jenkins was just a little upset as we went to the dressing room. "You guys aren't looking for the open man. You're not going to the boards. You're not getting back on defense. Why in the hell did we drive all the way out here to the middle of nowhere? I could have just called the Kirby coach and told him we weren't interested in going to Kansas City and we could have just hung 'em up and listened to them play on the radio. I'm thinking about calling the local police and having you guys arrested for impersonating a basketball team. You do understand that if we don't beat these guys, Kirby wins the district? I'm going to get some popcorn and you guys can sit in here and decide whether or not you're going to get off your asses and play ball."

No one said anything when Coach walked out, but we all knew it was time to play. In the second half, I don't think anyone on either team got a rebound except Suitcase. He was a man with a mission and everyone just stayed out of his way as he swept the glass clean. We all played incredible defense and we got a bunch of unexpected scoring from Chris, Jerry and Slugger. Rock and I just tried to get them the ball and when the final buzzer sounded we beat El Paso State 64 to 52.

Coach Jenkins tried to get us to sleep as much as possible on the van trip back home. When you put ten big guys in a small van, it's pretty hard to get much sleep.

We got back to Douglas Friday evening where we were met by a raucous group of students, which included mostly cheerleaders and football players. Revived by their enthusiasm, we were excited about playing the big game on Saturday afternoon.

Of course, Christine was in the group that met us as we arrived at the gym. When I walked her back to her dorm, she said she wanted to go out for a movie or something. I convinced her I was tired and would just like to go over to her dorm and relax for a while.

Christine held my hand as we walked. "Jim, do you really love any thing in the world except basketball?"

This question kind of pissed me off and I snapped back,

"Christine, basketball is just a game. What do you think I am...
some kind of dumb insensitive jock?"

"No, No, Jim, don't get me wrong. I think you're one of
the most sensitive guys I've ever known, but I have never seen
anyone love anything more than you love basketball. I love to
watch you play ball.... I wish there was something in my life, I
enjoyed like that."

"Most guys grow up dreaming about being a college
football or basketball player. But, I'm lucky. I grew to be six feet
four inches tall, have a little ability and an old man who taught
me the game. You should have seen us last night in El Paso. We
stunk the place up the first half and Coach was really upset when
we went into the locker room. Then we went out that second half
and we were beautiful... the game was beautiful. Slugger and
Chris couldn't miss; Suitcase was clearing the boards and the rest
of us were just playing great defense and supporting the three of
them. It's not like I need to be the star, but I do have to play. I
can't describe the rush I get when I go to the basket, get air borne
and know that I have about five or six options I can execute in a
split second before I come down. I can put the ball up with my left
hand, my right hand, or dish to two different guys in front of me
or behind my back. For those one or two seconds that I'm in the
air, I feel total control and freedom. Or, if I pull up for that jumper
from twenty feet and it hits nothing but the bottom of the net, I feel
like I own the world."

Christine stopped in front of her dorm and sat down on a
bench by the doorway. "Wow, I don't think I realized how much you
love it. What are you going to do when you get too old to play?"

"Don't think I haven't thought about it." I sat down beside her. "I hope I am good enough to make it as a professional when college is over, but I don't know. I've never played against Division I players except Tulsa and TCU and I don't guess they count."

"Even if you do make it as a pro, that couldn't last more than say…ten years…you will be thirty-two years old. Then what?"

"Why in the hell do you have to be so reasonable? I don't even want to think about the day when I can't play basketball."

"I think I want to be part of your future Jim. I just think you need to have some plans for life that extend beyond basketball."

"You're starting to sound like The Rock, but I know you all are right."

Christine smiled. "You better go get some rest…so we can beat Kirby tomorrow afternoon."

As we went to the dressing room to suit up for the completion of our Kansas City plan, The Rock started talking to everyone.

"Get your game face on Big Jim…leave it all on the floor Suitcase…we got to give 110% guys…let's go to Kansas City."

Although he had always been the team leader, when we hit the floor, he took charge of the game like no point guard ever took charge of a game. He passed with more authority, made some impossible plays look easy and the rest of us responded with probably our best effort ever. Kirby responded in a like manner and the best District 9 basketball game ever played was tied 70 to 70 with 10 seconds left on the clock. Kirby called time out to prepare for the final shot of the game. When they brought the ball in, they quickly set a screen for their best shooter and he took a 23-foot jumper with six seconds on the clock. As soon as he turned the ball loose, I sprinted toward our basket and as I looked back, I saw Suitcase come down with the rebound, flip it to Rock on the outlet and The Rock hit me with a perfect strike as I went in the air and slam dunked the Kangaroos to Kansas City.

When I came down from the dunk, a Kirby player ran into me and I fell to the floor and slid on my butt against the wall pads on the end of the court. Leaning back against the pad, I looked up at the scoreboard. Kangaroos 72--Visitors 70 and the time on the clock showed 00. The Rock was the first one there to pick me up as Christine and The Cheerleader came running behind him, their faces red with tears of excitement running down their cheeks. They started hugging us and only let go when the football players rushed onto the floor, hoisted all of us onto their shoulders and carried us around the court as the fans cheered. As we made our way to the dressing room, Coach Jenkins finally got us to sit down.

"You guys don't know how proud I am. It couldn't have been any better. We'll celebrate tonight but remember, we still have more basketball to play."

He then took the game ball from under his arm and said. "Who do you think should get the game ball?"

Before anyone had an opportunity to say anything, I said, "Coach, why don't we all sign it and you keep it in your office for us."

Rock agreed, as he said, "You keep it in your office, Coach

and anytime you have a team that isn't giving a hundred per cent, you show them this ball and tell what this team did tonight."

As we left the gym, headed for the SUB, The Rock cued it, I soloed it and the guys sang the chorus:

*Goodbye Ole Paint, I'm leaving Cheyenne.*
*I'm going to Montana, to throw the Hoolian.*

*We will take Coach Jenkins and he'll drive the van.*
*We're going to Kansas City, just as we planned.*

*Ride around little doggies, ride around them slow,*
*For the Fiery and Snuffy are raring to go.*

We didn't take the van, however and Coach didn't have to drive either. Chris Wright's dad, Howard, our most loyal fan who came to nearly every game, gave us an incredible present when we qualified for the National Tournament. He chartered a plane for our trip to Kansas City.

With the exception of Chris, it was the first time any of us had ever been on an airplane. Most of us were scared to death except Rock who was completely captivated by it. He spent most of the flight in the cockpit with the pilot. After we got to Kansas City he couldn't stop talking about it.

"Can you believe that plane ride, Big Jim? It was the most incredible thing I've ever done."

"Hell, I was scared to death," I said.

"You need to relax and enjoy it, Big Jim. I was in there with the pilot. He had everything under control. In fact, he was in total control. I can't wait for the flight back."

"I'd like to win a couple of ball game first." I said.

The trip home could have been pretty quick because we were eliminated in the first round of the tournament. After our run in District, our record had improved to 14 and 9, but it was the worst record of any team in the tournament. This meant we were the 16th seed and had to play the number one seed, North Kansas State College, the first round.

The "line" before the game had them as a 30-point favorite, but we did save our pride by playing a real gutsy ball game, coming up short by only 6 points. Coach Jenkins was proud of us and as we stayed to watch the rest of the tournament games, we held our heads high. We were all sophomores and the guys were all talking about winning it all next year.

As I watched the other games, however and saw the talent the teams in the semifinals and finals had, I knew we had to have at least one more player to get to that level. That player was going to have to be as big as Suitcase, as quick as The Rock and a great shooter. We could play on the level with the teams in District 9 and we might win one or two games in the National Tournament if we caught the right breaks, but none of us had the talent to carry the team to that ultimate level.

Even though we lost our only game at the National Tournament, the trip was the greatest adventure we had ever been on. We loved our flight home and Rock, again, spent all his time in the cockpit as the rest of us were already turning our trip to Kansas City into some of the most fantastic bullshit ever.

When we returned to campus, my preoccupation with basketball had caused my grades and love life to suffer a bit. My love life revived quickly because with Christine it was like a conquering hero had returned from battle, with all the lust and passion that goes with it. Granted, we were only gone four days, but I was grateful Christine was such a romantic. The professors, even though they were supportive of my basketball efforts, were not all that sympathetic with the fact that I had a mountain of makeup work to do. I did get it done and by late spring Christine and I were into a pretty serious relationship. At least it was the most serious romance I had ever been involved in.

Not only was Rock constantly on my butt about my plans for life, Christine now joined in. Christine's philosophy was a little different than Rock's, however. Where Rock's was based on "giving it back," Christine's was based on "getting it all" and mostly for her. She talked about me climbing the corporate ladder, building my own business, or going to work for her father.

When I shared her ideas with The Rock, he got almost as mad at her as when he told Whiskey to stick the basketball up his ass. He did know I cared for Christine and never let her know he was upset with her.

Our second year of college was nearly perfect, until the end of the school year. We won the district basketball championship, won the Mid-American Bowl in football, made our grades and both had love lives. We tried to get Slugger to fight Golden Gloves again. Since he had broken his hand the year before and now had a pretty serious girlfriend, he decided not to jeopardize his love life in the ring. Alex continued to publish *The First Amendment*, but after he started going to all the football and basketball games, he became totally consumed with sports and the paper became mostly a sport's page. The reporting even became somewhat credible. He came to every game and Coach Jenkins let him go on one road trip with us.

One of the fraternities had an all school party to celebrate the first anniversary of the burial of Katy, but The Rock and I were smart enough not to attend.

# Chapter Twelve

About three weeks before the close of our sophomore year, the guy on the desk in the lobby buzzed our room with a phone call. Students didn't have private telephone lines in their rooms in 1961 and if you received a phone call, it came to the main desk of the dorm and you had to walk to the lobby to take it. Rock went to take the call and then came back to the room and said it was for me.

"Who is it?" I asked.

"My Mom," he responded.

"What's she calling me for?" I quipped.

"Just take the call, Big Jim. She's got something she needs to tell you," Rock said.

When I got to the phone, Ethel said, "I am sorry I have to tell you this but Luther Jones found your dad slumped over in his truck on the Painter Lease this afternoon. Luther took him to the hospital, but Tom died before they got there. The doctor said he had a massive heart attack."

I asked her the stupid questions, "Are you sure?... How?... Why?"

I then realized I just needed to go home. Rock took the

phone and talked briefly to Ethel and then he hugged me. For all
we had been to each other, it was the first time we ever hugged.

I walked back to the room and began to pack my bag. The
Rock came in a few minutes later and started packing his too.

"What are you doing?" I asked.

"What does it look like I am doing? I'm going to drive my
best friend home to help him bury his dad."

"You don't have to do that. You'll miss class. I'll be okay."

"This isn't your decision, Big Jim. The Cheerleader and
Christine are going too." Rock said in a somewhat firm manner.

When we picked the girls up at their dorm, both The
Cheerleader and Christine were crying and for some strange
reason, I felt a need to comfort them. When you're twenty years
old, people you know aren't supposed to die. My grandparents
had all died when I was very young and my mom died when I was
ten, but I had never really thought about losing Dad.

As we drove, the girls asked questions about Dad and it
made Rock and me feel better to talk about the way he had taught
us to play basketball. About watching the fights with him on TV
and how he had all of those newspaper clippings taped to his
living room wall.

The Cheerleader had been to Ferguson with The Rock and
had met Dad, but Christine and I hadn't quite reached the point in
our relationship of meeting each other's parents. I knew Ferguson,
Oklahoma and the people she was about to meet were going to be
a total shock to her.

Christine had grown up in North Dallas and had spent

her childhood surrounded with a huge home, new cars, private schools and live-in domestic help. Her father was the chairman of the board of one of the largest banks in Dallas. She was an only child and had never lacked for anything. Because of all of this, I kind of felt sorry for her. There is no way I would have traded my parents or my childhood for hers.

It was midnight when we arrived in Ferguson and we drove to Ethel's house where she waited up for our arrival. She came out in the yard and hugged me as soon as I got out of the car. She then hugged Rock and The Cheerleader and Rock introduced Christine. After Ethel gave Christine her hug and told her what a great guy I was, we went in the house, where The Rock and I had spent a major part of our lives.

The house was a three room "shot gun" with three rooms built in a straight line. A small bathroom had been added on during the Forties. It was neat and clean with a wholesome aroma of food cooking in the kitchen. Christine had never eaten chicken-fried steak and fried potatoes with onions, so Ethel fed us probably the best meal Christine ever ate.

"There's nothing you can do till morning, but you can go to the funeral home first thing and make arrangements." Ethel said.

"I should have come home more. I haven't been home the entire school year. The last time I saw Dad, was in Tishomingo at Christmas." I said, trying to deal with my guilt.

"When you didn't come home for the holidays because you were playing ball, you did exactly what Tom wanted you to do. Your ball playing brought him one of the few pleasures of his life."

"At least he went quick and didn't have to lay in a hospital bed and suffer like Mom. He did love to watch Rock and me play ball. I wish he could have seen more of our games."

"He is really the reason we are playing basketball. But when I think of him, I'll always think about those fights we watched on Friday night TV." Rock said.

The girls listened as Ethel, Rock and I reminisced about Dad. About 2:00 P.M., Ethel said, "The girls can sleep on the couch here and you boys go to Jimmy's. You should go to the funeral home early tomorrow morning." Ethel was the only person in the world I allowed to call me Jimmy.

When we got to the house, it was open and was just as Dad had left it that morning. With the exception of more of my newspaper clippings taped to the wall, it was just as I had left it the previous summer. The house was similar to Ethel and Rock's except an additional bedroom had been added when Mom and Dad built the bathroom. There was also a washroom in the back that had been converted to my bedroom when I was about six. I was born in this house and until I went to Baker College, it was the only place I had ever lived.

Rock and I talked very little as we walked around and looked at the things we had seen a thousand times before, like Mom's picture, the chrome kitchen table, a trophy Dad got in high school for making all conference and a magazine picture of Oscar Robertson pinned above my bed. At this moment they all took on a special meaning – they were all that was left of Dad. No, I was all that was left of Dad.

I didn't sleep much and finally got out of bed about 6:00 AM and fixed breakfast for the two of us, just as I had done the previous summer for Dad. We dressed and went to the funeral home at 8:00.

Mr. Greer, the funeral director, greeted us at the door and told us if we wished, we could view Dad's body prior to making the funeral arrangements. As we stood in front of his casket and looked at Dad, neither of us said anything for about five minutes.

Rock put his hand on my shoulder. "That's enough Big Jim."

We then walked into Mr. Greer's office and sat down.

Dad and I didn't really have a church. Before Mom died, she took me to the Methodist Church nearly every Sunday, but Dad wasn't much of a churchgoer and as a result I wasn't either. Even though Rock called me "the religious nut," Ethel had taken him to the Baptist Church every Sunday of his life.

"Which Church would you prefer for the service?" Mr. Greer asked.

I thought about The Rock and me playing basketball as kids. "The First Christian Church," I said.

"Are you a member there?" Mr. Greer asked, knowing damn well I wasn't.

"No, but I spent more time in there as a kid than any other Church."

He then asked about where Dad was born, what year, his parents' names and other information related to the obituary.

"Is there any special music you would like to request?" he continued to question.

When Rock saw the blank look on my face he said, " 'Amazing Grace' is nice Big Jim...your Dad would like that."

We then set a time, selected pallbearers, finished other details and Mr. Greer said I should come by after the funeral and he would have my bill totaled. For some reason, this came as a shock to me because I hadn't thought about paying for final expenses.

I was sure Dad didn't have life insurance because he always said he didn't believe in it. I also knew, as a product of the depression, he didn't trust banks and didn't have a bank account. Mr. Greer had given me the personal items that were in Dad's pockets when he died and they consisted of an old pocketknife, a twenty-dollar bill, a dime and four pennies. When I checked at home under the mattress where he kept his money, I found $126.

When we got to Ethel's house, Mr. Burnett was there. He shook my hand and told me how sorry he was. Mr. Burnett kind of kept an eye on Dad. He was someone Dad could talk to and trust and they were, in an odd sort of way---friends. We talked about Dad for a few minutes; then I asked Mr. Burnett if we could go outside. As we stepped onto the porch, I asked, "How much does a funeral cost?"

When he told me eight or nine hundred dollars, I nearly choked. I explained to him my Dad's "estate," plus what I had was less than $200.

It was then Mr. Burnett eased some of my anxiety. "Jim, you're going to have more than a nine hundred dollar funeral bill because there are some other bills of your Dad's that need to be paid. The house and pickup are worth something and if you sell them, you'll be more than able to meet your obligations."

"I think Mr. Greer expects his money tomorrow," I said.

Mr. Burnett then calmly said, "Yes he probably does and he will offer to clear the bill for the deed to the house, but the house is worth at least twice as much as the funeral bill and you're not going to let him have it. We'll go to the bank this afternoon and I'll co-sign a note with you for enough to pay Mr. Greer. When you come home for your summer job, you can live in the house, clear your things out of it and sell it at the end of August."

On the way to the bank I asked Mr. Burnett why he would have to co-sign my note.

He simply said, "Because the bank doesn't know you as well as I do."

When we returned to Ethel's, people had begun to come by with food and condolences. This is something friends do in small towns. I don't think they do this in the cities. As I greeted old friends, Christine stood right there by my side and even though she had never been involved with working people and had never been in a house that humble, every person she met treated her with more dignity and respect than she thought was possible. I think for the first time in her life, she felt good about something other than herself.

The funeral was a comfort to all of us. The minister was a kind, well-educated man who seemed to know exactly what words to say. Rock was right about "Amazing Grace." Dad would have liked it.

We buried Dad next to Mom in the Ferguson South Cemetery. In Ferguson there was the South Cemetery and there was the North Cemetery. The working people were buried in the South Cemetery and the well to do in the North Cemetery. Because there were a lot more working people than well to do in Ferguson, the South Cemetery was much larger and it was where Dad belonged. In the future, even if I become the richest man in the world, the South Cemetery will also be where I belong.

When we got back to Baker College, there were only two weeks left in the semester and I was again behind in my class work. I had to work my butt off for finals but the time passed quickly as I prepared to go home, work and dispose of Dad's things. The Rock was going to the Navy summer training and it would be the first time since we were six we would be apart.

My relationship with Christine was about as good as it could be, but we decided we would wait until the fall for me to meet her parents. She couldn't quite understand why I had to go home for the summer, because paying off two thousand dollars worth of debt, really didn't register with her as anything significant.

The Cheerleader, Christine and I took Rock to the airport and he flew out of Dallas Love Field to someplace in Ohio for his summer camp. I, then, returned home to Ferguson to attempt to get my finances in order.

Coach Norm talked to me just prior to me leaving for the summer and asked if I would be head trainer for the football team that fall. This meant I would have to report back to school two weeks early for the beginning of practice. It was the second week in June when I got home, so I had a lot to get done in the next two months.

It was very lonely at home and I missed Dad, Christine and The Rock. I did meet Christine in Oklahoma City at The Cheerleader's home for one weekend and The Rock and I exchanged two or three letters. I was working fifty hours a week for the oil field construction company, but with my shortened summer, I was only going to make about five hundred dollars. I spent the first few evenings of the summer going through Dad's and my personal items and putting them into boxes. We didn't have much, but there were a few dishes, pots and pans, picture albums, old high school yearbooks and some tools.

I don't guess it was such a big job but as I sorted through things, I would dwell on obscure items and reminisce about Mom and Dad. I really could not remember Mom as well as I wanted to and the memories were not distinct occasions such as Christmas or my first day of school. When I opened a little jewelry box, which was about the only personal item of hers that remained, it was not the contents of the box that made me melancholy. A faint sweet odor radiated from the old keepsake and I felt almost as if she was in the room. It had been over ten years since she had died. I remembered her getting sick when I was in the third grade and Doctor Meadows telling Dad she had cancer. I didn't know what cancer was but knew it wasn't good. After a long and agonizing illness, I felt guilty when she died because of my relief for her and the end of her suffering. I was also angry with her for leaving us. As I watched Dad grieve, I tried to block everything out and pretend it never happened. I wasn't successful, however, because when I opened the little box some ten years later as a grown man…I let go of something I didn't even know I had harbored for half my life. I could see her in the kitchen in her apron and the odor of fried potatoes and onions seemed to fill the air. I could hear her voice as she sang those old songs from the "Hit Parade," and I remembered her putting a poultice of Vick's salve on my chest to help me sleep when I had a cold. For the first time since she died I did not feel angry about her death. I allowed myself to be glad she was my mom and to remember her, the way she deserved to be remembered.

As I went through Dad's things, I had feelings of sadness; his recent death was still very much on my mind. I could see myself dealing with it in a much healthier manner, however. Dad had fought in World War II as an infantryman in the Army. He never talked about it and I knew very little of his experiences. As I opened a box of old letters he wrote to Mom during the war and began to read them, I realized for the first time the great debt we owe to their generation.

I also realized for the first time how deeply he loved my mom. The focus of every letter was not the adversities he was encountering but how much he missed her. He expressed himself in those letters in a way I truly did not know he had in him. I wished I had found them before his funeral; we could have shared them with his friends.

Reading Dad's letters to Mom must have inspired me. I spent the remainder of the evening writing letters. I was at peace with myself as I wrote The Rock.

*June 20, 1961*

*Dear Rock,*

*Things are pretty lonesome without you around. Are you an Admiral yet? I know you aren't, but I bet you will be someday. I have been going through Mom and Dad's stuff and believe it or not it has made me feel better about them. They were pretty neat people and I am proud they were my parents. You were right that night in the snowstorm when you said, "There have never been two guys in this world that have been given more or enjoyed life as much as you and me. We have brains, talent and opportunities." We have all of this because we had good parents. I know Dad wasn't perfect but he was a hell of a good guy. I'll let you read some of the letters he wrote to Mom when you come home.*

*I have been playing in a few pick-up games at the park. Playing two years of college ball has made me pretty awesome out there with those high school kids. They aren't quite as good as those guys from Kansas at the National Tournament. I met Christine down at The Cheerleader's house last weekend. It was good to see her and The Cheerleader is about to die for you to come home.*

*I cleaned out Dad's clothes and gave them to the Salvation Army. I did keep that big heavy work jacket of his, just in case we get caught in another snowstorm. I am going to try to sell the pickup and the furniture and hold off till the end of summer to sell the house. If I don't get this stuff sold I am going to be in a hell of a bind. I see your Mom every few days. She said I could store a few boxes at her house after I get the other things sold. I look forward to getting this summer behind me and getting back to Baker College. If Coach Jenkins will go out and recruit us a "super stud," we just might make some noise next year.*

*Let me know about Navy life,*

*Big Jim*

It was the first week in July when I received Rock's answer to my letter.

*Big Jim,*

*You never cease to amaze me. I know I give you hell about not having any plans, but you always seem to take everything that comes your way in stride. There is no doubt in my mind that you will get all those things sold and will be back at Baker College next year hitting twenty-foot jumpers and bullshitting me about how good you are. I am glad you got to see the ladies in OK City and thanks for checking in on Mom.*

*That's something about those old letters you found.*

*Thanks for saying you will share them with me. You're right about our parents and even though I never knew my Dad, all of them gave us the things we need to make good lives for ourselves. As time goes on, I am more and more convinced that life is not about status, position, or wealth. It is about relationships. It is about our commitment to other people and their commitment to us. Just think about what our parents, Coach Jenkins, Mr. Burnett, Christine, The Cheerleader and all the guys on the team mean to us. You can't put a price tag on that.*

*You may not have a plan, but you do have great relationships and you are the best guy I know.*
*(Notice I said guy...remember I have a girl friend that's the best.) Get that stuff sold and I'll see you back in Kangaroo land.*

*Rock*

As I continued to sort, I kept out enough cookware, towels and such to last the summer and then stored the rest of the things in the shed behind Ethel's house. I put a For Sale sign on Dad's pickup and then started concentrating on selling the furniture.

A man came by a few days later and wanted to know what I was asking for the pickup. I told him $175 and he, of course, offered $150. One hundred and fifty was what I wanted, but if I had said that, he would have offered $125. We made a deal, but I had a deep sense of sadness as he drove Dad's old truck away. After consulting with Mr. Burnett, I ran a classified add in the *Ferguson Journal*, listing the house for $2,000. Mr. Burnett appraised the house for me and said it should bring at least $1,800. Again I priced it for a little more than I was willing to take.

We didn't have very much furniture but I thought it was worth at least $200. After no one showed interest in it for about three weeks, I asked a used furniture dealer to bid on it. When he offered me $35 for all of it, I kicked him out and took it to the Salvation Army along with Dad's clothes.

When a young couple with two little kids, offered $1,850 for the house around the first of August, I sold it and gave them possession the next day.

I moved in with Ethel for my final ten days of the summer and after I paid off the bank and Dad's other bills, I had about $200 plus what I had earned and saved from my summer job. It was going to be tough for me to make it through my junior year of college, but I'd find a way.

Those ten days I spent with Ethel were among the most relaxing and peaceful days of my life. Even though I insisted she not do it, she cooked for me every meal. She did let me buy some of the food, but under no circumstances would she let me prepare it. She told me about Rock's dad, how they met and how much Rock was like him. She also said Rock's dad and my dad were best friends in high school. Dad had talked about this before, but it was nice hearing her stories about them. Even though I had known her nearly all my life and she was like a second mother to me, I really didn't know much about her. I asked her why she and my

Dad never got together?

"Jimmy, your Dad was a good man who had a hard life and you know we did go out some. I even think he was finally getting over your mom. You know, he took me to that ball game in Tulsa and to Tishomingo to meet you guys last Christmas. We went out for dinner several times and I had started cooking some meals for him. I think with time we might have even got married, but we weren't given the time. I am grateful for the occasions I spent with him and I'll always regret waiting until it was too late to get together with your Dad."

As I drove back to Douglas August 14, 1962, I thought, *that dorm room in Austin Hall is the only home I have.* But before I allowed myself too much self-pity, I said out loud, "But it's a hell of a good home." I wondered if I would ever go back to Ferguson. I knew I would, just to visit Ethel.

# Chapter Thirteen

*"I ride an old paint and I lead an old Dan,*
*I'm goin' to Montana to throw a hoolian. "*

-

When I arrived at Baker College, I found I didn't actually have a home in Austin Hall. It was August 15 and the dorms wouldn't be open until August 27. I went over to Coach Norm's office and he told me I would have to move into the barracks with the football team until the 27th.

"The football team will not move in until tomorrow," he said, "So you will have the whole barracks to yourself tonight." Coach Norm then put me to work inventorying supplies and equipment. About five o'clock he let me move my things into the barracks and I could see it was not going to be a great night because the barracks were pretty big and I hated to be alone.

I called Christine in Dallas and she said she would drive up to see me. We made arrangements to meet in front of the gym at eight o'clock and since we hadn't seen each other in over a month, we were pretty excited. I was back on the same per diem allotment we had during the holidays for basketball, so when she arrived we went to my designated café for dinner.

"Will anyone be coming in the gym tonight?" She asked over dinner.

"No, I don't think so."

"I don't want you to have to stay in that gym alone…why don't I just stay with you?"

This seemed like a "hell of an idea" to me, so we went back to the gym.

Christine left about seven o'clock the next morning, wanting to leave before anyone else arrived. She wasn't successful, because later that morning, Coach Norm ask me, "What was that Blankenship girl doing in the gym early this morning?"

When I told him I didn't know, he just looked at me and smiled.

The football players started moving in about noon and were scheduled for their first workout at five o'clock. I spent the day getting the training room ready and had about 120 ankles to wrap at four o'clock. Coach Jenkins came in and helped me and we got them on the field by five. He told me he would help me until school started and then try to find an assistant trainer. This job as head trainer was going to be pretty demanding until football was over, but after that, I had my room and board made for the year. The team worked out two times a day at 7:00 AM and 5:00 PM. I spent my free time in the gym working out and shooting baskets. Coach Norm caught Jerry Miller playing one on one with me during an afternoon break and nearly had a stroke. Jerry was probably going to make All-American, as quarterback and

Coach didn't think much of the idea of him risking injury playing basketball.

When The Rock and I hung out in that old boxer's gym during high school, I worked out on the speed bag, did squats with the bar bells and jumped a lot of rope. I believed these activities improved my jumping, my coordination and my quickness and, as a result made me a better basketball player. I continued to do these things after we came to Baker College and the life I had during those last few days of August was perfect. I did my job, doing something I enjoyed, worked out, ate all my meals in a café, hung out with the guys and saw Christine every couple of days.

I moved into the dorm August 27th when it opened for new student orientation. The football team went to one workout a day and this cut my workload in half. Everyone would return on the 29th and I couldn't wait for The Rock to get back and to tell me all his Navy stories.

I was shooting baskets on the afternoon of the 28th when someone came up behind me and said, " Big Jim, I'll bet I can hit six out of ten free throws blindfolded."

I turned and said, "You've never done it before."

The Rock replied, "You lying son of a bitch."

We then, grabbed each other and hugged for the second time in our lives.

We played one on one for about two hours, laughing and talking the entire time. When we finished, I helped him carry his things into the dorm, where we cranked up Hank Williams and started our junior year at Baker College.

The Rock said the Navy training was pretty mindless and you didn't do any thinking for yourself. You just did what you were told and each day was filled with physical training and classroom activities with a whole lot of regimentation. He told me about one guy he talked out of going AWOL. He said the guy got so homesick he nearly lost his mind. Rock convinced him they were really only going to be there two months and if he left, it could screw up his whole life. Knowing The Rock, I bet he came up with some "hell of an idea" that kind of got the guy liking the place and he was probably home sick to see The Rock by the time he got home.

He told me about this other guy that went to a bar with them on a Saturday night, put a move on a local's girl friend and ended up in a hell of a fight. Rock found out later the only reason the guy put a move on the girl was to antagonize the local and he considered Saturday night to be a failure if he didn't get into a fight.

I think The Rock enjoyed the physical training and he was in good shape when he arrived. Good enough to kick my ass in one on one.

I didn't have much to report to Rock other than my sales negotiations on Dad's stuff. He was glad I had spent some time with his mom and was feeling guilty for not being able to spend much time with her himself. He flew into Oklahoma City when he returned from summer camp. The Cheerleader picked him up at the airport and they did spend a couple of days with Ethel.

All the guys were back and everyone had lots of new bullshit to report from their summer's activities. Most everyone had gone home and worked for the summer. Alex went to summer school in San Antonio and Chris worked as an intern in his dad's real estate business. Slugger worked every summer "measuring cotton." Measuring cotton was something the department of agriculture did, but I never figured out what the hell it was. Peters was at the same training with The Rock, but they were in different squadrons and never saw each other. All- American worked in Paul's Valley for a machine shop and got into a hot romance with the boss's daughter but broke up with her prior to coming back to school. He said he was going to have to find a different job next summer because the machine shop guy damn sure wouldn't hire him back.

A few days after classes started, The Rock and I were again in the gym playing one on one. We noticed a big, good looking black kid come in and start shooting at the other end. We stopped, went over and introduced ourselves. His name was Billy Joe Jackson and he said he was a transfer student from Eastern Arkansas Junior College. He also said Coach Jenkins told him about us, but he had been too shy to look us up.

Billy Joe was the first black student ever admitted to Baker College and, of course, was a little bit uncomfortable with the idea.

"So far, about the only thing I want to do is go home." Billy Joe said.

"We felt the same way when we first came to Baker College. We'll show you the ropes. Don't worry about it...Do you all want to play a game?" I said, not waiting for an answer.

"Here's the rules -- We play two on one, but the two man can only rebound. The guy who gets the rebound becomes the offense and keeps it as long as he scores or rebounds. And Billy Joe, if we work real hard, we can keep Rock on defense all afternoon."

Billy Joe was the greatest raw talent I'd ever seen. He was 6'5", could jump out of the gym, was quick as a cat and even though his mechanics needed some work, he could shoot a little.

When we finished, I asked him, "What dorm are you in?"

" Houston Hall," he replied.

"We've got to get you moved to Austin Hall as soon as possible," I said.

"Do you have a campus job?"

"I'm cleaning the science building," he responded.

"You need to check with Coach Norm and see if you can be my assistant trainer for the football team."

"I don't know anything about being a football trainer."

"It will take about thirty minutes of my intensive instruction for you to know as much as me," I laughed.

Billy Joe felt better about Baker College after that first meeting in the gym. We got him moved to Austin Hall, next door to The Rock and me and rooming with Alex. Coach Norm also gave him the assistant trainer's job. Billy Joe became a regular in our room with Hank, the slots and the bullshit.


The Rock and I had gone to a high school that integrated in 1956 and we had friends who were black. We were naïve enough to think after integration in '56, everything was right with the world and all injustices had been taken care of. One night, shortly after

Billy Joe moved in with Alex, we were in a bullshit session and Alex told us we needed to listen to Billy Joe's story about growing up as a black kid in segregated Arkansas. Billy Joe was reluctant to talk about it and told us the only reason he would was because we were the first white people he ever met that treated him as an equal. "You guys…everyone of you on the team and Alex…from the very beginning gave me the same respect you give each other. And you give me the same bullshit you give each other."

Billy Joe continued, "What Alex is talking about is; I went through grade school in a four room shack that didn't even have indoor plumbing. The teachers were black women and most of them hadn't even graduated from high school. They did their best and some of them were pretty darn good but it was hard for us to understand the white kids in brand new modern schools with fancy football uniforms and marching bands when the only thing we had were their hand-me-down textbooks and a path to the privy. We could not go to the public swimming pool or the movie houses. In fact, my dad got an old movie projector and showed us movies in the schoolhouse on Saturday night until the white school board decided it was taking too much electricity and made him quit. We were not allowed to go in the front door of the stores and shops and we drank at water fountains that said 'colored only'. When we integrated the schools, the only reason I was not totally rejected was the fact that I could play basketball. Hell, they shut down Little Rock High School for a whole year just to keep black kids out."

I guess we all already knew what Billy Joe was telling us but never had the courage to admit it to ourselves. I told Billy Joe,

"I feel bad and guilty for what happened to you and your family, but for as long as I live, you are my friend and you are going to get my respect...and my bullshit." The others nodded in approval as a tear ran down Billy Joe's cheek.

All the guys, The Rock, Suitcase, Chris, Slugger, Peters, Billy Joe and I played basketball every afternoon in the gym. Alex would even come over and watch. This was quite a turn around for a guy who wouldn't even go to a game the year before. One day early on, Billy Joe asked me, "What have you done to get to where you can jump so high?"

"My God man, you can jump higher than me. What did you do?" I responded.

"I'm taller than you... You get off the floor higher than I do... What do you do?"

"Squats and jump rope."

"Will you show me how to do it?"

"Sure and if you want, I'll help you with your shooting."

"What's wrong with my shooting?"

"Hey, your shooting's okay, but if you'll square up every time, spread your hands on the ball, keep your elbows in, release from your forehead, let the ball roll off your finger tips and follow through with your arm straight as a string and your thumb pointing down through the basket--you'll be a hell of lot better shooter."

Billy Joe started working hard on the squats, the jump rope and on the shooting. In him, we could all see that "super player" we needed to win it all and as a result, all of us worked harder.

After I helped Billy Joe with shooting the basketball,

The Rock decided my career plans should involve coaching and teaching, rather than art and the only way I could possibly "give it back" was by teaching kids to play ball. It was now harder for me to defend myself because Rock knew a hell of a lot more about coaching than he knew about art.

One night just before we went to sleep he came out with his "Big Jim, did you know that." As I waited for him to give me some information I cared nothing about, he surprised me with, "You probably know more about shooting a basketball than anyone I know."

"What the hell are you talking about?"

"I am talking about what you told Billy Joe about squaring up, spreading his hands, keeping his elbows in, releasing from his forehead, letting the ball roll off his finger tips and following through with his arm straight as a string and his thumb pointing down through the basket," he responded.

"That's pretty much how you do it."

"Yeah and you do it about as perfect as it can be done," Rock continued to compliment me. "And you can teach other players to do it. Billy Joe is almost perfect now and you understand the whole game, not just shooting. You're a natural teacher and that, Big Jim, is the way you need to 'give it back'."

Neither of us said anything for a few minutes.

"What do you think?" Rock asked, as he broke the silence.

"I think you would be a lot better shooter, if you'd keep your elbows in."

"Why did you wait till now to tell me," he quickly responded.

"Maybe I didn't want you to be as good as me."

"You lying son of a bitch." We both laughed and then went to sleep.

As Rock and Christine continued to talk to me about the future, I stayed pretty noncommittal with both of them, trying to maintain my carefree attitude. Christine was a senior and would graduate in the spring. I think she was truly in love with me and I was in love with her. Her demands on my future planning were becoming more urgent. She visualized us getting married the summer after I graduated, moving to Dallas and me following in her father's footsteps. At this point, I hadn't even met her father and had no idea how he felt about putting me to work or following in his footsteps.

The first two years I was in college, I thought college life would go on forever, playing ball and hanging out with the guys. I even harbored a dream that I was good enough to play professional basketball. After watching those really good teams and players in Kansas City, I knew I had only two more seasons of basketball left. The Rock was probably right about me pursuing a coaching career. He may have overestimated my potential as a teacher just as he overestimated my artistic ability but I did love playing sports, teaching others how to play and figuring out things like convincing Coach Norm to play Rock in that bowl game.

My course of study, however, was leading to a degree in business administration and even though I hated accounting and economics, I was interested in sales, marketing and management. I could see myself working as a salesman after graduation and even Rock admitted, with my bullshit, I'd be a natural.

What I never discussed with Rock and Christine was the difficulty I had making career decisions when I was concentrating on coming up with enough money just to finish school. I felt like I had enough to get through the junior year, but when it was over, I was going to have to rent an apartment for the summer and get a job that would allow me to save enough for my senior year. I had always worked in the summer but had never had to pay for room and board while I worked. I may have been stupid or just too proud, but I wasn't going to accept any gifts or loans from Christine or her parents. I would make it, but it would be on my terms and through my own efforts.

# Chapter Fourteen

The football team had a decent season, winning six, losing two and tying one. They did not get a bowl bid, but Jerry Miller made second team All-American and Billy Joe and I had a big time as the team's trainers. One day while the guys were working out, we were playing catch on the sideline. Coach Norm came over and in a kidding manner said, "You guy's wouldn't consider letting me get new trainers and you coming out for the team, would you?"

" We're getting our room and board to be trainers and we'll play on the team for the same," I said.

He laughed, "There's no justice. The best two athletes in school are the damn trainers, or I should say Billy Joe's the best athlete in school. Green, you're just the best coach. You don't think you could get The Rock out here to play defensive back do you?"

"I don't think so Coach"

"Get your asses back to work," he laughed. Coach Norm was a lot like Coach Jenkins. He knew how to make people feel like they were worth something. When I think about it, most of the people at the college were that way and that quality, I think, was the most important thing I learned at Baker College.

People in my life like Mr. Burnett, Coach Jenkins, Coach Norm and other teachers in high school and college continued to give me hope and encouragement. They did the same for The Rock and a thousand other kids. The Rock and I talked about it a lot, but his understanding of it was far greater than mine.

Christine and The Cheerleader's sorority was having their fall dinner dance at Texoma Lodge. We were excited to be their dates and looked forward to the event. The Rock and I always had a bit of a problem when it came to more formal functions. We really didn't have suitable clothes for such occasions. The only suit I had was the one I graduated from high school in, which was now too small and never was in style. We would usually borrow something from friends and I will always be grateful to Chris Wright for keeping me in a wardrobe during college. Rock, however, bought a new suit with his Navy money and wasn't going to have to borrow this time.

One day, just before the dance, Coach Jenkins overheard me ask Chris if I could borrow a sports coat. The next day, Coach called me in his office and said, "You have a pair of gray slacks don't you?"

"Yes sir," I said.

He then went over to the closet and took out a navy blue blazer and a pair of nearly new black shoes. "This blazer kind of makes me feel like a college kid and I don't wear it much, see if it fits you."

I tried it on and it was perfect. Coach then handed the shoes to me. "These shoes are too tight on me but I think they'll fit you. Why don't you take them too?"

I was so overwhelmed I couldn't say anything.

"It would probably be best not to say where you got this stuff because I'm really not supposed to be giving my ball players clothes, but I want you to know that I didn't give them to you because you're a player. Now get your ass out of here."

The sensitivity of Coach Jenkins was amazing. The way he handled himself and his ability to always say and do the right thing was something to be emulated. I am sure all of us would take this with us the rest of our lives and hopefully do things ourselves…worthy of emulation.

We officially started basketball practice around the first of November. We were thankful Whiskey got his Masters degree and was gone. When football was over in mid November, All-American Jerry Miller joined us. We, of course, never referred to him as Jerry Miller again; he was simply "All-American." Billy Joe was playing at a level that was almost mind-boggling and it became apparent after a few days that we had a hell of a team.

Each year when basketball season started there would be a few guys come out for the team who had never played much basketball, or who had played at a low level. In the fall of 1961 we had a bunch of guys come out for the team. I think it was because we had won the district and went to the National tournament the year before. Most of these new prospects were good guys and it became apparent to them in a few days they really didn't have much of a chance to play varsity basketball. Some of them quit, but others remained the entire season and were content to never suit up for a game and to contribute what they could as members of the practice squad. Those who stayed were our biggest supporters and loved just being a part of the group.

There was this one guy, however, Robert Caruth, who stayed out for the team for a while, but pouted everyday when Coach didn't practice him with the starters. He was one of the better walk-ons but was slow with pretty marginal skills.

Robert knocked on our door one night and asked if he could come in. He sat down on the edge of Rock's bed and said he thought he would quit basketball.

"If that's what you think you need to do," said Rock, "you need to tell Coach Jenkins, not us."

"I just thought you guys might help me work through it,"

"Work through what?" I said.

"Well, I think Coach has already decided that you guys who played last year and Billy Joe are going to get all the playing time this year and he won't give me a chance."

"Let me tell you something," Rock said. "Coach is going to play the group of people that he thinks can win ball games and if you get out there and work your but off instead of pouting around and feeling sorry for yourself, he might give you a shot."

"You don't understand," Robert argued, "Coach plays favorites and he won't play me because my family's wealthy and he favors you poor guys."

"Hold on man," I quickly responded, "he plays Chris

Wright and he sure isn't a poor guy. Let me say again what Rock said….If you get out there and work your but off, he might play you, but that's not guaranteed. He is still going to play the guys he thinks can win and that's the deal whether you like it of not…How much time did you spend shooting baskets in the summer when you were a kid?"

"I didn't shoot baskets in the summer did you? And besides what has that got to do with it?"

"I'll tell you what it has to do with it. I spent at least four hours a day every summer day for about ten years shooting baskets. That doesn't make me any better person than you, but it does give me an edge in making the starting lineup at Baker College. Don't come in here feeling sorry for yourself about not getting to play on the basketball team. You've got everything going for you. You've got money, good parents, good looks; you're smart, talented and you are attending one of the best colleges in the country. If you're so damn insecure, you have to start on the basketball team with absolutely no effort on your part, then you need to find a hole somewhere and crawl in it and die."

Robert said nothing as he stormed out of the room.

Rock leaned back in his chair, rubbed his chin and said, "Damn Big Jim, you were a little tough on Robert."

"I guess I was. But what the hell is a guy like Robert thinking? I just can't feel sorry for someone that has everything in the world going for him, coming in here whining about Coach Jenkins playing favorites to poor kids."

"I didn't say you were wrong, Big Jim, I just said you were pretty tough on Robert."

As it turned out, Robert did quit the team. I didn't feel very good about it and I realized I could have expressed my feelings to him in a more tactful and sensitive manner. I later apologized to him and he agreed I was tough on him but also told me he deserved it and probably needed it. We were not what you would call "buddies" after that, but we were friends and as time went on, he joked about the night I chewed his ass out.

We opened the season the Friday after Thanksgiving and, since they came to Douglas last year, we returned the trip to Rogers University this year. This meant we had Thanksgiving dinner on the road. A café in Texarkana fixed us a family style turkey dinner. We all held hands around the table and Coach Jenkins said grace. After we started eating, we were totally silent. I guess Coach sensed we were missing our families and wishing we were home.

"You know," said Coach, "my favorite Thanksgiving was when I was about twelve-years-old. We had a big family and we were in the middle of the depression. My folks were farmers as was all our family. Everyone came to our house for Thanksgiving dinner. There were aunts, uncles, grandparents, cousins and so many people we had to eat outside sitting on the ground. It was a beautiful fall day and I don't ever remember a better Thanksgiving."

Billy Joe said he could remember Thanksgivings just like Coach had described and they were also his favorites. All the guys then told about their favorite holiday times with their families.

"I think my favorite was the year before last when my Dad

and I had Thanksgiving with Rock and his Mom," I said. "It was our first time home from college and was just the four of us, but was really special."

"I have to agree with Big Jim on that." The Rock said, "but today is pretty special too."

We enjoyed seeing the Rogers' guys but didn't "fraternize" with them.  We found out real quick that we were a whole lot better with Billy Joe than we were without him. We were ahead by about 25 at half time both games. Coach would not run the score up on anyone and as a result he didn't even play Billy Joe or The Rock in the second half of either game.

As we played our first five or six games of the season, we blew people away by 20 or 30 points. We found ourselves ranked sixth in the nation and were enjoying huge crowds at home. The only problem was Kirby had picked up two junior college transfers and was ranked seventh. This was going to make for another dogfight in District 9 for the trip to Kansas City.

Christine decided the time had come for me to finally meet her parents. It wasn't like we could just jump in the car and drive to Dallas some Sunday afternoon to meet them. For reasons I didn't understand, we had to make arrangements a couple of weeks ahead of time to meet in a somewhat formal setting. I agreed to do whatever it took, so Christine found a Saturday night in December when we didn't have a ball game and arranged for us to have dinner at her parents' house.

Christine cleverly suggested I arrange to spend the night

at Chris Wright's parents, go home with Chris for the weekend and drive his car over to her house for dinner. She also made sure I had my blazer pressed and I borrowed a shirt and tie from Chris. I didn't realize at the time that she didn't want me to drive up in that old Ford and she was ashamed of my shirt and tie. When I got to her house, which was only a couple of miles from the Wright's, I felt real uncomfortable in Chris's car, shirt and tie. When I rang the doorbell, a woman in a black and white uniform opened the door and I was embarrassed when she called me sir and acted as if I was superior to her. She showed me to the parlor where Christine and Mr. and Mrs. Blankenship waited.

After Christine introduced us, Mr. Blankenship asked me to sit down in a large leather chair like his. Christine and her mother, sitting in similar chairs, stared at me.

"Well, Christine tells me you're a basketball player." Mr. Blankenship said, in a condescending tone.

"Yes sir," I replied.

"And she tells me your family is in the oil business in Oklahoma," he continued.

At that moment I cut my eyes at Christine. *Why did she think she had to lie about me to get her parents to accept me?*

Her father then continued, "She also told us your father passed away last spring and we want to express our condolences."

"Thank you sir,"

"Do you have brothers and sisters Mr. Green?" Mr. Blankenship inquired.

"No sir," I answered.

"Well who's running the family business while you're playing basketball?"

"I guess I am," I answered, "but it doesn't take much time."

Mr. Blankenship continued quizzing me about a bunch of right wing bullshit. I started trying to think of a way to get out of there without embarrassing Christine and her mother.

Finally, I stood up. "Mr. Blankenship, thank you for the invitation to dinner, but I think it might be best for everyone concerned, if I just excuse myself."

As I walked to the door, Christine followed and with tears running down her cheeks said, "I'm sorry."

"I know," I said. "I am too, but we both know that this is never going to work and we need to end it now."

She didn't try to stop me as I got in Chris's car and left.

I drove back to the Wright's and when Mrs. Wright answered the door she said, "Well Jim, you're in early, Robert's in the den. Why don't you join him?"

When I walked in the den, Mr. Wright said, "How did it go?"

"Not real well," I said, "I guess Chris is out for a while?"

"Yeah, I don't expect him home for a couple of hours," he said. "Do you want to sit down and talk about it?"

I thanked him and sat down. After all, I was stuck there until Chris was ready to go back to Douglas. "Mr. Wright," I said, "Christine Blankenship and I have been seeing each other since my freshman year. We really care about each other and I was thinking I wanted to marry her. When I went over there tonight, it was the first time for me to meet her parents. First of all, that big house, the fancy furniture and the servants blew me away. Then her dad said 'Christine tells me your family is in the oil business'. Christine had lied to them about that. I don't even have a family and my Dad, before he died, was a four hundred dollar a month hired hand in the oil field. That's as close as we ever got to 'oil business'. He kept on insulting and belittling me and I told Christine it was over and left."

"I know Christine Blankenship," Mr. Wright said, "and I can sure see how you might be in love with her. She is about the best-looking girl I've ever seen. I also know Paul Blankenship and he has lots of power and old Dallas money. Jim, I'm glad you got yourself out of that deal. Christine is the only kid he's got and he will never be satisfied with anyone she brings home."

"I should have known this thing wouldn't work. I guess I did know it but didn't want to admit it." I said.

Then, Mr. Wright, showing a great deal of discernment, said, "You probably need to talk to The Rock, don't you?"

"Yes sir, I guess I probably do, but it can wait till tomorrow."

"I need to look at some property in Douglas tomorrow. Why don't you take Chris's car back to Douglas tonight and I'll bring him up there in the morning." Mr. Wright offered.

When he insisted, I wasn't hard to convince and as I thanked the Wrights and told them goodbye, Mr. Wright said, "For what it's worth Jim. If I had a daughter and she brought you home, I would've thought she did pretty damn well."

I drove back to Douglas in about fifty minutes. When I got

to the room, the door was locked. I immediately knew something was crazy because we had never locked the door in three years. In fact, I didn't even have a key. When I pressed my ear against the door I could hear "If You Got the Money" playing on the record player. I knocked lightly on the door and whispered, "Rock, it's me." He opened the door enough for me to get in and then locked it again. The Cheerleader was sitting on my bed and they were eating cheeseburgers.

"What the shit is this?" I said.

"We thought you were gone for the night and thought we would just come over here and spend some quality time together," Rock replied.

"I didn't plan to be here," I said, "but you guys can get booted for this."

"Not unless you tell, Big Jim," Rock said, smiling at me.

I sat down and asked if they had another cheeseburger, then told them what happened in Dallas. Rock was sort of like Mr. Wright and was proud I was out of the deal. The Cheerleader said if Christine really loved me she would give up her family for me.

Rock quickly told her, "Carol, Big Jim would be the last person in the world to let anyone give up his or her family."

They consoled me for about an hour and at midnight I said. "Well we've felt sorry for me about as long as we need to. It's time for us to address the problem at hand."

"What's the problem at hand?" The Cheerleader asked.

"Getting you out of this dorm room without getting caught," I quickly replied.

We all stood up and laughed as The Cheerleader hugged

both of us at the same time and said, "I love you guys."

At Christmas break, we moved into the barracks, but Coach gave us three days off on the 24<sup>th</sup>, 25<sup>th</sup> and 26<sup>th</sup>. I went home with The Rock and The Cheerleader's parents invited Ethel, Rock and me to join them for Christmas dinner in Oklahoma City. Mr. and Mrs. Wilson were both teachers in the public schools, had a nice home in the eastern part of the city and their son, Ben, was a junior at Midwest City High School.

I have never been treated with more warmth and hospitality in my life. Mr. and Mrs. Wilson were wonderful people. Ben was a high school basketball player and we enjoyed swapping stories with each other. I kept thinking, how different it would be, if Christine's parents had been like the Wilsons. I also thought about last Christmas in Tishimingo with Dad. As I enjoyed being included in the Wilson's Christmas, it occurred to me that if I ever got to the point in life where I had a family and was able, I could sure "give it back" by inviting some kid without a family to dinner.

When we got back to the barracks on the 27<sup>th</sup>, we had to prepare to travel to Dallas and play in the Cotton Bowl Small College Basketball Tournament on the 29<sup>th</sup>, 30<sup>th</sup> and 31<sup>st</sup>. The tournament was a part of the Cotton Bowl celebration, which included a parade and, of course, the big football game on New Year's Day.

We didn't stay in a cheap motel in Dallas. We stayed in a pretty nice downtown hotel and ordered all of our meals from the hotel restaurant menu. The tournament was played in the Automobile Building at the fair grounds. The building was long and narrow and had six basketball courts set up side by side with temporary bleachers running the length of the building. There was a field of sixteen with some of the best small college teams in the Southwest. Three or four games were played at the same time with other teams warming up or working out on the remaining courts.

We played Liberty College from New Orleans in the opening round Thursday morning and won by ten. We played the second round that evening and beat Central New Mexico. Friday morning The Rock, Suitcase and I asked the front desk to call Peters's and Slugger's room and tell them there was a news reporter in the lobby doing a story on the tournament. He would like for them to come to the lobby in their uniforms to take some pictures. We hid behind the couches in the lobby as those dumb asses stepped out of the elevator in their basketball suits and asked everyone if they had seen a guy with a camera.

We played the semi-final game that night against Houston Methodist and didn't play very well, but we won in overtime. Coach kind of chewed our asses out about our prank that morning and not having our game faces on. But Coach couldn't help himself; he thought the prank was funny as hell. In the finals we played Northern Oklahoma and had to play well because they were ranked second in the nation and were damn good. As the game progressed neither of us ever led by more than five points. The score was tied something like eighteen times and with five seconds on the clock, we found ourselves down by one with the ball and a timeout. When we brought the ball in, Rock was to hit

Billy Joe inside for the final shot. Northern Oklahoma doubled up on Billy Joe and Rock caught Chris going across the middle and hit him with a perfect pass. As Chris went up for the shot, an Oklahoma guy came over his back and buried him in the floor. There was now no time on the clock with Chris going to the line to shoot two free throws. Northern Oklahoma called time out to try to "ice" Chris. When we came to the bench there was nothing the rest of us could do but watch.

Coach Jenkins said to Chris, "Son, you can go out there thinking about how bad you're going to feel when you miss or how good you're going to feel when you hit. What's it going to be?"

"I'm going to be feeling good, Coach," Chris quickly replied.

As he took the ball for his first attempt, we knew if he could just hit one, we were in overtime.

He bounced the ball lightly two times, then put it in the air for what seemed like thirty minutes before it hit "nothing but net." We all cheered, but Chris didn't even look back as he took the ball bounced it two times and hit the game winner.

Winning the Championship from such a strong field gave us confidence and we knew we had arrived at the level we had been seeking. As the Champions, we rode on a float in the parade and nearly froze our asses off. We also were guests at the football game and were impressed with the huge crowd and talent of those major college football players. For most of us, it was the first big time game we had ever been to. We had so much fun in Dallas; it was hard for us to go back to Douglas and start classes for the second semester.

We played East Texas Christian at their place the second week in January. We won by about thirty points. Everyone got to play and we were in high spirits when we went into the dining room at the Piney Woods Café. After all road games, Coach would reserve a large table at a local restaurant and pre-order either fried chicken or chicken-fried steak. As we sat down and started drinking our iced tea, there were a few other people sitting in booths and smaller tables around us. I noticed a short, middle-aged man get up from his table, walk over to the cashier's desk and start talking to a guy who appeared to be the manager.

The manager came over to our table and said loudly to Coach Jenkins, "I'm sorry sir, but the Negro boy will have to be served in the kitchen."

We looked around at each other; then Coach looked at all of us and said, "What do you guys think?"

Rock immediately said, "I think that if Billy Joe's eating in the kitchen, we're all eating in the kitchen." At that point The Rock stood up, picked up his iced tea and walked toward the kitchen.

Without hesitation the rest of us, including Coach Jenkins, picked up our tea and followed The Rock.

The kitchen wasn't that big and it was pretty obvious they were going to have a hard time serving our dinners in that limited space. In about two minutes a policeman arrived. Coach Jenkins told him we would leave and take our business down the road, "To a place that will treat all my players with the respect they deserve."

Just as we started out the back door, the policeman said to

me, "I don't know why the shit you guys are making such a fuss over that big nigger."

I hit him in the mouth as hard as I ever hit anything in my life. He stumbled backwards, knocking pots and pans all over the kitchen.

He quickly pulled out his gun and said, "You, big boy, are under arrest for assaulting an officer of the law." He actually kind of slurred this because his lip was split and beginning to swell. He handcuffed me, put me in his police car and took me to jail while Coach Jenkins and the guys followed in the van.

When I got to the jail, they fingerprinted and booked me. Coach Jenkins demanded they let him post bail, but to no avail. They told him the Municipal Judge would hold a hearing at ten o'clock tomorrow morning and if the judge wanted to set bail, he certainly could.

Coach put the team up in a motel and told them, "We're not going home without Green."

I spent the longest night of my life, certain I would be fined, given jail time and kicked out of school. I had screwed my whole life up in about one second.

When they took me to the courtroom the next morning, Coach Jenkins and the team were already there. Mr. Wright and a man I didn't know were also there. When I caught Rock's eye, I could tell he had been crying and Rock very seldom cried.

The police officer came in shortly and his lip was pretty ugly. There was a man with him who I assumed was the prosecutor.

The judge then came in and without looking up read out

loud. "We are here to examine the case of the State of Texas and Officer William W. Thompson vs. James L. Green. What does the State have to offer?"

The prosecutor stood and reviewed what had happened at the Piney Woods Café the previous night. He was pretty accurate in his account except he said my "actions were unprovoked." He also failed to mention what Officer Thompson said prior to me hitting him.

The judge then said, "Who represents Mr. Green?"

The man with Mr. Wright rose and said, "I do, your Honor." He then, introduced himself as James Sadler, my attorney.

Mr. Sadler made a few very brief but concise points. He told the judge, "according to several eye witnesses, Officer Thompson, just prior to Mr. Green hitting him said, 'I don't know why the shit you guys are making such a fuss over that big nigger'. " He went on to concede I did strike Officer Thompson, but "I don't think your Honor can say it was unprovoked."

For the first time the judge looked up and said, "Would you please take the stand Mr. Thompson?"

After the officer was sworn in, the Judge asked "Did you say; 'I don't know why the shit you guys are making such a fuss over that big nigger'?"

Officer Thompson, without hesitation, said, "Yes, I did your Honor."

The Judge then asked, "How do you feel about that?"

"I don't feel very good about it, sir and I owe the young man I said it about an apology," Officer Thompson replied.

The Judge then told the Officer to step down and asked me

to take the stand.

After I was sworn in the judge quickly asked me, "Do you have a history of hitting people, Mr. Green?"

"No sir, I don't,"

"Have you ever hit anyone before?"

"Yes sir, but I've never hit anyone that didn't need hitting."

I looked out at The Rock and he was cringing and rolling his eyes.

"Why did Officer Thompson need to be hit?" the judge continued to question.

I thought for a minute, "Judge, I heard Officer Thompson apologize for what he said and I know he is really ashamed of saying it, but Billy Joe Jackson is my friend. We play ball together, we study together, we eat together and on road trips he sleeps in the bed next to me. He, his parents and his grandparents have put up with comments like Officer Thompson made all their lives and sometime it has to stop. I don't guess I should have hit Officer Thompson, but it was just a way for me to try to stop it."

The judge asked, "If you were in the same situation again, what would you do?"

Again, I thought for a few seconds, remembering I had taken an oath to tell the truth, "I would probably hit him again."

"Good for you," said the judge. "CASE DISMISSED!"

I saw a wave of relief wash over the faces of Coach Jenkins and the guys and they looked like they were going to start cheering, but they restrained themselves. Officer Thompson came up, shook my hand and said, "You're a good guy Jim Green and if

I ever say something like that again, someone needs to hit me."

On the way home, the guys were again in good spirits, replaying all the courtroom drama and giving me hell for saying, "I never hit anyone that didn't need hitting." I had dealt with the police and the judge, but knew I still had to deal with Dr. Odem. I thought he would be sympathetic with my motives but wasn't sure he would condone my actions.

Dr. Odem had told The Rock and me when we buried the kangaroo he never wanted to see us in is office again. We were tense that evening and when we heard nothing from Dr. Odem, I began to think he wasn't going to take action. The next day while dressing for practice, Coach Jenkins walked in with Dr. Odem and my heart sank.

"You guys sit down for a minute, Dr. Odem has something he wants to say to you," Coach announced.

Dr. Odem seemed out of place in the locker room and I thought it was probably the first time he had ever been in one. He stood in front of us and began by saying, "Coach Jenkins and Mr. Wright have given me a full account of what happened the night before last. I want you young men to know that I have never felt more pride in Baker College than I do for the way you stood up for our convictions. Bigotry and hatred are demons of our society and you are to be commended for standing up against them." He continued, "Although we are not going to take any action, I have to say we cannot condone the violence displayed by you, Mr. Green."

There was dead silence for a few seconds and then The

Rock stood up and said, "Dr. Odem, prior to the night before last, Jim Green probably never made a distinction between the color of Billy Joe Jackson's skin and his."

"What is your point, Mr. Riley?" Dr. Odem asked.

"My point sir, is if the whole world was like Jim Green, there wouldn't be any bigotry and hatred," The Rock said.

Dr. Odem loosened his necktie, took it off and then shucked off his coat.

*What's he going to do, challenge Rock to a fight?*

Dr. Odem laid his coat and tie on the bench and looked at Rock with a penetrating gaze, "Your point is well taken Mr. Riley, but as president of this college, I can't condone violence. But if you will allow me to talk to you man to man, I'll tell Jim Green I'm glad he hit the son of a bitch."

We then took the floor for our work out. Dr. Odem came out, laid his coat and tie on the bleachers and stood at half-court and watched us for a while. At one point a ball rolled to his feet, he picked it up and shot a two handed set shot from mid-court that hit "nothing but net." I hadn't seen anyone shoot a two-handed shot since I was in the fifth grade, but he was perfect and knew exactly what he was doing. We all stopped and stared.

Coach Jenkins said, "Dr. Odem hasn't been a college president all his life. I understand he was a pretty good college basketball player back in the Thirties."

Dr. Odem smiled, picked up his coat and tie and as he walked out, said, "You guys see if you can get us back to Kansas City."

*We got all pissed off and got in a fight.*
*The policeman was sorry, 'Cause he knew we were right.*

*Ride around little doggies, ride around them slow.*
*For the Fiery and Snuffy are raring to go.*

# Chapter Fifteen

By the last week in January, we were fourteen and 0 with nine games left to play. Eight of those would be district games that again would determine who would go to Kansas City. Kirby was fourteen and one and we were ranked fifth and sixth respectively in the national poll. This year was different than last year. We still would be well matched, but both of us were much better than we were in '61. Billy Joe made the difference; Chris Wright had become an effective sixth man with The Rock, Billy Joe, Suitcase, All-American and me starting. Chris performed well off the bench because he could play any position but The Rock's. When he came in for The Rock, I went to the point guard and he took my forward position. Slugger and Peters didn't see much action but were supportive and never complained. I really liked to play the point guard and often thought if I was as quick as The Rock, there might be a place for me in professional basketball. But I was not as quick as The Rock and there was no way I ever would be, so I accepted my fate -- I would have to work for a living.

This team was the greatest team anyone could ever hope to play on. We had size, talent, great coaching and cohesiveness beyond belief. Suitcase and Billy Joe were awesome on the boards. With the exception of Suitcase, all of us could score and everyone could hit the open man with the ball.

When Kirby came to Douglas for our first meeting with each other, we were both three and 0 in District play. We prevailed 64 to 60 in an exciting game. If we won the rest of our games, we would return to the national tournament. But we still had to play Kirby in Midland, where they were tough.

As everyone had predicted, the season came down to that final regular season game in Midland and if we won, we would finish the season undefeated and be on our way to Kansas City. We had several fans make the trip to West Texas and we were pumped for the game.

It followed the same pattern as the final game the year before with The Rock hitting a buzzer beater to put the game into overtime. In the overtime Billy Joe took the whole team on his back and carried us to a 76 to 71 win. With about five seconds to go in the overtime we had the ball, Coach Jenkins called time out and I wondered, *what the hell for*, as we walked to the bench.

"We are up five and this game is over," Coach said, "We've won the district, we're going to Kansas City and we're happy, but when that buzzer sounds, let's show these Kirby folks what 'class' guys we are. You know they really deserve to go to Kansas City too."

The Rock passed the ball to All-American. He held it and

when the buzzer sounded, we shook each other's hands, then began shaking the Kirby guy's hands and giving them the praise they deserved. The crowd rose to its feet and gave both teams a standing "O."

Mr. Wright again chartered a plane for us to go to Kansas City and we were more comfortable with the flying than the previous year. Rock spent most of the time in the cockpit and told me for the first time he was going to try to get into flight training after he got his commission. He just kept adding to his plan and I still didn't have a one.

We were not the number sixteen seed for this year's tournament. We were the number four seed and this meant the tournament officials expected us to get to the final four. We went to Kansas City to play at that ultimate level and to win it all. Perryman University from Ashton, North Carolina was the number one seed and had been ranked number one all season. They had two 6' 10" guys and had beaten five or six major colleges. They were an overwhelming favorite to sweep the tournament.

We had no trouble with thirteenth seeded Eugene College in the first round and then avenged our loss from the year before, against North Kansas State College. They had lost a couple of players to graduation and we won the game by eight.

We were now in the final four and playing the semifinal game against an awesome Perryman University squad. We had watched them play their other two games -- they were frightening. I don't think we went into the game with the confidence necessary to win, but we were committed to giving Perryman a hell of a battle. The game took every ounce of energy we could find. When Billy Joe fouled out with two minutes left, we were down by two and there was not enough left to overtake Perryman. We lost, but we played the best game a Baker College team had ever played and we were proud of our efforts.

Perryman won the final game in a blow out and we won the third place game by fifteen. We knew we had the second best team in the nation, but never second-guessed Perryman ranking as number one.

After the final game, all the teams gathered on the floor for the awards presentation. They first named the All-Tournament Team and the first name they called was mine. Of course, all the guys cheered as I went out to get my trophy. I stood there and listened to the other nine all-tournament selections and when Billy Joe's name wasn't called, I felt embarrassed. If we were to have only one player selected, it should be him and I wondered if this was some more racist bullshit.

Then the PA announcer said, "The most valuable player for the 1962 National Tournament is Billy Joe Jackson of Baker College." I had never felt so proud in my entire life.

When we returned to Baker College, there were about two months left in the school year. Most of the guys now had girlfriends, so with the exception of Billy Joe and me, they all had their time committed for the rest of the school year. After my recent failures in the love department and my tight financial situation, I swore off women. Billy Joe didn't have a girlfriend because, even though Baker College was working on justifying the racial injustices of the past, it was not ready for interracial dating.

Alex tried out and got the lead role in a college production of *Hamlet*, so his time was committed to rehearsal. He did show me a few guitar chords and left his guitar in the room so I could practice. Some other guys donated a few albums to our country music collection and it now included not only Hank Williams, but also Hank Thompson, Lefty Frizzel and some "Gun Fighter Ballads" by Marty Robins. Billy Joe and I tried to sing some of these songs and learn the chords on the guitar. We only knew one three-chord progression, so we did all the songs in C.

Both of us also started making better grades and it was actually looking like I might get a 3.0 for the second semester. Billy Joe was a history major and like The Rock planned to teach and coach when he graduated. His grades were on the bubble the first semester but he was also up around the 3.0 range this semester.

After a couple of weeks of practice, we performed the songs for the guys and they sang with us. We weren't very good and that bunch of guys knew about as much about music as The Rock did about art, but we thought we were great.

Billy Joe and I went to the opening night of *Hamlet* to support Alex. We laughed on the way over to the play about how cultured we were getting, going to plays and learning to play a musical instrument. Alex was great and we decided we would go back the second night.

The next afternoon a crowd was in the room, singing and having a good time when some of them started making fun of

Alex's acting. Alex became uncomfortable and when Billy Joe stood up and told them to lay off Alex, things got quiet. Billy Joe had never been very assertive, except on the basketball court, but when the big guy got up and started defending his roommate, he got everyone's attention.

"Big Jim and I went to the play last night and it was great and Alex was great. Alex comes to all our ball games, tells us how good we are and writes about us in his paper. His talents are just as important as ours and the least we can do is respect them."

All was quite, then Rock stood up and said, "Here's the deal, we're all going to the play tonight and we want you to 'break a leg' Alex."

"What's this break a leg shit, Rock?" I quickly responded.

"It's what you tell actors before a performance. Like good luck, let's go get 'em, you know like when Coach is trying to fire us up before a game."

After Alex assured us The Rock wasn't bullshitting us, we all told him to "break a leg" and started making plans to go to the play.

We went together and sat on the front row. It was the first play most of the guys had ever seen. For Billy Joe and me, however, it was our second. I'm sure we made Alex nervous sitting on the front row, but he was great and when it was over, we kept applauding until he got three curtain calls. We waited for Alex in the lobby after the production and we all walked back to the dorm talking about how good the play was. We even went in the room and spent about an hour rehashing the merits of Alex's performance. We were all trying to act like some kind of intellectual giants. Of course, we didn't know shit, but it didn't matter.

When The Rock and I were little kids, among our many adventures was setting up track and field meets in the backyard at Dad's house. We had a straight away down the alley we used for sprints and also built some hurdles and dug a jumping pit. We drove nails about one inch apart into two boards and made standers for the high jump and pole vault. We found some old cane poles and used them for the cross bar and vaulting pole. The pit was also used for the long jump. We actually called it the broad jump and I always thought it was really a stretch to make this term politically incorrect. Dad got us a big bearing from the oil field for a shot but discouraged us from including the javelin and discus in our track meets.

We invited all the neighborhood kids and spent summer days competing with each other in what we called the Ferguson Olympics. We even made medals from tin foil and, surprisingly, were sensitive enough to make sure each participant got one.

Rock was good in all the events and I was particularly good in the high jump. I started out jumping like everyone else using a natural technique call the "scissor." It was simply jumping over the bar in an upright position, leading with your right leg and following with your left. I saw a film clip of the real Olympics at the movies and the high jumpers were using a technique I later learned was called the "Western Roll." Simply stated the Western Roll was just going over the bar head first and landing on your right shoulder. I started practicing and it wasn't long before I was dominating the high jump at the Ferguson Olympics.

I never got an opportunity to participate in a real track and field meet until we were juniors in high school when Ferguson High put together its first track team. A bunch of guys went out for the team and of course none of us had any coaching. As a result we were not real successful as a team but Rock did win a few medals in the 440-yard run. That's the 400-meter dash now. After some coaching and reading some articles in "Scholastic Sport" about the great Soviet Union high jumper, Valerie Brummel, I experienced some success late in the season.

During our senior year I won the gold in several big meets and got sixth in the state meet. It wasn't a major accomplishment but not bad for a self-taught guy who learned all he knew about the high jump from "Scholastic Sport."

It was the spring of our junior year at Baker College when Coach Norm, who in addition to being head football coach was also the track and field coach, said to me, "Green, why didn't you tell me you went to state in the high jump?"

"Going to state in the high jump isn't that big a deal in Oklahoma. You don't have to be that great."

"How high did you get?"

"Six two."

"Six two! Hell, six four won our district last year. You have your ass over here for track workouts Monday afternoon."

"But Coach, I haven't jumped for three years and track season is already half over."

"That's your fault and besides high jumping is like riding a bicycle. You know damn well that if you got something you can contribute to Baker College, I'm going to see that you contribute it. You might just get us a medal at the district meet."

I knew it was pointless for me to argue and if I didn't show up Monday afternoon, he would find me and drag me to the track.

"Okay Coach, I'll see you Monday."

When I told The Rock about my conversation with Coach Norm and my decision to go out for track, he laughed his ass off. He told me it served me right for getting him in that bowl game when we were sophomores. He also said Coach was right and it was my responsibility to represent Baker College if I had something to contribute. When he started laughing again, I told him he better shut up if he didn't want me to tell Coach about him running the 440 in high school. "You wouldn't do that...yes, you would," he said as he stopped laughing.

I started working on playing "Good Bye Ole Paint" on the guitar; Billy Joe knew all the words. In fact, he knew all the real verses. The Rock had never sung but one verse and except for the ones I wrote, it was all I knew.

The Cheerleader had a surprise birthday party for The Rock over in the lounge at her dorm. All the guys were there with their girlfriends and as a special treat Billy Joe and I did the real verses of "Good By Ole Paint."

When we finished, Rock's response was, "Big Jim, what's a hoolian?"

"I don't know."

That night, just before we went to sleep, The Rock said, "Big Jim did you know that a hoolian was also called a rendezvous and was a gathering of frontiersmen, mountain men and local Indians in the Northwest, during the 1800's. They would designate a date and place, some time in the summer and by word of mouth, everyone would get the news and congregate at the chosen spot. People would show up with food and whiskey to sell or trade; prostitutes would come in and they would spend about a week having one big party. They would trade things with each other, eat, drink, make music, dance and whore." He then continued, "It was also a big loop made with a lariat, or when you bring a steer down from the front of his horns without twisting him. And that Big Jim is what that guy in the song was going to Montana for, 'to throw the hoolian'."

I surprised him "Yeah Rock, I knew that."

"How did you know it?" Rock quickly shot back.

"I asked Mrs. Akins in the fifth grade,"

"And she told you what I just told you?"

"Pretty much," I said, "except for the part about the whores and the steer."

"Why have you always told me that you didn't know?" he questioned.

"I don't know, Rock, I guess maybe I just wanted to know something that you didn't and always just kind of bullshitted you about it."

Neither of us said anything for a minute and then he said, "I'm sorry, Big Jim."

"What are you sorry for?" I said.

"All of that 'know it all', 'did you know stuff'," he replied.

"I shouldn't have told you I knew.... And don't quit the 'did you know stuff', it's about the only way I get information," I concluded.

We laughed for a moment and then he said he had "a hell of an idea." His idea was pretty simple, but I liked it. He proposed we define a hoolian as an outdoor party with food, beer and music. He further proposed we have the first annual Baker College hoolian at Lake Texoma two weeks from Saturday. "We'll find a beach and tell the guys to bring food and beer and stuff to trade. We'll camp out and get Alex and Billy Joe to bring the guitar. We'll set aside a whole night for singing and bullshit."

"What about the whores?" I asked

"This will be a Mrs. Akins' version of a hoolian," he replied.

Coach Norm was right; high jumping was like riding a bicycle and coupled with the fact that I was three years older and stronger, I was jumping six two in a few days. He did know a little about coaching high jumpers and by the time the district meet rolled around, I had won a couple of dual meets and placed second at a big meet at East Texas State. I was going six four and six five and this was in the days before foam pits and "the flop." The flop is where you go over the bar backwards headfirst and land on your neck. It was not invented until they had the big foam pits. We were going over the bar head first and landing on our shoulder in a sand pit. I was not motivated to fall much further than six and one half feet straight down under these conditions.

At the East Texas State meet, I met Stan McCool. Stan McCool was a World Class long jumper from SMU. World Class meant he would probably medal in the next Olympics. He was a celebrity as a long jumper but about at my level in the high jump, which he also competed in. He wiped out the field in the long jump and as he walked over to compete with us, every one around the high jump pit whispered, "That's Stan McCool."

The high jump field got down to Stan, a guy from Sam Houston State named Jake Campbell and me after the bar got to six two. When you get down to two or three jumpers in high jump competition, there is a lot of dead time because the bar is going up in half-inch increments and they give you plenty of time to rest between jumps. As we were sitting on the ground resting after all of us cleared six three, Stan asked, "How come I haven't seen you at any meets before?"

"Because, this is my first meet," I said.

"Have you been injured?"

"No, I've only been out for track a couple of weeks."

"One of the other guys told me you play basketball for Baker College."

"That's right."

"I don't think you can ever become a great high jumper if you don't quit basketball and concentrate on jumping."

"You're up McCool," the official running the high jump shouted.

Our conversation was halted, as we both cleared six three and a half along with Jake. High jumping isn't like you're competing against the other jumpers, you're just trying to see how high you can go. In those days we didn't try to get some kind of psychological advantage and always cheered for each other as we cleared the bar.

When we sat back down, I followed up on Stan's comment about quitting basketball. "Look Stan, basketball is the love of my life and high jumping is something I do just because that big guy over there told me to do it," I said, pointing to Coach Norm who was standing near by talking with some other coaches.

I continued, "I respect the hell out of guys like you who dedicate themselves out here and reach the level you have reached because I've tried to do the same thing in basketball. It's probably a little late for me to decide to be a track and field star."

"Yeah, I know what you're saying and I have made a pretty strong commitment in the long jump but really only do the high jump because I'm already here and I enjoy it. I enjoy getting to know guys like you."

We both cleared six four and waited as Jake missed three times and was out. We shook his hand and congratulated him as the officials raised the bar to six four and a half. Stan was a good guy and I was glad Coach Norm had made me go out for track. Stan cleared six four and a half on his second attempt. I missed it twice and heard Stan say, "Way to go" as I cleared on the third try. Both of us went out on six five and Stan won the gold because of fewer misses at the previous height. As I stood on the presentation stand beside Stan and Jake and they hung our medals around our necks, I thought about what Rock wrote in that letter a couple of years ago, "Life is about relationships."

The district track meet was held in Abilene the last weekend in April and it involved the same schools that were in our basketball district. Coach Norm's goal for me was to get a medal at the district meet and pick up a few points for the team championship. My first place finish didn't pick up enough points for the team championship, but it did qualify me for the Division II National Championships in Indianapolis. I was the only Baker College "trackster" who qualified. I placed fourth in the national meet, didn't get a medal, but had the time of my life as Coach Norm and I flew to Indiana, saw all the sites and roomed together for three days. I did jump six five and a half and Coach was convinced I could win the gold next year.

Even though our group never desired or received official status on campus, at some point during our sophomore year we did get a name. We were known as the "Round-ballers." Billy Joe was the only person we ever added to the group, so it consisted of eight basketball players and Alex. We never referred to ourselves as the Round-ballers, but the other students did.

We never sponsored a dance or dinner party and we didn't have an intramural football team or other things the Greeks did. We did get solicitations for our opinions on various college issues and I think most everyone liked and respected us.

The politics of the campus centered on the fraternities and sororities. Power struggles were constant as they tried to elect their brothers and sisters to positions in student government. The ultimate compliment came to us one night during the spring of our junior year. Jess Coleman, president of the Tri Delts and Bob

Roberts, president of Omega, knocked on our door. Rock and I were sitting at our desks as I yelled, "It's open."

"You two are a pretty unlikely pair." Rock commented, when Bob and Jess walked in.

As the two of them sat down on the edge of my bed, Bob said, "Wait until you here what we have to say."

"Who are you guys going to support for student body president?" Jess quickly asked.

"I haven't given that one a hell of a lot of thought," I said.

"Well, here's the deal guys," Jess continued.

"Those damn Sig Gams are going to run Bill Potts and we don't have anyone in either of our groups who can beat him. He is going to spend about a thousand dollars of his old man's money and if he gets elected, this place is going to be a joke."

"You've lost me Jess. We understand your dilemma, but what can we do about it?" Rock said.

"What you can do Rock, is you can run against Potts," Bob replied. "You're the only person in this school who can beat him and we can guarantee all the Kappa, Alpha, Omega and Tri Delt votes for you. The Round-ballers sort of transcend all the fraternity stuff and you're the only group on campus besides the Sig Gams that can elect a candidate."

At this point, I'm saying nothing and Rock only says, "Thanks for your confidence guys; I'll let you know in the morning."

After Bob and Jess left, neither of us said anything for

about fifteen minutes and then for the first time I could remember in our relationship Rock asked for my advice, "What do you think I should do, Big Jim."

I initially came out with some dumb ass thing like "a man's got to do what a man's got to do." Then I told him, "You have always preached that 'giving it back' stuff to me and it seems like this might be a chance for you to give it back. What's it going to be?"

"You're right, Big Jim. Do you think I can get elected?"

"Hell yes," I said, "Who would vote against you?"

"What can my platform be?" he questioned.

"Giving it back," I responded.

"Great idea, Big Jim. I'm appointing you as my campaign manager right now."

Even though I focused all of my artistic talents on posters for The Rock and passed out cards to everyone on campus, the campaign wasn't that big a deal. Everyone loved The Rock and they loved The Cheerleader, who we now referred to as the "First Lady of Kangaroo Land." Rock destroyed Potts in a campus forum one night in the SUB and then defeated him 856 to 138 in the election.

The summer was fast approaching and I didn't have a clue about where I was going to live or work. I made application at several places in Douglas, but the job market was tight and it seemed most companies weren't hiring. All the guys knew I was looking for work and one morning Slugger came by and said his dad had a friend in Seymour, Texas, who was looking for a hand for the wheat harvest. He said his dad's friend had a couple of combines and trucks and had contracts with farmers to cut wheat from North Texas to Nebraska. Slugger said he understood it only paid a dollar an hour, but you worked about ten hours a day, seven days a week and your room and board was free. I quickly figured it up and at $10 a day for 80 days, I could make $800 and with my room and board paid for, I could save most of it.

Slugger told me the man's name was Gus Holt and he lived at Route 1, Seymour, Texas. I sat down and wrote Mr. Holt the following letter:

*Dear Mr. Holt,*

*Ken Chapman of Howe, Texas told me you were looking for a harvest hand for the summer. He said you paid a dollar an hour but you worked about ten hours a day, seven days a week and room and board was free. If this is the case, I would be interested in applying for the job. I am currently a junior at Baker College in Douglas and I am majoring in business. I have worked at summer jobs all my life, can drive a truck and operate other equipment. I can go to work on May 27 and will be able to work until August 29. Don't worry about me quitting and going home in the middle of the harvest, because I won't have a home until August 29 when I start back to school. I am 6'3" tall, weigh 185 pounds, know how to work, can play the guitar a little and made the All National Tournament basketball team this past year. If you need to check references you can contact Mr. Walter Burnett, Principal, Ferguson High School, Ferguson Oklahoma and Coach Ralph Jenkins, Baker College, Douglas, Texas.*

*Thank you,*
*Jim Green*
*Baker College*
*Douglas, Texas*

In about ten days I received the following reply from Mr. Holt:

*Dear Mr. Green,*

*The job pays $1.15 per hour and you will get in about 70 hours a week. Room and board is free but it is kind of like camping out. Bring 2 or 3 pairs of jeans, 2 or 3 long sleeve shirts, socks, underwear and personal items and meet me at the grain elevator in Vernon, Texas on May 29th at noon. Unless I hear otherwise from you, I assume we got a deal. See you on the 29th.*

*Gus Holt*

I was plenty relieved when I got Mr. Holt's letter. I knew it was going to be a tough summer, but if everything worked out, I would have enough to make my senior year. Since I didn't have to be in Vernon until the 29th and Rock wasn't leaving for his Navy summer camp until June 1st, we decided to have our hoolian on the night of May 27th. We could go watch our senior friends graduate, then head for the lake.

I really went to graduation just to see Christine and to say a final goodbye. Christine and I talked several times after our break up but had never gone out together again. Graduation was in the chapel and it was the first time I attended the event. We sat at the back. It was an impressive ceremony. The professors all marched in first, dressed in their black robes, mortarboards and hoods displaying the school colors of their highest degree. The seniors then followed in their robes and hoods, all exhibiting the Baker College red, white and gold. There was a welcome by President Odem, the presentation of awards, a speech by someone who was important, but I don't remember his name and then the seniors were awarded their degrees.

When we left the chapel, the graduates were standing in small groups with their parents and friends, laughing, hugging and taking pictures. The Cheerleader, The Rock and I walked over to where Christine had congregated with her family and friends to give her a hug and congratulate her. She introduced The Cheerleader and Rock to her parents and then said to them, "And you've met Jim."

Her smart-ass dad immediately said. "Yes, how's the oil business Mr. Green?"

I quickly came back with, "I got out of the oil business, Mr. Blankenship and I'm getting ready to go into the wheat farming business."

The Rock and The Cheerleader dismissed themselves. I could tell The Rock was about to bust out laughing. I hugged Christine one more time, told her goodbye and never saw her again.

The hoolian was perfect, the night was beautiful, there was plenty of beer and the only food we had was hot dogs. I don't think anyone did any trading and I am sure there were no whores. Alex, Billy Joe and I took turns playing the guitar while everyone sang. We did a few duos and solos, but, mostly, it was all of us singing around the campfire. In reality the hoolian was just a wiener roast with beer. It was good enough for us as we sang songs and told stories till the sun came up. Billy Joe learned all the verses to those "Gun Fighter Ballads" by Marty Robins and really impressed us as he sang "The Strawberry Roan." It's about five minutes long without one repeated line.

As we sat around the campfire and the hour got late, Slugger said, "I think we better get some sleep."

"Do we have to go sleep?" Peters quickly ask.

"Why wouldn't we?" Slugger responded.

"I just didn't know we were going to sleep out here," Peters shot back.

"What's the matter?" All-American said. "Are you afraid of the dark?"

"I'm not afraid of the dark, but I'm afraid to sleep outside," Peters confessed.

Some of the guys started giving Peters a bad time and Rock intervened, "You guys lay off Peters, we are all afraid of something."

Someone said they were not afraid of anything and insisted he knew The Rock had no fears. The Rock responded by telling us some of the things he was afraid of.

"I am afraid of a lot of things," he said. "I am afraid of making a C on a test. I don't know why I'm afraid of it, but it probably keeps me from making very many C's. I am afraid of something bad happening to my mother, Carol and other people I care a lot about. I am afraid of the devastation of war and to be honest with you, I'm a little afraid of going to sleep outside. Peters isn't by himself on that deal. When you go to sleep outside, you are vulnerable to forces that aren't there behind closed doors."

"Well I'm damn sure not afraid of making C's," I said. "In fact C's are basis of my academic goals." After a good laugh from the guys I continued, "I am afraid of war and bad things happening to people I care about. I think that the thing I'm most afraid of is being alone. When I went home that summer after my Dad died and lived in the house by myself, I couldn't stand it. I'd stay out in the yard talking to the neighbors till as late as they would let me. I would go to town and look for someone to talk to and try to pick up girls to spend the night with me. Not for sex, just to keep from being alone."

"Until I met you guys I was afraid of nearly everything and I don't believe Big Jim didn't pick those girls up for sex." Billy Joe said as everyone laughed and agreed with him. "Seriously, I was afraid to go into a café, walk through a white neighborhood, or just take a trip. I don't think I was afraid of getting physically hurt as much as I was afraid of being rejected and made to feel inferior. The thing I'm most afraid of now is disappointing my family. I have a good chance of graduating from college and no one we ever knew has done that. I guess it's sort of like Rock being afraid to make a C. This fear is going to motivate me to be successful."

All-American then admitted he, too, had a few fears. Like Billy Joe, he was scared to death he wouldn't please his dad. Everything he did was to try to win his dad's approval. So far he wasn't sure he had ever done it, but his fear would keep him throwing touchdown passes and hitting twenty-foot jumpers. "You know that game we had at home last year with El Paso State when I got twenty-one and hit eight of ten from the field and five of five from the line. Do you know what he said to me after the game? He said, 'Billy Joe got twenty-four'." Hell, I made All-American quarterback in football and all he could say was, 'You better be glad you had those good receivers.' I guess it's selfish on my part, but just one time I'd like to hear him say, 'I'm proud of you son'."

Alex admitted he was afraid of a lot of things but not things we might expect. "The other people in the speech and drama department think I'm afraid of you guys and afraid of being rejected by you because I'm not a jock. But they don't really know you all and I have never in my life been more secure and comfortable with a group of people than I am with you. I am afraid I might not be good enough as a newspaper reporter. It is a tough business and to make it with a big-time paper is almost impossible. I don't know what I'll do if I fail because it is my only dream in life."

"You'll make it Alex," Suitcase said. "You're good and I'll bet you end up as editor of one of the best papers in the world…as long as you don't stop being afraid of not making it. I am afraid of the same things the rest of you are plus… scared I will never be able to find a woman willing to marry someone as big and clumsy as me."

Slugger probably was the most secure person of the group because his biggest concern was the feelings of others. He wasn't as self-centered as the rest of us, but he also admitted he had many of the same fears.

I think the biggest "fear surprise" was when Chris said, "I am afraid of not being wealthy."

"What in the hell are you talking about?" Rock quickly questioned.

"I have been wealthy all my life and I guess my dad will see to it that I always am. But I can't be satisfied with my parents providing for me all my life and making my own way goes beyond making a living. I must do at least as well as them, which means I have to accumulate a fortune on my own. My greatest fear is not being able to do this."

We all knew nearly everything about each other and that night we pretty well shared every detail of our fears and hopes. I don't think a group of guys could have been closer. Basketball had brought us together, but our relationship wasn't about basketball, or how wealthy our parents were, or the color of our skin, or how good-looking we were, or how smart we were. The relationship was about integrity, values and commitment. We were a bunch of guys who loved each other and found it difficult to imagine not being together.

The next day The Rock and I stored the things we weren't taking for the summer in the gym. I made arrangements with Billy Joe and Coach Norm for Billy Joe to report to football workouts on August 15. He would take care of the trainer duties until I got there to help him on the 29th.

Billy Joe was going home to Arkansas to work in a poultry plant for the summer. The Rock and I told him if he would take me to Vernon to catch the wheat harvest and take Rock to Dallas to catch his plane, he could drive the Ford home for the summer.

# Chapter Sixteen

On the morning of May 29$^{th}$, I put my wheat harvest clothes in a duffel bag and said goodbye to The Cheerleader and The Rock. Billy Joe and I then headed to Vernon, Texas. It was a two hour and thirty minute drive to Vernon and Billy Joe and I were so worn out from talking and singing at the hoolian, we didn't say much. We got to the grain elevator about 11:30 AM and when I saw a pickup truck drive up with "Holts Custom Combining---Seymour, Texas" painted on the door, I knew my latest adventure was about to begin.

I got my bag out of the back seat and we walked over to Mr. Holt's truck. Mr. Holt was a tall lean man, about forty-five years old, with a weathered look from working hard in the sun. I introduced Billy Joe and Mr. Holt asked him if he wanted to "hire on" also.

Billy Joe told him thanks, but he had a summer job in Arkansas.

I told Billy Joe goodbye and to take care of the Ford; I threw my bag in the truck and got in with Mr. Holt.

He said we were setup to start cutting for a farmer about five miles north of Vernon tomorrow morning. We got acquainted on the way out to the farm and he filled me in on what the routine would be. "Remember where the grain elevator is, because you're going to be taking wheat there in the morning."

When we got to the farm, Mr. Holt had set up headquarters about a hundred yards from the farmer's house. His equipment and all we would need to make our trip north were at the site. There were two combines, two wheat trucks, a camper trailer the Holts lived in and an old school bus the hands lived in. He introduced me to his wife, Beth, who was a pretty lady with a nice smile. She was busy frying chicken on a portable stove. She told me she would be doing all the cooking, laundry and paper work for us and hoped I wasn't too particular about what I ate. He then introduced Juan Ortega and his son Carlos. Juan worked for Mr. Holt full time and Carlos was a senior at Seymour High School.

Mr. Holt then explained that he and Juan would operate the combines, Carlos and I would drive the trucks and Beth would "try to keep all of us in line." We then went over to the school bus and Mr. Holt said, "This is your home for the summer."

The bus had a make shift bathroom on the back with a large water tank mounted on the roof. There were two bunks on each side, near the middle of the bus and there was room at the front to transport the cook stove and other supplies. I threw my bag under one of the bunks and went outside where Beth was serving lunch (but they called it dinner and the evening meal was supper). It didn't take but a minute to figure the "board" part of this road trip was going to be great. She served fried chicken, mashed potatoes, gravy, green beans, biscuits and peach cobbler. The barbecue from Smokey's then became the second best meal I had ever eaten and would be far down the line before the summer was over.

Juan and Carlos gave me a crash course about how to maintain and operate the truck, what to do when I went to the elevator and how to deal with on the job situations. Juan's English wasn't very good, but it was a hell of a lot better than my Spanish. Carlos served as an interpreter for us and I was impressed with the ability of the three of us to communicate.

A typical day on the harvest involved getting up at 6:00 AM and eating a huge breakfast of eggs, ham, potatoes, gravy and biscuits. We would then gas and service the equipment and usually wait about an hour for the wheat to be dry enough to cut. You didn't cut the wheat as long as dew was on it. Carlos and I would then follow the combines to the field and they would start cutting, making circular passes as the combined wheat fell into the bin behind the operator. I drove the truck for Juan and Carlos drove for Mr. Holt. When Juan's bin filled, he would give me a hand signal and I would pull along side of him and he augured the wheat into the truck. We went through this process several times before filling the truck. With truck fully loaded, I would then drive to the elevator. I pulled onto the scales at the elevator and gave them the name of the farmer who owned the wheat. They then weighed the loaded truck, tipped it up to dump the wheat and then weighed the empty truck. They wrote me a receipt and I hurried back for another load.

I usually made five or six trips to the elevator everyday, with a break to eat at noon. Most of the time it would be dark when I got back to headquarters at the end of the day.

Mr. Holt and Juan would have usually finished showering when Carlos and I got in, so we just washed up and all of us sat down in folding lawn chairs to eat. We'd talk about our day and plan the next day, even though there wasn't much planning to do. Everyday was pretty much the same as the day before as we traveled north. Beth's food was out of this world and the boredom of sitting in the truck and watching that combine make circles was compensated by our anxious anticipation of our next meal.

After supper, Carlos and I showered and then came back for another glass of tea. We all sat in a circle in the lawn chairs and as time progressed told jokes and stories and talked about our dreams. It was kind of like the bond we had on the basketball team back at Baker College. We were a group of people working for a common purpose and we had to know and trust each other to get the job done.

After we left Vernon, Texas, we set up in Western Oklahoma for about three weeks cutting for several different farmers. It was while we were there; Mr. Holt went to the camper one evening and brought out an old guitar.

He handed the guitar to me, "You told me in your application you could play this. Let's hear it."

"I remembered saying I could play a little, but if you all know any Hank Williams stuff and will sing along, we can probably get to where we think we're pretty good."

After that first night with the guitar, we would do a couple of songs most every night at our after supper social hour. I think Juan's English improved as a result of the singing and I know

I started learning Spanish as I lived in those tight quarters with Carlos and him.

After about two weeks on the wheat harvest, I was about as home sick as a guy who didn't have a home could get. I missed Baker College and all the guys. After supper and singing one night, I stayed out in one of the lawn chairs and wrote The Rock.

*June 10, 1962*

*Dear Rock,*

*This wheat harvest deal isn't all that bad but I sure miss you and the rest of the guys. I guess your summer is going about the same as last summer and know it is probably tougher on you to be away than it is for me. I don't have a girl friend to miss but I wish I did. The people I am working with are great and you wouldn't believe the food. Mr. Holt (the boss) has an old guitar and we sit around every night and sing a few songs and tell stories. I live with a guy named Carlos and his dad Juan in a damned old school bus. Juan doesn't speak much English. He is learning a little, however and I am learning some Spanish. You would really like the group. Mr. Holt and Juan operate the combines and Carlos and I drive the trucks. Beth, Mr. Holt's wife, is the great cook I was talking about and the six of us are spending about twenty-four hours a day with each other. We do see the farmers we're cutting for and Carlos and I see the guys at the grain elevators. I get plenty of time to think, sitting in that truck twelve hours a day. I have been*

*trying to figure out how I can "give it back" but haven't had much luck. The Navy thing is good. I should have done it with you. There might be a little more purpose to my life if my thoughts went beyond playing basketball. I bet that damn Billy Joe is taking out his hometown girl friend every night in the Ford. I hope he is working out some. I'm sure not. But I do think we can win it all next year so you better report back to school in good shape. Mr. Holt said that if I needed to get a letter, we would be at Homer Perkins farm at Rt. 2, Buffalo, Oklahoma, in about three weeks. Send me a letter there and they will get it to me.*
*Big Jim*

When we set up to cut for Homer Perkins, in Buffalo, Oklahoma, at the end of June, we found he had left the country. His wife said he disappeared about a month ago, leaving a note saying the farm was hers and he wasn't coming back. She told Mr. Holt the wheat still needs to be cut and she would be grateful if he would transfer the contract from her husband to her. Mr. Holt didn't give a damn who the contract was with and we started cutting the next day. She did ask Mr. Holt if he had a Jim Green working for him and said a letter came for him a few days ago. As I got parked in the wheat field and waited for Juan to cut the first load, I opened the letter and read it four or five times.

*June 18, 1962*
*Big Jim,*

*I hope this letter finds you. Somehow I don't*

*have much confidence sending mail to Homer Perkins in Buffalo, Oklahoma. It sounds as if you are having an interesting summer. You are right; I am missing Carol more than I did last summer. The training is going okay and I do feel good about it. I think it is really an honor to serve in the Navy. When I think about the price my Dad paid for this country, I am proud to be a part of it. I am also impressed with what you are doing. What could be more American than working in the "bread basket" of the world? Your contribution there and the great experiences you are getting are pretty significant. Sometimes I can't believe how lucky the two of us are. You know damn well you are going to end up being a coach and that is how you are going to give it back. It is all right for you to spend your time thinking about basketball.*

*Big Jim, you are about the best friend a guy could ever have and I know sometimes I give you a hard time. You don't realize how proud I am to be your best friend. I can't wait for the summer to be over and to be back in Austin Hall. This will probably be the last letter from me this summer because you will be long gone from Buffalo, Oklahoma, before the next one could get there.*

*Rock*

Mrs. Perkins was a real attractive woman, about forty years old and from the start kept smiling at me. The first evening, after supper, while we were singing, she walked over and ask, "Can I join you all."

"Sure," Mr. Holt said.

I gave her my chair, put the guitar strap around my neck and walked over to lean against the pickup fender. "Do you have any special requests?" I ask her.

"Do you know, 'Your Cheating Heart'?" She smiled.

"Do we know, 'Your Cheating Heart'," I answered, as I struck the C cord and everyone joined in.

We did several songs together and she smiled at me the entire time.

It was obvious she was lonely and enjoyed having us around, as she came by and joined us every evening after that.

"I think Mrs. Perkins is trying to get you in the sack," Mr. Holt said one morning.

"I don't think so," I said, "she's just a little lonely."

"Don't let Beth or the boys catch you sneaking in the farm house." He laughed.

We finished cutting Mrs. Perkins's wheat about noon on a Saturday and decided not to move to the next location until Sunday morning. Mr. Holt let me take the pickup to town on Saturday night and I thought I might catch a movie or something. Just before town I noticed a little roadhouse with a few cars in front and I decided to go in and have a cold one. I sat down alone at a table, ordered a beer and as I listened to Johnny Cash on the jukebox, I heard someone say, "Mind if I sit down." When I looked up it was Mrs. Perkins. I nearly shit. She sat down, started buying my beer and as the evening wore on, we laughed, danced and had a good time. When she asked me to go home with her about eleven, I remembered what Mr. Holt said about "not getting caught in the farm house," besides she was twice my age, so I told her I better pass.

She left and about twenty minutes later I did too. When I got in the pickup, she was sitting on the passenger side. My "good judgment," was telling me to get out of this deal, but since I'd had a few beers and hadn't had a date since Christmas, when she unbuttoned her blouse, my lust took over for my "good judgment" and the rest is history.

In July we were hauling wheat to an elevator in Dighton, Kansas and the operator was an old man they called "Toggle." Toggle was loud, crazy and full of bullshit. They said he had operated the elevator for years and anyone who ever drove a wheat truck had a story to tell about him. One afternoon on our last run, Carlos was in front of me at the elevator and Toggle had this deal. He gave you a quart of beer, if you could drink it from the time they started tipping your truck until the truck was back down, the beer was free and you got a bumper sticker that said "TOGGLE'S TRUCKER." It takes less than a minute to dump a wheat truck.

I told Carlos not to get into this because if Juan and Mr. Holt found out, they would kill him. I was glad he took my advice and was also glad when his truck got out of sight going back to headquarters, because I was going to try this deal.

I did it and got my bumper sticker, but the next morning when Mr. Holt said, "Green, I need to talk to you," I knew I was in trouble. Most of the time Mr. Holt called me Jim and only when I was about to get my ass chewed, did he call me Green. "This isn't my first wheat harvest, Green and if you ever pull anything again, like you pulled at the elevator yesterday, you'll be hitch-hiking back to Texas."

I hung my head, apologized and assured him I would "keep my nose clean." As Mr. Holt started to walk away he said, "Just for the record, Jim, I got a TOGGLE'S TRUCKER sticker in '47."

This road trip was the longest I had ever been without shooting a basketball. When we set up in western Nebraska, late in the summer, I was delighted to find a hoop nailed to the side of a barn with an old basketball lying on the ground. One morning when the wheat didn't dry till about eleven, I went over and started shooting. It wasn't long before Mr. Holt, Beth, Juan and Carlos were over shooting with me. Carlos was a high school player and was pretty good and I could also tell Mr. Holt had played a little ball in his younger days. It was the first time Juan had ever picked up a ball, but he loved it. Beth was actually the best of the bunch and Mr. Holt told me she had been a real good high school player. We all had fun and laughed a lot as we did something other than cut wheat for the first time in about two months. When we quit to go to work, Mr. Holt walked to my truck with me and said, "You can damn sure shoot that basketball."

"That's about all I can do," I replied.

He then said, "I don't know about that. You play a good guitar, drive a pretty good truck, speak a little Spanish and tell a good story. What more could a man want?"

I smiled at him, "You're right and if I had a good woman like you've got, everything would be perfect. Hell, Beth can even play basketball."

When we finished our last contract, we were in Scottsbluff, Nebraska and it was August 24th. It took us over four days to get everything "roaded" back to Texas and we got back to the grain elevator in Vernon about noon on the 28th. Mr. Holt paid me for the summer and my check was $856. He told me Beth could drive my truck on back to Seymour and he would take me to the bus station in Vernon, where I could catch a ride to Douglas in time to start classes tomorrow.

I told Beth thanks for the great cooking, hugged her and then told Juan and Carlos goodbye. When we got to the bus station, there was a bus leaving at 1:00 P.M. and Mr. Holt bought my ticket. I walked back to the truck with him. He wished me good luck, then reached behind the seat and handed me his guitar and said, "I want you to have this. You did a hell of job this summer and this is kind of a bonus."

I thanked him, shook his hand and caught the bus to start my final year at Baker College.

# Chapter Seventeen

*"My foot's in the stirrup, my pony won't stand,*
*Goodbye, old partner, I'm leaving Cheyenne."*

It was 3:45 P.M. when the bus pulled into the Douglas station. It was about a mile from the bus station to the college and since no one knew I was coming, I walked to Austin Hall carrying my duffel bag and guitar. When I got to the room, Rock had already moved both of us in, but he wasn't there. I went next door and Alex was sitting at his desk typing the first 1962-63 *The First Amendment*. We greeted each other and talked about our summers. He said Rock was working in the library, but the doors were locked and I couldn't get in. He told me Billy Joe was over at the gym taping ankles for football practice.

When I walked into the training room Billy Joe was taping All-American and Coach Jenkins was taping this big lineman named "Tiny" Myers.

I said, "I don't know if you guys can ever get this job done without me."

Coach Jenkins pitched me his roll of tape. "It's about time you showed up Green," then shook my hand and told me it was good to have me back, as he walked out.

I shook Billy Joe, All-American and Tiny's hands and asked Billy Joe if he put new tires on the Ford.

"No" he responded, "but I fixed the radio."

"Did I ever tell you the story about the time All-American broke all those passing records? All of us were listening to the game and that radio broke on the last play."

"No more than ten times," Billy Joe said.

He asked All-American if the story was true.

"I don't know, I wasn't in the car. I was breaking all the records."

We laughed and bullshited to the point Tiny threatened to whip my ass if I didn't finish taping him.

As Billy Joe and I finished the taping, I heard someone down the hall loudly say, "How's the wheat farming business, Big Jim?"

I hollered back, "It's better than the damn Navy," and when The Rock walked in, I grabbed him as we shook hands. He then went with us to tend to the football team, as we caught up on each other's summer adventures.

I had been kind of envious of Rock last year. He came back after the summer and had this new group of friends. I, of course, went home and took care of the family business last summer. This gave him a group of people who I didn't know and I didn't know anyone he didn't know.

Last year he told me about the big guy from Pennsylvania

who got in a fight every Saturday night and the kid from Maryland that got real home sick. This year when we told each other about our summers, I was able to tell him about Mr. Holt, Beth, Juan, Carlos, the elevator operator in Kansas and that good-looking farmer's wife from Oklahoma. We mostly told stories about the people we had met and didn't really talk much about our jobs. We were glad to be back together and as we started our senior year, I suppose we were felt more mature, because there was a little less bullshit and country music.

Each year the first chapel service was the opening convocation for the school year. All students were, of course, required to attend and the faculty would march in wearing their full regalia as President Odem, the dean of the chapel and the president of the student body sat together at the altar as the principal speakers for the program. It was not hard for me to believe Rock was president of the student body, but the emotions I felt when I saw him up there with Dr. Odem and the dean were overwhelming. It had only been three years since The Rock and I had sat in this same service, fresh out of Ferguson High School, wondering if we could make it at Baker College.

When The Rock stood, stepped up to the podium and said "Fellow students, welcome to the one hundred and thirteenth year of Baker College," I wanted to stand and cheer but refrained, not wanting to spoil this great moment for the best friend a guy ever had.

As president of the student body at Baker College opportunities for accomplishments were limited because Dr.

Odem called all of the important shots. The Rock, however, was instrumental in establishing the honor code he learned from his Navy experience and he diluted the control of the Greek system in the college social environment. He also made a powerful statement about "giving it back" which shaped the image of Baker for years as it was incorporated into the goals and mission of the college.

Early on in the year, The Rock and The Cheerleader got concerned about my love life and tried to fix me up with several girls. It wasn't that I didn't also have concerns about my love life, but the ones they kept trying to fix me up with, were mostly "silver spooners" and I had already been there.

One night just before we went to sleep Rock said, "Big Jim, did you know that?"

I interrupted him. "I know that sixteen-year-old girl from Van Alstine, who I gave the whirlpool and rub down to, isn't sixteen anymore."

"What the hell are you talking about?" he said.

"She's working in the office in the art building and she is in the new freshmen class."

"The freshmen class here at Baker College?" Rock questioned.

"No, the freshman class at Harvard ... of course it's the freshmen class here."

"Is she a silver spooner?" Rock then asked.

"Rock, I told you she was working in the office in the Art Building.... Silver spooners don't have campus jobs."

"They don't," he said.

"To be so damn smart, Rock, sometimes you have to be the biggest dumb-ass in the world."

He then started laughing and asked me if I was going to take her out.

I told him I had already asked her out and I was taking her to the movie tomorrow night and then maybe back over to the SUB for a dance or two. The college had a little theater that showed old movies once a week and it was free. *Cat On A Hot Tin Roof* was playing. I told Rock, "I can get to know her a little better before I invest any money in her."

Sandra was a little embarrassed for flirting and giving me her phone number when she was in high school. I assured her if The Rock hadn't talked me out of it, I would have called her then. As the evening went on, she liked the movie. We had a good time dancing in the SUB and I asked her out again. It was kind of nice to have a girl around and in a few weeks we were seeing a lot of each other. The thing I liked best about her, other than her long legs, was I had been kind of infatuated with Beth Holt from the wheat harvest and since they both played high school basketball, Sandra sort of turned me on.

Sandra's parents were working people in Van Alstine. Her dad was a mechanic and her mother ran a beauty shop. She was a great high school basketball player, but in 1962 there were virtually no opportunities for a girl to play beyond high school. Her goal was to be a high school coach, however, and her major was physical education. Over six feet tall, with long blond hair, a great smile and an athletic body, she was a desirable catch. She was a good student and on a "grant and aid" package, working as a secretary for the art professors. I think she was impressed with me not just because I was a senior basketball player but because of my artistic abilities. Working for the art professors really didn't make her an art critic, however. Sandra was fun, had a good sense of humor and besides reminding me of Beth Holt, also reminded me of a poor Christine.

During the late Fifties and early Sixties, I don't think college students watched very much television, at least we didn't watch much at Baker College. There were TVs in the lobbies of all the dorms and one in the SUB. Other than watching Bill Mazeroski hit that homerun that beat the Yankees in the 1960 World Series, I don't remember much TV prior to the fall of 1962. In October 1962, when they discovered Soviet missiles under construction in Cuba, we did watch TV. President Kennedy put up a naval blockade and demanded the Soviets get all of their weapons out of Cuba. I guess this was the closest the world ever came to a nuclear war. From October 22, when President Kennedy announced "The Crisis" to the American people until October 28 when Nikita Khrushchev agreed to have the missiles removed, the art classes, basketball and hoolians became very unimportant in our lives. It wasn't like we had a fear of having to go to war. It was a feeling of despair and a fear of the whole world being destroyed. We were a generation that had been raised in a time of fun and prosperity with only a vague threat of war. This vague threat was now near reality.

We sat glued to the television, eager for any glimmer of hope, talking very little to each other and thinking about nothing but our doomed futures. When Khrushchev caved in and "The Crises" was over, I had the greatest sense of relief in my life. During that seven-day period, "The Crisis" interrupted nearly everything in our lives. We just went through the motions as we started basketball practice.

The football team experienced the same lethargy. They won their game on the Saturday of that week but it was the most unemotional athletic event I ever witnessed, with neither team giving a damn about who won or lost.

After our fears were relieved on the 28th, the college had a talent show in the SUB to celebrate. We were feeling good and since we now had two guitars, we entered the show. Alex and I played the guitars and Billy Joe found an old tambourine some place and he banged it around as the guys sang, "On A Honky Tonk Hardwood Floor." We didn't win first prize but did win what they called the "constellation" prize, which was Milky Way candy bars for everyone.

The football guys were having a hell of a year and thanks to surviving that lack luster game during "The Crisis," they were undefeated. Billy Joe and I made a good team of trainers. I had picked up enough from Clyde that first year to have a basic knowledge and as we worked with the coaches and the team doctor we became pretty knowledgeable.

This year while the guys were working out, Billy Joe and I started punting the ball back and forth to each other and since we both had some athletic ability and lots of spring in our legs, we could boom that ball out there pretty well. Coach Norm told us one day if he didn't already have a good punter, he would make one of us come out for the team. Little did I know, but this would let The Rock get his revenge on me for having to play in that bowl game.

He still drove the cheerleaders to all the games and when we were out of town for a game, he would hang around on the sideline.

The last game of the regular season we played in Abilene and our punter got roughed up and strained his leg during the first quarter. His replacement "squibbed" one off his foot for about fifteen yards in the second quarter. At halftime as Coach Norm headed to the locker room he passed by Rock, who said to him, "Big Jim, could do the punting the second half."

"I was thinking about Billy Joe," Coach replied.

"Big Jim's better," Rock answered.

I wasn't better than Billy Joe and The Rock knew it. He just figured Billy Joe was too valuable to the basketball team to risk his life out there.

When we got to the dressing room, Coach Norm didn't ask me if I would do the punting the second half. He told me I would. I told him I had never had a football uniform on in my life.

He said, "You're damn sure going to have one on in about five minutes and then you're going out there and taking some practice snaps from the center." He also told me when I went in the game, I'd better "kick the hell out of that football."

Coach Norm was 6'4", weighed about 300 pounds and had played linebacker for the Detroit Lions. I knew from my track experience I didn't have the option of telling him no.

As the second half progressed, we didn't get into a punting situation and I thought I had "dodged the bullet." We were ahead by one point with about two minutes left in the game. We had the ball, but were inside our own five-yard line. After three plays up the middle and gaining nothing, it was fourth and ten on our own three and not only was I going to have to punt, I was going to have to punt from the back of the end zone.

The punt wasn't very pretty; it was low and sailed to the left of the punt returner. When he didn't field it, it took a Baker College bounce and rolled dead on their twenty. They failed to move the ball and we went undefeated for the season. In the only football play of my life, I had a 77-yard punt. As we left the field, I told Rock he wasn't the only football star from Ferguson, Oklahoma.

The football team got another bid to play in the Mid-American Bowl and, of course, the whole school was excited about this. It wasn't the best thing for the basketball team because it meant we wouldn't have All-American till after Christmas. Coach Jenkins would be preoccupied with football and Billy Joe and I would have our time stretched pretty thin.

Starting our final basketball season at Baker College, our hopes were extremely high. We had only lost one game the previous year, finished third in the nation and had everyone back. This was going to be the year we could win it all. We won most of our games prior to Christmas, but were not as sharp as we had been the year before. We kept having injuries like The Rock turning an ankle and missing a couple of games and we didn't have All-American. The only aspect of the team that was an improvement over the previous year was Billy Joe. He had worked hard all summer and was even more awesome than before.

I continued to see Sandra through the fall, but I didn't allow the courtship to get very serious. I knew that after I graduated and she was still in college, it would be hard to maintain a relationship. With basketball and football seasons going on at the same time, my time was pretty limited and our romance was kept on a pretty light note.

The realization we were going to graduate in a few months and we were going to have to fulfill some kind of military obligation, was also on most of our minds. Just prior to the Cuban Missile Crises there was a problem in West Berlin and the Texas National Guard was called to active duty. This made the six-month National Guard thing not very attractive. I was really beginning to regret not doing what Rock did with the Navy and it was too late to do it now.

In the fall of 1962, with Berlin and "The Crisis" our military build up was at its highest level ever. By the time we would graduate, test ban treaties were signed and the arms race slowed. We didn't know this in the fall of '62, however, and we were looking for the best avenues to serve our country.

In early December, Coach Jenkins introduced me to a friend of his from World War II named Thomas Powel. They had served together in the Army Air Corps in the South Pacific and his friend was now a recruiter for the Air Force. Major Powel told me about a program the Air Force had similar to Rock's Navy program. Instead of going through basic training in the two summers before you graduated, you did basic training after graduation, then went to Officer's Candidate School. He told me after I got my commission, I would probably be assigned to the Armed Force's European basketball team and spend my military career playing basketball around the world. He gave me applications to fill out and told me I would know in about two weeks if I was accepted. I would have to take a physical in late spring and if I passed, I would be sworn in as soon as I graduated.

As I took all of my Air Force information and the application back to the room, I was pretty excited. The Rock, delighted with the idea, wanted me to start filling it out right then. He helped me with the application to officer training in the United States Air Force. When I got my letter of acceptance, we were even more excited. He said he would get off my back about not having a plan, for at least the next four years and by the time we got out of the service, we would have enough stories and bullshit to last the rest of our lives.

# Chapter Eighteen

During the Christmas break, we traveled with the football team to Springfield, Missouri, December 27th and reported to the Cotton Bowl Tournament two days later with the basketball team December 29th. The football guys won their game and finished their season as the only undefeated team in the history of Baker College. "All-American" made All-American again and the team was voted number one in the nation by a couple of polls.

We did not win the Cotton Bowl Tournament and blamed our second place finish on injuries and not enough preparation time. We did believe by the time district play rolled around we would be back to our 1962 form and could make a serious run at the National Championship.

By the end of January, Rock's ankle healed, All-American was back on the team and Billy Joe was having a super year. We were ranked eighth in the national polls and were regaining our "championship" focus. Kirby, however, was undefeated and ranked fourth in the nation and when they beat us by two in the first round of district--we had our backs to the wall. We now had to beat them in Douglas the last regular season game to force a playoff.

We believed the National Championship was between Kirby and us. We were both better than Perryman had been last year. We had Billy Joe, but they had two players nearly as good as him. There was not another team in District 9 that could compete with either of us, so everything was riding on the games we had with each other. Even though they had beaten us in Midland, we fully expected to beat them in Douglas and then be favored to win a play off game on a neutral court. As it was the previous year, both teams were among the top three or four in the nation, but only one could go to Kansas City.

In work out, the day before the big game, we were confident we would win and return to the National Championships for the third straight year. We were having the best practice I ever remember. Passes were crisp and on the money, every shot was falling, we were high in the air on rebounds and I think we were at our peak level. Near the end of the workout, however, Billy Joe sprinted for a loose ball and I heard a loud, sickening "pop." From my trainer's experience, I knew immediately that he had snapped his hamstring; Kansas City was now just a pipe dream.

We stopped practice and as Coach Jenkins took Billy Joe to the clinic, we all followed. Coach and I helped Billy Joe back to a diagnostic room. The doctor confirmed our fears. When I went back to the waiting room, the guys, with a look of despair on their faces asked, "Can he play?"

"In about six weeks," I said and their hearts sank along with mine.

As we went to the locker room before the game on that Saturday in February, I guess we all knew this would be our last game. I tried to pump everyone up. Billy Joe, standing there on his crutches, tried, Coach Jenkins tried and The Rock tried.

Rock did get us to the point where we were not going down without a fight. He got us angry about our bad luck. We took the floor and we had a hell of a game. Without Billy Joe we couldn't come close to matching up with them man for man. Coach moved me to Billy Joe's spot and Chris Wright took mine. We stepped up on defense and I had the offensive game of my career with the other guys on a mission just to get me the basketball. Shots were falling and I was in a zone. We played the perfect game through the first thirty-six minutes and with four minutes and fifteen seconds to go in the game we were tied 58 to 58. With four minutes on the clock, I went up for a rebound and coming down, I was hit and twisted on my right leg as my foot touched the floor. I grabbed my knee and knew I had torn it all to hell. *God why did you pick now for me to get my only injury as a ball player?*

The guys watched in dismay as they carried me off the floor, but they didn't let up. As I sat on the bench with that ice bag on my knee, I had never seen a bunch of guys play with so much courage. Kirby doubled up on Rock and Chris, however and we couldn't generate enough offense to win the game. We kept fouling, trying to get the ball back and Kirby hit all their free throws.

With about a minute to go, Coach started taking the guys out, one at a time. Our crowd stood cheering and Coach met and hugged each one. The Rock was the last to come off and sat sadly beside me till the buzzer sounded. The sadness was not so much about losing, as it was about playing our last game together.

With the loss of that game, we were dejected -- we had failed to reach our goal of a National Championship. But, we couldn't think of one thing we could have done differently that would have changed our fate. Billy Joe would heal in a few weeks and the NBA would probably draft him, but the rest of us would never play again and if we did, nothing could ever compare, to those glory days at Baker College.

In athletic competition, literally millions of young kids dream of reaching the goal of a state, national or world championship. Some have the talent and work hard enough to at least have a shot at reaching their goal. Just one miniscule event that happens in a split second can prevent the goal from ever becoming a reality. The event may be a bad pass, a shot missed by a fraction of an inch, a poor call by an official, or a hamstring-pull the day before the big game. In any case, if a team or player avoids all of these adversities, it is only by the grace of God. And only a very small number ever realize that ultimate goal.

Kirby won the National Championship in 1963 and had Billy Joe not pulled that hamstring, we probably would have won it. But he did and we didn't. The pursuit of the goal, however, is what makes great players, great teams and great games. I will forever be grateful for my opportunity to have been a part of it.

What was important about playing basketball at Baker College, however, was not how great we were or were not. We would have never approached greatness as a basketball team, had

Billy Joe not been a superstar. We would have still developed the same love for each other, the same bonds that would last our entire lives and the same values that made us all good people. Each guy on that team was special for many reasons other than basketball abilities. I would never consider trading my place on that team with a place on any other team in the world.

Most of us came from pretty humble beginnings. All-American came from a working family in Oklahoma and just like The Rock and me, found at an early age, that he could realize his dreams through athletics. All-American was "All-American" and had tremendous ability that he developed with hours of shooting a basketball and throwing a football. Some people thought he should try to "walk on" in the NFL, but like me, he knew his limitations. Because he was as slow as Christmas, he had no aspirations of playing professional football. He majored in physical education at Baker College and planned to either go to physical therapy school or try to get a fellowship in PE at some graduate school. He had always been a basketball and football hero and loved it. He was good looking and confident as hell, which made him the heartthrob of all the ladies. On the football team, he was the leader and had it not been for The Rock, he would probably have been the leader on the basketball team. From the first day at Baker College, All-American had been an important part of our lives.

Slugger was the most considerate person I ever met. He always made you feel like you were important and was genuinely interested in what was going on in everyone's lives. He majored in history and government and planned to pursue a masters after we graduated. Slugger's GPA was the highest on the team which was pretty damn high, considering Rock was on the team. His only priority as a member of the team was for the team to succeed. He played a lot when we were sophomores but as a junior and senior was pretty much in a support role, but was no less important to the team. I think Slugger's value system became a part of all of us and as a result we all became better men.

Suitcase was quiet and when he first came to Baker College he was self-conscious about his size. He never became a loud or real talkative person but as he started setting those rebounding records, his self-esteem improved significantly. When Suitcase did say something, it was usually fairly important and he was pretty articulate. He was a government major and planned to go to law school from the beginning. His dad worked for a refinery in Houston and Suitcase's goal in life was to become a lawyer and improve the working conditions for guys like his dad. He was the most consistent and dependable player on the team and, for his sake, it was probably a good thing Rock's "hell of an idea's" were never too illegal or immoral because, had they been, Suitcase would have gone along with everyone of them.

Peters was the most "gung ho" guy I ever met. Coach or Rock could get him so fired up; you needed a straight jacket to contain him. There were a lot of ball games he never played in, but he was in every game as he encouraged the rest of us. After he split his head open when he was a freshman, Coach wouldn't let him jump off Suitcase's back any more, so he started leading the team on the floor prior to the ball games. He would take off, at about 100 miles an hour and dribble the ball to our end and bank it off the board, the rest of us would follow, continuing to tip the ball against the board, then Billy Joe would finish it up with a "monster" slam dunk. Peters took off so fast, the rest of us had to sprint to keep up with him. We kept telling him to slow down, but the roar of the crowd excited him so much, he didn't. One night, he took off and we didn't. He dribbled the length of the floor not knowing he was alone and put the ball on the backboard. When he turned around and saw what we had done, he looked back at us and mouthed, "You bastards." The rest of us might drink a beer now and then or even smoke a cigarette or two, but Peters walked the straightest line I had ever seen. He majored in chemistry, was pretty damn smart and never missed an assignment or a day of class. He was in the same Navy program with The Rock and Rock said he was absolutely perfect for the Navy. He loved being part of the team and the team wouldn't have been the same, without him.

Chris Wright, of course, was our only "silver spooner." He made no apologies for it. He didn't have the same kind of growing up experiences the rest of us had, but he loved all of our stories and wished he could have been part of them. Chris majored in economics, was going to graduate school for a degree in finance and we were all sure he would be independently wealthy by the time he was thirty. Chris's father, Howard, was important to all of us and was the most compassionate and benevolent man we had ever known. Chris was just like him. When I was strapped for money our junior year, he would have given me money, but would not dare insult me with the offer. He was a hell of a player and loved the game more than anyone. His presence on the team enlightened all of us about a world beyond slots, country music and bullshit. However, no one enjoyed the slots, country music and bullshit more than Chris did.

Billy Joe's background growing up was not that much different than ours. However, the rest of us hadn't been faced with all of the racial bullshit. Billy Joe went to a segregated school until he was a high school freshman. The elementary schools he attended were marginal and he had difficulty catching up in high school and college. He did catch up and not only Billy Joe, but also all of those black kids that integrated the public schools in the Fifties and Sixties, should be given medals for accomplishing what they did under such adverse circumstances. Billy Joe had amazing athletic ability and his work ethic made him the best college player in Texas in 1963. He was what made us a great team, but looking back on it, his warm friendship was all that really mattered.

It was remarkable after we lost to Kirby, the final game of our careers, the number of students who came by our room and expressed their appreciation for our commitment to the basketball team. Somehow they made the "Round-ballers" part of what they thought was good and right about the world. This became more important to us than a national championship or some superficial ego boost. We were able, through the Baker College community, to feel a sense of true success and accomplishment.

The Rock and I were grateful for being a part of this team. We were grateful for Coach Jenkins and we knew we had not disappointed him. We also had a strong work ethic and we had a strong value system ingrained in us by our parents and our teachers. We knew what we encountered with this team over the past four years was special and everyone did all they could for us to be successful. We cherished our days at Baker College as the most significant of our lives.

My knee had some torn cartilage and possibly ligaments and the doctors told me I would eventually have to have it repaired. It did mean I wouldn't play any more basketball, or win the national high-jump championship and I didn't pass the Air Force physical. This put my life back to the "no plans stage," but The Rock didn't get on my case about it. He knew I was concerned as I started making applications for jobs. He continued to be my biggest supporter in my efforts to find my place in the world.

The Baker College liberal arts degree was wonderful for those students who were planning medical school, law school, or other graduate studies. It also was tremendous training for business executives and general leadership roles in society. Training for entry-level jobs in the work-world was really not there, however. My plan, when it included the Air Force, probably would have worked out real well, but that didn't materialize. The necessity of finding a good job in the work place was going to take some luck.

I believed my education and background were going to afford for me, in the future, many opportunities for roles of leadership and high-level responsibility. But not many companies or institutions were looking for twenty-two-year-old CEOs. I was not sure what I wanted my future to be, but knew, at some point, opportunities for fulfillment and "giving it back" would emerge.

The Rock always had a plan, but I think he was too modest

to share the part of the plan I believed would be reality. He always talked about teaching and coaching and he probably would do this for a while, but at some point, I was convinced, he would realize another calling. I would not be surprised if Rock ended up as the governor of either Texas or Oklahoma, or a senator or secretary of state, or even President. He was exceptionally bright, the strongest leader I have ever seen, had the best liberal arts education available and had tremendous charisma. He was preparing for a tour of duty as an officer in the US Navy and was a planner and visionary with the compassion and foresight to solve significant problems. The only thing that would prevent The Rock from eventually being elected to high public office would be either him declining to run, or stupidity on the part of the electorate.

I had a lot of crazy things going through my head as I thought about our futures, but my assessment of Rock's future wasn't crazy. I even thought I should have stayed with Christine and let her dad bank roll a political campaign for The Rock, but decided a right wing jerk like him probably would never support The Rock. I thought I could make a lot of money on my own and maybe get The Rock elected governor.

The Rock had never mentioned any political aspirations to me, but I knew he could reach platitudes of significant proportions. One of my major achievements over the past four years was confidence in my ability and my friend's abilities. I honestly believed we could do anything in the world and do it better than anyone else.

There were only two months left before graduation and as others finalized their plans for jobs, graduate school, or military service, I began a job search with very little time and very few ideas. I didn't have the option of moving home for a while and trying to find myself. I could move back to that school bus with Juan and Carlos, but it wasn't what I had in mind with a college degree. The military buildup had subsided and this made the job market extremely tight. My choice of a college major wasn't the best in the world because there was a flood of business majors out there looking for jobs. The art minor wasn't much help either.

To tell the truth, my favorite course at Baker College was "Introduction to Philosophy." In fact, I liked it so much I took it twice. Rock, of course made an A in it the first time and took a couple of other philosophy courses. We spent a lot of time discussing these courses in our bullshit sessions and developed a little bit of philosophical insight. There was not a real high demand for philosophers in the job market, however and if there was, they probably wouldn't hire anyone who failed Introduction.

I did one smart thing in my preparation for the real world and it was totally by accident. My sophomore year, as I enrolled in art classes, I did several studies in architectural design and Dr. Leslie suggested I take a course or two in engineering drawing. The courses were in the math department and I took two of them. I had already taken six hours of required math so this gave me a total of twelve hours in math.

It became apparent in my job search, if everything else failed, there was a big demand for technical people and I probably could get a job as a draftsman. The thought of sitting at a drafting board all day was not appealing, but it was more appealing than sitting in that wheat truck.

As I fretted and worried about my future, Sandra wasn't ready for life to get serious and our relationship became one of "just friends" with the possibility of something else in a couple of years.

The Rock prepared to leave for Officer Candidate School the first week in June and The Cheerleader was hired by the Dallas Public Schools to teach second grade beginning the fall of 1963. She planned to go home to Oklahoma City for the summer, teach summer school there and then return to Dallas. She would share an apartment with one of her sorority sisters, who was also going to teach in Dallas. The Rock and The Cheerleader had all of their plans in place. They were not engaged, but they planned to marry during the summer of 1964 with her getting a teaching job wherever he was stationed.

All-American got an assistantship at SMU in their graduate program in Physical Education and would be moving to Dallas and starting school in June. Chris Wright planned on attending graduate school at SMU and Suitcase was admitted to their law school. The Dallas Morning News hired Alex and, believe it or not, he was going to be a sports reporter.

Slugger planned on a June wedding and his fiancée, Brenda, who was a teacher, wanted to find a teaching position in Norman, Oklahoma and put him through graduate school at OU. Peters was in the same Navy program with The Rock and would also attend Officer's Candidate School.

The most exciting event that spring was Billy Joe being drafted by the Detroit Pistons and receiving a $10,000 signing bonus. He invited all of the guys to the signing ceremony in the gym lobby. His parents stood beside him and the press snapped pictures. We all had lumps in our throats, as Billy Joe signed the contract.

They had a table set up with a podium in the middle. Billy Joe and his parents sat on one side of the podium and the Piston's coach, Bob Spradling, and Coach Jenkins sat on the other side. All the guys from the team plus Alex and the sports writers sat in three rows of folding chairs in front of the table. The lobby was packed with students and local fans that were all standing.

Coach Jenkins went to the podium first, "I would like to welcome all of you to this very important event in the history of Baker College. Billy Joe Jackson just signed a contract with the Detroit Pistons of the NBA." Coach paused as the students and fans gave a huge and long ovation. "Everyone here knows what Billy Joe has meant to Baker College basketball. Everyone here also knows that what's happening to him today, couldn't happen to a better guy." Again, Coach paused as the crowd gave their approval.

Coach Jenkins then introduced Coach Spradling who in turn, asked Billy Joe to come to the podium and he helped Billy Joe into a Detroit Piston warm-up jacket. This was met with another thunder of applause.

Billy Joe then took the podium, "This public speaking scares me to death," he began, "but Rock told me to just focus on the guys from our team and pretend I'm just talking to them. That's what I'm going to try do. However, you didn't tell me you guys were going to be sitting with those sports writers,

Rock." The crowed laughed and Billy Joe relaxed a little as he continued. "I want to thank Mom and Dad and Coach Jenkins and everybody here at Baker College. But most of all I want to thank the guys that everyone calls the 'Round Ballers' -- You're the best roommate in the world Alex – what a friend…. I've never met any better folks than Chris, Slugger and Peters…. Suitcase, you got be the toughest guy in the world. I hope the Pistons have some re-bounders as good as you…. All-American – what an athlete and what a guy…. Big Jim, you taught me every thing I needed to know about playing the game -- and Rock, you taught all of us everything we needed to know about everything. I thank everyone here and I promise I won't let you down."

Billy Joe's speech made us all feel special and important. It was a big deal for all of us -- just to be a part of someone realizing his most cherished dream. When it was over, the Piston's coach told me Billy Joe had told him that I was a hell of a player and he was sorry about my knee. He said if it wasn't for that injury, they might have been able to sign me too. I felt flattered by the coach's compliment but knew I couldn't play in the NBA even if I had the healthiest knees in the world.

Rock came in one afternoon with some interesting information he picked up over in the PE department. There was a high school basketball/math teacher's job in Bonita, Texas, posted on the bulletin board. Bonita was about sixty miles west of Douglas and had a high school with about 260 students. The Rock wouldn't give up on me being a coach and said, "Big Jim, you've got to check this thing out."

I told him, "You know I don't have a teaching certificate and I don't think any of those schools will hire non certified people."

The Rock said, "I talked with some people in the education department and they told me there is such a shortage of math teachers, schools are hiring teachers on emergency permits with bachelor's degrees and twelve hours of math. These teachers are going back to school in the summers to get certified."

Coaching basketball and teaching looked pretty good at this point in my life, even though I knew my ability to teach math was pretty marginal. I went over to the gym and told Coach Jenkins what Rock told me. He said that he would check with the education department and if they thought there was a possibility for this to materialize, he would call Bonita and check it out.

The next afternoon Coach Jenkins told The Rock to have me come by and when I did, he told me he had made some calls and the Bonita Athletic Director wanted me to come over there and talk to him the next afternoon.

As I drove home from my interview in Bonita, I toyed with the offer they had made, but wasn't very excited about accepting it. That night Rock was anxious to hear about the interview. I told him they offered me the job, but I didn't tell him much more. I said I wanted to sleep on it. "We'll go over to Coach Jenkins's office in the morning and I'll tell you and Coach about it at the same time and let you all help me decide what to do."

As Rock and I sat in front of Coach Jenkins's desk, I

thought about that first trip to Douglas, four years ago and us sitting in this same place as Coach told about all the virtues of Baker College. Coach pointed me in the right direction then and I was confident he would point me in the right direction now, as I told The Rock and him about the job in Bonita.

I told them that when I got there, I went to the Athletic Director's office in the field house. He showed me around the school and then took me back to the office. He started the interview by telling me the responsibilities of the job. They included coaching high school basketball, junior high football, junior high basketball, junior high track and teaching four sections of junior high math. He then asked me if I had played any football. I told him about that one game where I went in to punt and when he started asking me football questions, I think I surprised him with how much I knew. He then lectured me on things like not starting basketball until football was over, not opening the gym for the kids to shoot during the summer and not allowing kids to play basketball unless they also played football. The man seemed to be completely paranoid about basketball. Never once did he ask me a question about my abilities as a basketball coach, or a math teacher. If I were an educator, I'd hope I might think math was as important as football.

As soon as I finished talking, Coach Jenkins said, "Jim, you want The Rock and me to tell you what we think and my advice is pretty simple. Bonita, Texas, isn't any place for Jim Green. What do you think Rock?"

Rock said, "I think you nailed it, Coach."

Coach Jenkins then said, "Not all teaching and coaching

jobs are the same and if you want to coach, I'll help you find a good job." He also said, he thought he could get my grant and aid extended for a year and I could come back and get my teaching certificate and be his student-assistant coach.

I thanked him and then told Coach and Rock I learned something on my trip to Bonita that was a "reality check." I said, "Given my situation, I don't think I can consider teaching next year. If I take a teaching job in the public schools, do you know when I will get my first pay check?"

"September 30," Coach Jenkins understandingly replied.

"That's four months. And you have about $150," Rock said, realizing my problem.

Coach Jenkins then asked me if I thought I would be interested in a sales position. I told him I had some interest and thought it was the avenue I probably needed to pursue.

Coach thought for a moment, then said, "There's a guy I played ball with at Oklahoma A&M, who's in the wholesale furniture business in Dallas. Let me give him a call and tell him what a big bullshitter you are." The Rock and I laughed as Coach Jenkins tried to come through for me, one more time.

When I went back to the room that afternoon, I could hear the guys laughing as I walked down the hall. The Rock had always talked about what a bullshitter I was and I guess he was right. I did embellish and exaggerate big stories like the "kangaroo burial" and the "snowstorm." To Rock, however, every event was an adventure, a "hell of a story," and he embellished everything. As I walked into the room, he was telling about my interview at Bonita and he had that Athletic Director, overweight, wearing a sweat suit, chewing tobacco and spitting into a coffee can. Even though I hadn't turned the job down yet, he told the guys that when I was offered the job, I told the Athletic Director to shove it up his ass.

The Rock and I had certainly had our share of adventures and stories and as the years passed and we told about them over and over, some of them reached unbelievable proportions. At one time, I told him he should write a book. He told me I should write one too, but I needed to read one first.

Neither of us had a brother, but I think our loyalty and dedication to each other exceeded that of most brothers. My dad's death hurt Rock as much as it did me, tearing up my knee probably bothered him more than it did me and my job search was as important to him as it was to me.

It was about two weeks before graduation when my job search ended. Coach Jenkins called me over to the gym and told me his buddy Lyle Robinson, from Oklahoma A&M wanted to buy my dinner at the Cattleman's in Dallas that night. The Cattleman's was the best restaurant in Dallas and guys like me just dreamed of going there. Coach told me Lyle was a great guy and if I just showed up and was myself, he thought Lyle might have something for me.

Even though I couldn't afford it, I drove to downtown Douglas and bought a new shirt and tie. The shirt was a blue oxford cloth, button-down, with a box pleat in the back and a locker loop. It was just like all the other guys wore and identical to the one I had borrowed from Chris Wright. The tie was a red and blue stripe. When I put them on with my gray slacks, blue blazer and shined black shoes, I thought, *Christine sure would be proud of me.*

I arrived at the Cattleman's on time and Mr. Robinson met me in the lobby. He said he recognized me because he had seen a couple of my college games. He ordered us a pitcher of beer and the "two biggest steaks in the house." We started talking about Coach Jenkins, playing ball and old jocks we both knew. Immediately, I knew I liked him and was hoping he felt the same about me.

Evidently, he did because when we finished those two steaks, he said, "Do you think you can sell furniture?"

When I told him I thought I could sell just about anything, he said, "Here's the deal…. You'll be given a territory that covers northeast Texas. You'll call on furniture stores in all those little towns and believe me, there are a bunch of them. There are not many big stores, so your orders will be small, but there will be a lot of them. You'll travel three days a week and work the showroom here in Dallas two days each week and one weekend a month. You can go to work on June 1 and I'll train you for one week. Then you'll 'hit the road' on your own."

As I was taking all of this in, I thought, *this sounds great, I wonder what it pays.*

He continued, " I'm going to pay you $300 per month plus a 2% commission on your sales which should average about $500 a month the first year, depending on how hard you work. I'll also furnish you with a new car, pay all your travel expenses and you'll be covered by our group health insurance."

"Let me get this straight," I said, "If I make $500 a month in commissions, that will be a total of $800 a month, plus a car, expenses and insurance?"

"That's the deal," he said.

"Where do I fill out the application?"

"Son, you don't have to fill out an application. You're hired. Do you want the job?"

"Yes sir," I quickly answered.

"Good. Then we have a deal and here's enough to help get a place to live and move down here." He reached in his pocket and gave me a check for $200 payable to *Jim Green*. He said he had a feeling we would make a deal so he made the check out ahead of time.

As I drove back to Baker College, I don't know if I had ever felt more relief and excitement in my entire life. Not only did I have a job but I also had a good job, working for a great guy and making more in one month than I did the whole summer on the wheat harvest. I also had $200 "walking around money" in my pocket. Is Rock ever going to make some great bullshit out of this?

Rock was, of course, just as excited as I was. He did tell me, however, he was never going to let me off the hook about "giving it back" and somehow I had to teach some kids out there how to shoot a basketball. We only had two weeks before graduation and since we'd spent all our time the past six weeks trying to find me a job, we needed to concentrate on having some fun.

# Chapter Nineteen

Rock compiled a list from our basketball game programs of all the senior guys who we played against in District 9. He sent them an invitation to the second annual "Baker College Hoolian," which was to be held the weekend after graduation. As he planned the hoolian, I didn't have the heart to tell him the only thing Mrs. Akins told me was, "a hoolian is a big loop in a rope." I figured he had bullshitted that part about a big party but his hoolian could be what ever he wanted it to be.

The college held the sports banquet just before graduation. This was a time when all the teams and players were recognized for the past year's accomplishments. Prior to the banquet, Coach Jenkins called all the guys over to the gym for us to vote on the basketball team's most valuable player. Since we had a guy who had just signed an NBA contract, there wasn't much doubt who the MVP should be. I got the award our sophomore year, Billy Joe got it our junior year and we voted to give it to Billy Joe again for 1963.

I'm sure Billy Joe was thinking about the time Rock said, "If Billy Joe's eating in the kitchen, we're all eating in the kitchen." He stood up and said, "If Billy Joe's getting the award, we're all getting the award."

At the Banquet they presented the MVP award to the whole team. We all went to the front to receive it and all of our names were engraved below the inscription "Baker College--1963--Most Valuable Basketball Player." We, in turn, presented the award to Coach Jenkins with The Rock making the presentation.

The football team received much deserved praise at the banquet because of their undefeated season, number one ranking and bowl game win. Coach Norm, at the end of his presentation of the football players' letter jackets, said he had two more jackets to present and then did a really nice thing. He told about The Rock playing defensive back in that 1960 bowl game and me punting in the 1962 game. He then presented both of us with football jackets. All- American got the award for "Best All-Round Athlete" every year and, of course, deserved it for his accomplishments in both basketball and football this year. When the banquet was over, I kidded Coach Norm for not considering The Rock and me for best all-round.

"I still can't believe you let Big Jim talk you into playing me at defensive back in that bowl game," Rock said.

"It's hard to believe I ever listened to any of Big Jim's bullshit, but I want to tell you guys something. I have never enjoyed two people in my life any more than I have you two. I hope life is good to you and you know if you ever need anything, all you have to do is call me." Coach Norm said.

"You've already done more for us than we deserve," I said, "and giving us these letter jackets was pretty special. Thanks for everything, Coach." I said, as I reached to shake his hand, but instead grabbed the big bear and hugged him.

The last week before graduation, The Rock, The Cheerleader and I spent a lot of time talking and I suppose got into a kind of melancholy mood. We were excited about graduating and for The Rock and me, it was a pretty big deal. Both of The Cheerleader's parents were college graduates and it was pretty much expected she would get a degree. No one from Ferguson, except for maybe Mr. Burnett, ever thought Rock and I would finish college.

As we talked about our plans, we swore that whatever happened, we would all pursue some life adventure together in the future. I still didn't have a long-range plan but I did have a job and for the first time in my life, I might get enough financial security to make some plans. We all grew up a lot since that first varsity game when we were freshmen and we were all grateful for the bonds and friendships we made. At Baker College, the people made all the difference and Mr. Burnett was right when he told us some four years before that we had a wonderful opportunity. We believed we had taken advantage of our opportunities.

Mr. Burnett and his wife, Alice, brought Ethel to our graduation. It was the first time Ethel was ever on campus and she was proud and impressed. The morning of the event was perfect. The sun was shining and there was not a cloud in the sky as we gathered to line up in front of the chapel. The faculty marched in front of us in their multi-colored regalia, as we formed a line, two abreast in our robes and hoods of red, white and gold. The Bachelor of Arts graduates had red and white hoods and the Bachelor of Science graduates had red and gold hoods. Since the only difference between the two degrees was a foreign language, only the people from business administration wore the red and gold. I thought since there were only about twenty of us out of a class of about two hundred, it looked like we were sort of special. I also thought back about my decision to major in business so I wouldn't have to take a foreign language and now at graduation, I spoke better Spanish than most of those who had taken four semesters of college Spanish. I guess not all education takes place in the classroom.

Rock and The Cheerleader both graduated cum laude and Mr. Burnett told me later when he told Ethel what cum laude meant, she was the proudest person he had ever seen. I graduated "without honors" but was just as proud and I wished my mom and dad had lived to see this.

As we congregated outside after the ceremony, with our degrees in our hands, we looked at them for the first time, as our friends and families took pictures. It was nice Mr. Burnett and Alice came. They stood by me and I figured out years later, their purpose for being there, wasn't so much to give Ethel a ride, but to support me on this very important day. Coach Jenkins came over and the three of them enjoyed renewing their old friendship. Coach Jenkins looked pretty impressive in his cap and gown with the orange and black Oklahoma A&M hood.

It was good to see Billy Joe's parents again and they were even more proud of their son's college degree than they were of his basketball contract. Most of the other parents had been to ball games over the years. Mr. Wright had been to nearly all of them and Slugger's mother had cooked once a week for us our freshmen year. The other parents had not met Ethel, however, and she had the time of her life as they told her how great The Rock was.

The hoolian was set for the next night after graduation and then The Rock was going home for a few days before he left for OCS. I had already been to Dallas and All-American and I rented an apartment together on Gaston Avenue. I said goodbye to The Cheerleader, but I would see her again when we took Rock to the airport on June 6th. We planned to say our other goodbyes after the hoolian.

When we showed up on the beach for the second annual hoolian, nearly every senior in District 9 was there. Everyone had just graduated and we were feeling pretty special. Since we didn't know each other that well, we had tons of new bullshit for each other. There was lots of beer, a lot of hotdogs and this time, some trading. Trading mostly was negotiations between two items such as a Kirby baseball cap for a Wesleyan workout shirt or a Baker sweatshirt for a Harden windbreaker. Alex and I played the guitars 'til our fingers were sore, as we sang old songs and learned new ones. The hoolian was more than a wiener roast this year and it was one of the best times of our lives.

Except for those Rogers guys, we never got to know the opposing players. Sometimes when we played, we would have our pre-game meals together and talk a little bit, but for the most part the only times we saw each other was in the "heat of battle." We found the other guys had some of the same stories we had. The Hardin guys all went to the kitchen one time when a café refused to serve the black guys on their team; however, none of them hit a policeman. Nearly everyone had done that warm-up play where the little guy jumps off the big guy's back. The Kirby guys said they tried it in a game one time.

I met this guy from Wesleyan named Art Billings who had written a whole book of poetry. He had some good stuff and said he was impressed with all the verses of "Ole Paint." I think he was just being kind, but I asked him not to tell The Rock if he was serious. Some of the guys found out they were going to work for the same companies or were going to the same graduate schools. Life-long friendships were formed at the second annual "Baker College Hoolian."

The day after the hoolian was our last day at Baker College. As we packed and I carried my stuff to the car, The Rock and I were kind of quiet. We agreed I'd take care of the slot machine and record player for the two of us. He was going to ride home with The Cheerleader and she would bring him back to Dallas next week. I would take our car to Dallas and as soon as I got my company car, I would sell the Ford and send him half the money.

As we loaded my things, he said, "What happened to the one-legged flamingo?"

"I traded it at the hoolian," I said.

"Traded it for what" he said, in a concerned tone.

"For a poem Art Billings from Wesleyan wrote,"

"That flamingo might be valuable someday,"

"The poem might be too, besides, it's my plan for life," I said.

He asked if he could read it and when I handed it to him, he read it out loud:

*"He came from Oklahoma, about forty years ago.*
*And was tall and lean and gentle and talked real soft and slow.*

*He helped other people, just doing what was right.*
*And he loved little children and ladies of the night.*

*He went to Church each Sunday, out of love not out of fear.*
*And if Jesus came a calling, he'd offer him a beer.*

*The boy said, 'Old man, what's you doing, why are you wastin' time?'*
*He said, 'Son I'm just a country poet, looking for a rhyme'. "*

Rock said, "You did good Big Jim, it's a good plan."

I then told The Rock, "I'll see you next week." And I moved to Dallas.

# Chapter Twenty

*"When I die take my saddle from the wall,*
*Put it on my pony, lead him out of his stall.*
*Tie my bones to his back, turn our faces to the west,*
*And we'll ride the prairie that we love the best."*

As I drove south on Highway 75 to Dallas, I remembered that August day in 1959 when The Rock and I drove down Highway 99 from Ferguson to Douglas. I was still in that old '52 Ford and probably as naïve and ignorant as I was in '59. The difference, however, was this time I knew I was naïve and ignorant and I guess that's what a college degree is supposed to do for a man. I think the realization of your own ignorance is the mark of an educated person.

I recalled, in great detail, those first few weeks at Baker College and laughed as I remembered Dr. Odem chewing our asses out over that damn kangaroo and The Rock and I thinking there was no way the college could account for chapel attendance.

I remembered the first varsity ball game, Christine and how I felt life couldn't possibly get any better than this. I wondered what would have happened if Slugger hadn't broken his hand and had gone to Chicago and beaten Cassius Clay. That would have changed some history. I remembered talking Coach Norm into playing Rock in that bowl game and how tight my ass was drawn up last year when I had to punt in that game.

I laughed when I thought about those alarm clocks going off in the organ pipes and when Slugger and Peters came down to that hotel lobby looking for the photographer. I could see Rock picking up his iced tea and going to the kitchen at the Piney Woods Café and still couldn't believe I hit that policeman. I replayed the Perryman game in the national tournament trying to figure out if there was any way we could have won and how proud I was when Billy Joe got the most valuable player.

I could still hear the "snap" when Billy Joe tore his hamstring before the Kirby game and what if I had worked harder and hadn't tore my knee up, I might have had a shot at the NBA. I wished I had studied harder and made better grades.

My love life during my college days was pretty limited and shallow. I was attracted to Christine because she was uninhibited and beautiful. Attracted to Sandra because of her long legs and Mrs. Perkins was pure lust. I guess my relationships with the opposite sex were not very fulfilling. In fact a Freudian psychiatrist could probably win a Nobel Prize with a case study on me.

Except for the past two summers, I'd spent my entire life with The Rock. I think the idea of us not being together bothered me more than anything else. His relationship with The Cheerleader made him less dependent on me than I was on him. I was smart enough to realize, however, that spending the rest of my life living with The Rock was not a real healthy idea and it was probably time for us to pursue life on our own.

As I drove into Dallas, I liked the idea of living in the big city, even though I had never lived in one. The traffic bothered me, but I figured I would get accustomed to it. The prospects for fun and excitement seemed to be infinite and I became excited as I made my way to Gaston Avenue.

Gaston Avenue was the place to be for young, single men and women out in the world for the first time with a good paying job. The entire street was lined with newly built apartment houses and on weekends there was a party or two in each one. Many people who started their careers living on Gaston ended up meeting their mates for life and finding life's great opportunities there.

When I walked into my apartment, it was my second time there. The first time was the previous week when All-American and I rented it. It had two bedrooms, two baths, a living area and a kitchen. It was completely furnished and everything was brand new. It also had a central air and heat system. It was the first place I'd ever lived with air-conditioning. To move in, we had to put up a $100 deposit and pay the first month's rent, which was $150. After we paid this, $125 of my "walking around money" was gone.

All-American wasn't coming until the next day and I was

alone as I moved in. Rock and The Cheerleader were bringing the pots, pans and dishes I had stored at Ethel's, so I didn't have much to carry in. I sat the guitar in the corner of the living room, thinking it looked kind of decorative there and put my clothes in the closet and dresser drawers. On top of my dresser, I carefully placed my All-National Tournament trophy, my MVP trophy from 1961, Dad's All-Conference trophy, the picture of Mom, a picture of The Rock and me when we were eleven and my Baker College Degree. As I sat down on the bed and looked at that shrine of my life, I never felt lonelier.

Except for the summer I spent in Ferguson getting rid of Dad's things, I had never been alone. The feeling was different in Ferguson, because I knew the neighbors and had lived there all my life. It had been emotional as I left The Rock and Baker College. Even though I felt like I should be excited about my new beginning, I was just as scared and unsure as I was the first day The Rock and I had left for college. I needed to report to work the next morning and I looked forward to starting my new job, if for no other reason than not being alone.

I looked through the paper and found a big sale advertised at a local department store and decided if I didn't buy some clothes, other people were going to get pretty sick of seeing that blue blazer. After taking a few wrong turns, I found the clothing store and bought a sports coat and a couple of shirts and ties. This pretty well exhausted my "walking around money," but I had enough left to survive until I got paid.

I stopped at a grocery and picked up a loaf of bread, some milk, cereal, peanut butter and paper plates. After my dinner of two peanut butter sandwiches and a glass of milk, I turned on the record player and spent my first night in Dallas listening to Hank Williams and Lefty Frizzel. I picked up the guitar, just before I went to bed and sang a few verses of "Goodbye Ole Paint," but it was hard because The Rock wasn't there to give me the cue.

*When they left Baker College, they followed their maps,*
*The Rock joined the Navy and Big Jim sold lamps.*

*Ride around little doggies, ride around them slow,*
*For the Fiery and Snuffy are raring to go.*

# Chapter Twenty-One

I snapped awake at 5:00 AM and couldn't go back to sleep. I arrived forty-five minutes early for work and there were a couple of people already there. I got acquainted over coffee and when Mr. Robinson showed up at 8:00 AM, he took me on a guided tour of the offices and the showroom, then introduced me to everyone. I even got a small office, which I wasn't expecting. I spent the morning filling out paperwork and at noon, Mr. Robinson, who insisted I call him Lyle, took me to lunch.

In the parking lot, he stopped beside a new Ford Fairlane 500, gave me a set of keys and said, "Let's take your car."

I had never driven a new car in my life and this one was mine. At least, mine, as long as I worked for Lyle.

That first afternoon on the job, Lyle started my training, which dealt with the logistics of the job and product awareness. Lyle told me over and over, to be successful in sales, you have to know your product. That first day, I started learning about furniture brands, how the furniture was made and details about beds, tables, couches and, of course, lamps.

When I returned to the apartment at the end of the day,

All-American was there and already moved in. The first thing we did was go to the parking lot and I took him for a ride in the Fairlane. He was starting graduate school the next day and didn't have a car. His dad brought him to Dallas to move in and he had planned to ride the bus back and forth to SMU. While we were on our test drive, he asked what I was going to do with my old car and in about five minutes I had sold it to him for $140. I took him down to the parking lot at work; he drove the Ford back to the apartment and paid me as soon as he walked in the door. It was nice to keep the Ford in the family. It worked for All-American because he would only be driving a few miles a day and he loved the old car about as much as we did.

That night Suitcase, Chris Wright and Alex showed up. Suitcase and Chris were waiting for summer classes to start at SMU and Alex had already started to work for The Dallas Morning News. Suitcase and Alex shared an apartment just down the street from us, while Chris lived with his parents. We ordered some pizza and Alex brought the beer. As we ate, drank, bullshitted and sang songs, we realized things hadn't changed all that much. However, we did miss The Rock, Peters, Slugger and Billy Joe.

Billy Joe showed up a couple of days later. He was driving to Detroit on Sunday in his new Pontiac convertible. He purchased new cars for himself and his parents with his bonus money. He also bought some new clothes and they weren't sale clothes from a department store like mine. He looked great in those "high-dollar threads" and that blue convertible. We, of course, gave him hell about being rich and famous. He stayed with All-American and me and didn't leave until Saturday. We thought it was pretty cool having an NBA rookie "crashing" on our couch.

On Friday, as I finished the first week on the job, Lyle felt like I needed to get my "feet wet" and scheduled appointments for me with several stores in East Texas for Monday, Tuesday and Wednesday.

The Cheerleader brought Rock to Dallas on Saturday and I was to take him to Love Field to catch his plane early Sunday morning. She stayed a couple of hours, then said her goodbyes and returned to Oklahoma City. Because they were both in the same class at Officers Candidate's School, Peters was on the same flight with Rock to Ohio. His dad brought him to Dallas on Saturday. With the exception of Slugger, the whole gang was again together.

The Rock and I didn't have much of an opportunity to talk, but we both realized when we saw each other again, I would be settled into my job and he would be an officer in the US Navy. His training was to be completed by November 30 and he expected to be back in Dallas around the first of December. We agreed to write regularly and if I ever got a phone, maybe we could call each other.

Billy Joe moved over with Suitcase and Alex for Saturday night. We said goodbye to him, as Suitcase and Alex said goodbye to Rock and Peters at the end of the evening. Early Sunday morning All-American and I took The Rock and Peters to the airport and after they boarded, we went up to the observation deck and watched as their plane took off. I found myself anxious for the next six months to pass and for me to be on top of the terminal watching The Rock return.

Early Monday morning I left for East Texas to see if I could sell anything. Along with my training the previous week, I had taken home all the literature, booklets and sales pamphlets I could find. There was good information about my furniture in them, but with all the guys around, I hadn't studied them as much as I had intended to. I called on a store in Canton and two in Tyler that first day and spent the night in Tyler on Monday night. The people I called on were nice. One guy was a big basketball fan and had actually seen me play against East Texas Baptist in Marshall. He bought more than the goal Lyle had set and as I finished the day, I had exceeded my goals for the three stores I called on.

Lyle told me to stay at the best motels, to eat well and not be bashful about taking customers out for a meal. I did take one of the guys in Tyler to lunch. Those East Texas motels looked pretty much the same. In fact, they were mostly like the ones Rock put all those drawings in. That first night on the road I spent most of my time finishing up the paperwork on my orders and studying my product information material.

I called on stores in Kilgore and Longview the next day and that night, after I did my paperwork, it occurred to me I had failed to give The Rock his half of the money for the Ford, so I wrote to him.

*June 4, 1963*
*Rock,*

> *I told you I sold the Ford to All-American but I didn't give you your seventy bucks. Sorry, but it's enclosed. We did okay on that old car. If you don't count*

*those thousands of hours of labor, we drove it for five years and sold it for more than we had in it. I guess I should have given Billy Joe a couple of bucks for that radio tube he put in, but hell, he drove the damn thing all last summer.*

*I'm in a motel in Long View, Texas and have just finished up my second day on the road. As you always said, I could sell iceboxes at the North Pole and I've had a pretty good first two days.*

*Rock, I want you to know I am really proud of you and what you're doing. All of those dreams you had, when we were kids, are working out just like you planned. I haven't forgotten about "giving it back," but I still need some time to decide how to do it.*

*Let me hear from you and if you will send me the cue, I'll write a verse of "Ole Paint."*
*Big Jim*

On Wednesday, I called on a store in Marshall and caught a store in Minneola, then one in Terrell on my way back to Dallas. The guys who were left in Dallas agreed we didn't need to party every night so All-American and I attempted to get into some kind of responsible lifestyle as he started classes and I finished up my first real week on the job.

I spent the next two days on the showroom floor, had several customers and made some pretty good sales. My commissions that first week were over $200. Lyle was pleased and I thought I was the richest man in the world.

We settled into a routine of working hard all week and partying hard on the weekends. Except for the one weekend a month I worked, I spent Friday and Saturday nights drinking beer and dancing in some club, or at one of the many parties on Gaston Avenue. I also met a lot of good-looking young women who were doing the same thing. Most of them were airline hostesses flying out of Love Field. We actually called them stewardesses back then. My job continued going great. I was making a little money, had several girlfriends and for at least the summer of 1963, I didn't think life could get any better.

I did miss The Rock and looked forward with great anticipation to his letters. In his first letter to me, after I sent the money for the Ford, he wrote:

*June 10, 1963*
*Big Jim,*

*I got the money. Thanks for taking care of that. After selling that stuff of your dad's, you're getting pretty good at disposing of community property. However, don't sell the slot machine or record player; we may need them for a future adventure.*

*They keep us pretty busy here so I spend most of my writing time on letters to Carol. She writes me everyday, but don't you start that shit.*

*It seems our time at Baker College went by too quickly, I wonder how we are going to feel when October 15 rolls around and we're not starting basketball practice. I don't know if I can get by without passing that ball to you and watching you bury a jumper.*

*I'm proud of you too, Big Jim. I've never seen anyone who could take more bad shit and land on his feet than you. I'm happy you finally have a place in life that gives you a little bit of security with a little less financial pressure. You still know more about basketball than anyone I know and you're the best damn teacher I've ever seen. I know you will find a way to share this gift with others.*

*"Goodbye Ole Paint... I'm leaving' Cheyenne ... I'm going to Montana... to throw the hoolian."*
*Rock*

The summer of 1963 continued with work, parties and airline stewardesses. It didn't take long to decide this life wasn't going to last over the long haul and I wrote to Rock seeking his counsel.

*August 12, 1963*
*Rock,*

*Sorry, I haven't taken your cue and written a verse to "Ole Paint" but I have figured out I can't write a verse unless there is something to be excited about. There are plenty of good things going on in my life but no "hell of an idea" adventures, so I guess I'm going to have to wait for you to come home to write the next verse.*

*We got a telephone, so if you will send me the number where I can reach you, I'll give you a call. Our number is JL5-5127; if you get a chance, call me.*

*I should be feeling pretty good. I bought a TV, a garment bag for my traveling, some new clothes and have a checking and savings account at a bank downtown. I honestly enjoy my work and like meeting and bullshitting with all of those people. The parties and the girls I've met, however, are not all that fulfilling. I think if I met the right lady, life might be better.*

*I hope your training is going well. I know you miss The Cheerleader, but you all will be together soon and when you come home, make sure I'm included in some of your plans.*
*Big Jim*


The Rock called me as soon as he got my letter. It was the first time we had talked on the phone since we were in high school. He told me I needed to hook up with The Cheerleader's roommate as soon as they moved to Dallas. I knew her from college and I told Rock she was a semi-silver spooner. He told me I needed to forget that silver spooner shit and try to accept people for who they are. I assured him I would consider it.

The Cheerleader's roommate, Teresa Moss, was pretty good-looking. I didn't know her all that well and I think they tried to set me up with her before. The idea of going out with her wasn't out of the question, so I decided I would play it cool for a couple of weeks and then ask her out.

When The Cheerleader and Teresa moved to Dallas in the

late summer, they rented an apartment in the same complex with All-American and me. About a week after they moved in, I wrote The Rock.

*September 3, 1963*
*Rock,*

*While I was "playing it cool" and waiting for the right time, that damn All-American was buying flowers and "riding off into the sunset" with Teresa. It looks like I'm back to square one.*

*Guess who I ran into the other day? I was working the showroom floor and this guy who looked familiar, came up and said, "Welcome to the real world, Green." It was Moose, the guy who played for Harden when we were freshmen. He's managing a furniture store in Burkburnett, is married and has a couple of kids. He bought a bunch of furniture from me and when we went to lunch, he insisted on paying, as a peace offering for giving me that black eye. Man, that was a great night when we beat them, I scored all those points, met Christine and you got to third base with Cheerleader for the first time. By the way, Moose still remembered my name.*

*Big Jim*

When The Rock wrote back, he told me, the game when we beat Harden was a hell of a night and I was correct on all of my recollections except the part about him and The Cheerleader. On that he said I was a lying son of a bitch.

The Dallas Cowboys were a new and struggling NFL franchise in 1963 and they gave away a lot of tickets just to get fans in the stands. Lyle always had tickets and gave me four of them for the Dallas/Cleveland game. I took All-American, Teresa and The Cheerleader to the game and it was the game Jim Brown broke all those rushing records against the Cowboys. He got so tired of running, he finally sat down on the ground and leaned back against the stadium wall in exhaustion.

After the game we walked to a little café over by the Cotton Bowl. It was over dinner, The Cheerleader and Teresa told me about a girl they were teaching with.

"Jim, there's a girl named Patricia Lecerno who teaches across the hall from me," The Cheerleader started. "She went to college at East Texas State and this is her first year to teach. We really think you would like her."

"What does she look like?" I asked.

"I think you put a little too much emphasis on looks, but she happens to be really cute."

"How do you know she would be interested in me?" I questioned, showing a little interest.

"We've told her all about you and she really wants to meet you. Do you know where Kaufman is? It's a little town about twenty-five from here." Teresa said.

"I know where Kaufman is. I call on a store over there. What does that have to do with me going out with her?" I said.

"Just information Jim, it's where she's from," The

Cheerleader said, "don't get uptight."

"Sorry," I said. And then thought, *this is good information. If she's from Kaufman, she's a small town girl. And if her name is Lacerno, she's probably not a silver sponner.*

"Have you ever seen her?" I asked All American.

"Yeah, I met her last week and if you pass on this one, I think you're going to be sorry." He replied.

"Why don't you try to get tickets to next week's Cowboy's game and 'Pat' can go in my place." The Cheerleader said.

I agreed with the plan and told them I would check with Lyle for tickets.

Not only did I take Pat to the football game Sunday, I took her out the next Thursday, Friday and Saturday nights. On the following Monday night, when I was on the road, I wrote The Rock:

*October 1, 1963*
*Rock,*

*I guess The Cheerleader told you about Pat. I've been out with her four times and plan to see her again Thursday night. I think I kind of like her. She has cold black hair that just kind of shines and the most beautiful eyes, I've ever seen. Her smile makes you happy just being around her. The Cheerleader told me she was "really cute." What this meant was she is about the sexiest girl in the world. She loves sports and country music and she is not all wrapped up in herself. I'm not sure what "self-assured" means, but I've heard you intellectuals talk enough, that I think she is self-assured. Her grandparents came from Mexico, but her parents never spoke Spanish at home and get this, she says my Spanish is better than hers and her parents are going to be real impressed with me.*

*The Cheerleader told her all of those old stories about us and her sense of humor is just as warped as ours. She has a bunch of great stories of her own. I can't wait for you to meet her.*

*Big Jim found a lady and the lady is good.*

*He wrote Rock about her, as soon as he could.*

*Call me and we will sing the chorus over the phone. By the way, am I self-assured?*

*Big Jim*

Again The Rock called me as soon as he got my letter and started off with the chorus of "Ole Paint." Anyone who heard us singing together on the phone would have been sure we were absolutely nuts. He told me it sounded like I more than "kind of liked" Pat and from what Carol told him, Pat liked me too. Just before he hung up, he told me anyone who could write and sing over 100 verses of "Ole Paint," had to be self-assured, or the craziest son of a bitch in the world.

All-American and I went to the homecoming game at Baker College. Half of our old gang was living in Dallas, so the only ex-students we saw, that we weren't seeing everyday anyway, were Slugger and his wife, Brenda. Brenda was pregnant and we were pretty excited about the prospect of being "uncles" or "God-parents" or something.

It was the first time I had ever seen a Baker College football game that All-American wasn't playing in and I could tell he was agonizing, kind of like I would be the first time I saw the Kangaroo basketball team play without me. After the game, we went by the locker room and said hello to Coach Jenkins and Coach Norm. As we drove back to Dallas, we were a little sad because we were no longer a part of college life.

As Pat and I dated, my life seemed to take on a little more meaning and going to clubs and parties together was fun. We went to another Cowboy's game and when basketball season started in November, I took her to the first Baker College home game. As I watched those guys play, just as I expected, I ached to be out there.

I also started dragging her to high school basketball games and as we watched, I wanted to go out there and teach those kids how to pass, dribble and shoot. The coaches weren't that bad, but I was angry that somewhere along the way, no one had taught those kids fundamental basketball. If they're going to spend their time playing, they should be taught to do it right. My anger was mostly selfish, because when a guy shot a ball right, I could feel it in my own body, as if I had made the shot. Just like when I had watched Billy Joe Jackson shoot, I could actually feel that ball rolling off of my fingertips.

As Pat observed me agonizing over the games, she started talking to me about considering coaching in the future. I even talked to Lyle about it. He told me I was the best salesman he had, but if I thought I needed to do it, he would support me all the way -- just that I shouldn't wait too long. He shared that he had felt just like I do when he first got out of college, but he went into business and never had the guts to give up the money.

November 22, 1963, started great for me as I worked the showroom floor and sold a big order to a guy from Mesquite. President Kennedy and his wife were visiting Dallas. They got in the President's limousine with Governor John Connally and his wife and led a motorcade through downtown. I listened to the radio account as the President's car passed just a few blocks from where I was standing. "The president's car has just reached Dealey Plaza and is turning right from Main to Houston Street... It is taking the 120-degree turn onto Elm... and now passing the Texas Schoolbook Depository...Oh my God, they're shooting. The president's been hit."

The drama that unfolded during the next few hours and days was incredible. I had a feeling of despair and guilt. I was only a few blocks away and for some dumb reason thought I should have prevented it from happening. I felt guilt for being so caught up in my own little life and guilt for not "giving it back."

I also thought about the Democratic Convention of 1960, when Dad and I cheered as John Kennedy won the nomination and how optimistic we were when he defeated Nixon and was inaugurated in 1961. I remembered the anxiety of the missile crisis and the relief of the arms agreements. The whole world was affected by the assassination and to some extent, I guess it would impact us our entire lives.

With the shock and sadness of the President's death still hanging over us, Americans gathered round Thanksgiving tables. I spent Thanksgiving Day with Pat's family. It was the first time I met them. The shadow that was cast over the whole Nation made the occasion pretty somber. Pat's parents were wonderful hosts in spite of the circumstances and made me feel welcome. It was like last Christmas at The Cheerleader's home and I was reassured by the presence of good, hard working people whose main focus in life was their family and support of each other.

It was only a few days before The Rock would come home. Of course, The Cheerleader was excited beyond belief and I wasn't far behind her. We were eager to see him and anxious to hear where his orders would take him.

The Cheerleader, Pat, All-American, Teresa and I went to the airport to pick him up. All-American and I went up to the observation deck to watch the plane land. The Cheerleader was afraid that we couldn't get back to the gate in time to greet him, so she, Pat and Teresa waited there. The plane was on time -- as my wish of six months ago was fulfilled. I had a lump in my throat as that big jet touched down and we hurried to the gate to meet The Rock.

When The Rock came through the gate, he looked like a million dollars in that officer's uniform. The Cheerleader ran and grabbed him so fast and they remained embraced for so long, I thought the airport would close for the night before they turned loose of each other. He finally let go and hugged and greeted the rest of us. Even though it was their first time to meet, he hugged

Pat like he had known her for years. He said, " After all the things you guys told me about Pat, I feel like she's part of the gang."

I took the whole group to the Cattleman's for dinner. It was a really nice feeling to be able to do this and even though I knew The Rock and The Cheerleader wanted to be alone, I don't think they would have missed it.

Rock broke the good news. He was selected to go to flight school in Pensacola, Florida. The bad news was, he had to report to Pensacola in six days. We thought he would be home for at least two weeks and were disappointed he would only be here three days. Then The Cheerleader would take him to Ferguson to spend a long weekend with Ethel and he would catch a plane out of Oklahoma City for Pensacola.

I took a day off work so The Rock and I could drive up to Douglas and see Coach Jenkins. He told us he had recruited a bunch of good freshmen and they reminded him of us when we were freshmen. We told him he better find another Billy Joe if he wanted that new bunch to ever do anything big. He was real proud of both of us. He kept up with me through Lyle and, of course, The Rock being an officer in the Navy and going to flight school just blew his mind. He said it meant everything to him that all the guys on our team turned out to be such good men. He also said it was more important than any of the games or championships. Then he said, "You'll know what I mean someday Rock and you will too Big Jim, if you ever get in this business."

The night before The Rock and The Cheerleader left for Oklahoma, they went out alone for the evening. About midnight, they knocked on our door and got both All-American and me out of bed. The Cheerleader held her hands behind her back and said they had a surprise for us. She then thrust her left hand out and showed us the most beautiful diamond on her ring finger.

"We're getting married," she excitedly proclaimed with Rock standing there, smiling the whole time.

"When?" I asked.

"June 20th in Oklahoma City ...Will you be my best man?"

" Absolutely," I said. " I don't know who else would do it."

All-American and I hugged The Cheerleader and shook Rock's hand. We sat up half the night helping them plan their wedding.

The Rock's stay was too short. We did spend that day in Douglas and All-American, Chris, Suitcase, Alex and I took him out one afternoon for a couple of beers. Before he left, he asked me if I would go to Ferguson and have Christmas with Ethel. I told him I would, but I knew he was trying to find a Christmas for me, as much as he was trying to take care of his mom. He and Pat really hit it off and he told me if I let her slip away, I'd be the dumbest son of a bitch who ever lived.

# Chapter Twenty-Two

The week after The Rock left, I was in a bookstore across the street from the showroom. I had started picking up magazines and other light reading material to occupy my time in those motels when I was on the road. As I was browsing that particular day, I made two significant finds. On the cover of *Professional Basketball* was a group of the "Five Most Promising 1963 Rookies." One of the five was Billy Joe Jackson. I read the article in the bookstore aisle and then bought all ten copies. Walking out, I noticed a book on display titled, *Leaving Cheyenne*. I glanced at the book and found the title was taken from "Ole Paint" and thought I probably needed to read it. I purchased the book, planning to start it on my next road trip.

I gave copies of the magazine with Billy Joe on the cover, to all the Dallas guys and mailed one to Coach Jenkins, Slugger, Peters and The Rock. The next Monday night I was in a motel in Paris, Texas and I started *Leaving Cheyenne*. I read it in one sitting and when I finished at 2:30 AM, I wrote The Rock:

*December 20, 1963*
*Rock,*

*I finally read a book and it's my Christmas present to you. You won't believe it. The title is from "Ole Paint," and the guy who wrote it, seems to be like you or me or one of the guys. His name is Larry McMurtry and he's from Archer City, Texas. We've been through there; it's about twenty miles south of Wichita Falls and looks kind of like Ferguson. The story could also be about us and it's eerie how, as I read it, I felt it was you and me experiencing those adventures.*

*I think this is McMurtry's second book and he couldn't be much older than us. We've got to meet this guy someday. I'm really going to be pissed off if you've already read it, because it's the only important thing I found first.*

*From the book:*
*"My foot's in the stirrup, my pony won't stand.*
*Goodbye, old partner, I'm leaving Cheyenne."*

*Merry Christmas,*
*Big Jim*


Pat and I went to dinner two days before Christmas and exchanged presents. She gave me a black leather briefcase with my initials on the tab and I gave her a black leather briefcase with her initials on the tab. We thought this was the funniest thing that ever happened and knew it was bound to be some kind of good omen. She was spending Christmas with her family and I gave her a poinsettia to take to her mom. I left early the next morning for Ferguson to spend Christmas with Ethel. I looked forward to going to Ferguson; I hadn't been there in a year.

Ethel had lunch prepared when I arrived and we were both happy to be together on Christmas Eve. Little sacks of cookies decorated with red bows and ribbons were under a small Christmas tree in the corner of the living room. After lunch we played Santa. I bought some candy and then drove Ethel all over Ferguson, delivering the cookies and candy to shut-ins and children from her church. She said she would like to go to the Christmas Eve service that evening and asked if I'd take her.

The First Baptist Church was the largest church building in town and when we walked in, it was the first time I had been to Church, except for my dad's funeral, in a long time. It was a beautiful building with burgundy carpet, oak pews and stained-glass windows. A pulpit stood high in the center of the altar with a choir loft behind it. A small Christmas tree stood in front of the pulpit, with a nativity scene on the side. Ushers gave each person a candle as we walked in and when the service began, Mrs. Akins led a group of children to the choir loft. After they prayed, another group of children re-enacted the "Christmas Story." The choir sang several carols and the Minister preached a brief sermon. Then we sang "Oh, Holy Night" in unison, as we passed the fire of our candles, one to another. They turned off the lights in the church and, as we all stood singing and holding our lighted candles, I felt warmth I'd felt very few times in my life.

I took Ethel out for dinner after the church service. There were not a lot of eating establishments in Ferguson, so we went downtown to an old café that had been there for years and we both had "homemade" meat loaf.

On that Christmas Eve in 1963, I spent the night on the same couch Rock had slept on growing up. On Christmas morning I went to the car and brought in my present for Ethel. Ethel had never had many nice things in her life so I bought her the nicest table lamp my company sold. I had wrapped it in a big box and when I gave it to her, you would have thought I had given her a home in Beverly Hills. She immediately put it on a table, plugged it in and turned it on.

She then apologized as she gave me a small, but nicely wrapped package. "This is not very much but I think you'll like it."

I did like it. She had framed a 5" X 7" picture of Rock's dad and my dad, standing by an old '28 Ford.

Ethel cooked Christmas dinner for the two of us with turkey and dressing, potatoes, gravy, sweet potatoes, green beans and cranberry sauce. As we enjoyed our meal and each other, I thought about that Thanksgiving when she and The Rock had Dad and me over. I also thought about how much Ethel meant to me and what a wonderful Christmas this had been.

When I left that afternoon, Ethel made me take a plate of turkey with me. After a noticeable amount of hesitation, I did something I'd never done before -- I told her I loved her. She cried and told me she loved me, too. I hugged her and then got in the car. I drove by Dad's old house on the way out of town and was pleased the new owners had painted the house and planted some trees. At home, I put the picture Ethel gave me on the dresser with my other treasures.

On January 15, 1964, Teresa had a birthday party for All-American at our apartment. All-American was the first of our group to reach twenty-three years. Teresa baked a cake and, of course, Alex brought a bunch of beer. The Cheerleader and Pat were there, along with Alex's date and Chris, Suitcase and their dates. About nine, the cake was gone and we were working on the beer. I played a Marty Robins' song on the guitar and everyone was singing along. The phone rang and All-American took it in his room. In a moment, he came out and told me it was Ethel Riley for me; she sounded upset. The only other time I got a phone call from Ethel, it was bad news and I hurried to the phone. When she spoke, I froze in fear of what she had to tell me.

She said, "Jimmy, a young man from the Navy… came by today and brought a letter saying that Rockford's plane had crashed…and… and Rockford was killed." Carol stood beside me and knew by my expression what the news was.

She started screaming, "No…No…No…No."

I held Carol, as I asked Ethel if anyone was with her. She said Mr. Burnett and Alice were there. She gave the phone to Mr. Burnett. He quickly told me Rock was going up for a solo and there was a malfunction. He went down right after take off. It happened so fast; Rock probably never knew it. I asked Mr. Burnett to stay with Ethel and we would be there as soon as possible.

The next few minutes went by in slow motion as I sat on the bed. I watched Pat help Carol to my room as the others stood in disbelief in the living room. I then got up to tell Carol the scant details Mr. Burnett had relayed to me. Pat took charge of the situation, as I slumped on the bed holding the crying Cheerleader. Pat came back a few minutes later and whispered that the others were leaving. I went in, embraced them and agreed to call them as soon as we knew more. Pat urged me to pack my bags while Teresa helped Carol get her things ready. Pat even called Lyle, who was very sympathetic. He said I could drive the company car to Oklahoma and assured her he would tell Coach Jenkins about Rock. Pat then went home to pack, saying she'd be back in twenty minutes.

When Pat returned, I convinced her it would be best for me to drive and she could sit in the back with Carol. It was now 10:00 PM and we would not get to Ethel's until about 2:30 AM. As we drove, no one said a word. Carol's sobbing was the only sound in the back seat. When we got to Douglas, a flood of memories rushed through my mind, but I couldn't shake the feeling of unreality. My mind replayed my entire life and The Rock was always there.

After we passed through Douglas, all of those old landmarks, from our travels back and forth to Ferguson, kept appearing. At the little gas station outside of Durant, I thought of the time The Rock bought those 300 bananas. In Tishimingo, when we passed Smokey's I thought, *The Rock really liked the pinball machine better than he like the barbecue.* I wondered why he had to die. Was there anything I could have done? I didn't know how Ethel would ever get over this? The U.S. Navy had taken the two most important people in her life.

I agonized with Carol and thought about, how happy she was when she showed All-American and me her engagement ring. I wondered if The Rock ever read *Leaving Cheyenne.*

We were half-way home, when Carol spoke for the first time, "Jim, what do you think he was thinking, while that plane was going down?"

I said, "I don't think he had time to think and I am going to make myself believe the last thought he had was about you." She started crying again. I didn't know if I should have said it.

About 2:15 AM, we passed the spot where Rock and I had built that fire. I cherished that night we spent together in the Ford.

We got to Ethel's about 2:45 AM. The Burnetts stayed with us until 3:30 when Mr. Burnett encouraged Ethel and the girls to try to get some rest and told me the front door would be open at his house if I decided I needed to sleep. Four Navy officers would escort Rock's body back to Ferguson the afternoon of January 17 and we would have his funeral January 18.

Pat finally got Ethel to bed about four in the morning and about 4:30, she and Carol fell asleep on the couch. I picked up a package of cigarettes that were on the table, put on my coat and went out and sat on the front porch swing. I never had been much of a smoker but it sort of seemed like a time for a cigarette. I sat there in the cold and smoked and wished I could just talk to The

Rock one more time. I wanted to cry but didn't. That old macho bullshit wouldn't let me.

About seven, Pat came out and sat beside me. I thanked her for taking care of us. She didn't say a lot, somehow she knew I had to work through this myself. I told her I kept thinking, if we'd never left Ferguson, if we hadn't gone to college and if Rock hadn't joined the Navy, he would still be alive.

"But Jim, those guys who didn't leave Ferguson may live to be old men, but Rock lived more in his twenty-two years than they will in a hundred." She said.

"I'm sure glad I was a part of his twenty-two years." I replied.

At about eight, Pat went back in and made a fresh pot of coffee and I drove downtown and got some donuts. After a donut and a cup of coffee, I went up to Mr. Burnett's to shave, shower and get ready for the day. When I got back, Ethel and Carol were also getting ready for the day. Mr. Greer called from the funeral home and said he would come over about ten to make the arrangements. I told him I would find out what Ethel and Carol wanted and I would come up this afternoon to tell him. I wasn't going to put them through the stress of talking with him.

As the day progressed, a steady stream of people came by with food and condolences. Even though this brought back old memories and many tears, it was a comfort.

I did go to Mr. Burnett's that night and slept some. The next afternoon there was a knock on Ethel's door. It was Peters in full officer's dress. I hugged him and we held each other tight. When we parted, he told me he and three other officers had escorted The Rock home; and his body was at the funeral home. Peters, stationed at Virginia Beach, had requested to be part of the escort as soon as he heard about Rock. He was a little more formal with Ethel and Carol as he told us at least two of the officers would be with Rock's remains constantly until his burial and they were "requesting the honor of giving a military salute at the graveside."

The guys were going to be pallbearers. Mr. Burnett brought in some cots and asked Coach Jenkins and them to stay at his house. With the others and me he had a houseful. It was good for me to have them all together the night before the funeral. Peters joined us late in the evening. Even though we were somber, we were glad to be together.

At 2:00 PM on January 18, 1964, Mr. Greer drove Ethel, Carol and me to the Ferguson First Baptist Church to say goodbye to Rockford William Riley. When we pulled up in front of the church, an overflow crowd stood on the lawn and lined the sidewalk. As we walked into the church, it was just as I remembered it from Christmas, but instead of the small Christmas tree in front of the pulpit, Rock's casket set there draped in the American flag. Mrs. Akins' choir filled the choir loft and the minister sat in a chair near the pulpit. Peters and the other three Navy officers sat erect on the left side along with Chris, Slugger, Alex, Billy Joe, Suitcase and All-American.

Ethel and Carol told me exactly how they wanted the funeral. I had given their requests to Mr. Greer. The only thing I questioned was the Children's Choir and the only reason I questioned it was, I knew they'd sing "Ole Paint" and I thought Rock might think that was a little corny, but the real reason was, I didn't know if I could handle it.

The minister opened the service with a prayer and the choir sang "Amazing Grace." Ethel had asked me to read the obituary and I went to the pulpit. *Rock is probably laughing his ass off right now with "the religious nut" in the pulpit.* I took the obituary from my pocket and read,

> **Rockford William Riley** *was born May 13, 1941 in Ferguson, Oklahoma and died January 15, 1964 in Pensacola, Florida.*
>
> *He attended the Ferguson Public Schools and graduated from Ferguson High School in 1959.*
>
> *He received his Bachelor of Arts Degree, with honors from Baker College in 1963.*
>
> *He was an officer in the United States Navy.*
>
> *He was preceded in death by his father, William Riley and is survived by his mother Ethel Riley of Ferguson, his fiancé Carol Wilson of Dallas and a host of friends.*

I looked up from the paper and wasn't sure if I was supposed to say anything else, but continued, "Rockford William Riley was far more than we can put on a piece of paper and far more than we can express in words. He was, what he was, because of his mom, Carol, the Ferguson schools, Baker College, the Navy and all his friends. However, all I am and all I will ever be is because of Rockford William Riley…. the guy I called The Rock."

I sat down and Ethel squeezed my hand, giving me her approval, as she brushed the tears away with the back of her hand. The minister followed with his message. When he finished and the children started singing "Ole Paint," I lost it and for the first time since my mother died in 1951, I cried.

The guys carried Rock's casket out of the church and we took him to Ferguson South Cemetery to bury him beside his dad. At the cemetery, there was a tent erected over his gravesite and Ethel, Carol and I sat in folding chairs in front of Rock's casket with the guys standing behind the casket. The minister read a scripture, the Navy officers fired a salute, played taps, folded the flag that draped the casket and Peters presented the flag to Ethel. The minister said a final prayer; the guys removed their boutonnieres, placed them on Rock's casket and one by one embraced Ethel, Carol and me.

The guys, Coach Jenkins and Mr. Burnett came over to Ethel's after the funeral. It was the first time Slugger and Billy Joe met Pat, but the house was crowded and they didn't stay long. Around nine, Pat and Carol insisted I go up to Mr. Burnett's and spend some time with the guys.

I could hear them laughing just before I walked in the house but when I walked in they all stopped. They said they had decided to have a hoolian, so they bought some beer and were telling stories about The Rock. I told them, "The Rock would get a kick out of you guys having a 'cold one' with Mr. Burnett and Coach Jenkins." I asked for a beer and sat down on the floor between Slugger and Chris. I listened as they told about Rock hanging my drawings in those cheap motel rooms and the time he told Whiskey to stick the basketball up his ass. They recounted the Piney Woods Café, when Rock led us all to the kitchen.

In jest, Billy Joe said, "I don't know why you guys made such a fuss over that big nigger."

Coach Jenkins said, "You better be careful Billy Joe, Big Jim hit a guy for saying that one time."

"Yeah, I know Coach, I was there, remember." Billy Joe said.

Slugger and Peters told about the time The Rock and I trained them to box in the Golden Gloves and I hoped Rock was looking down from somewhere, enjoying this. I knew, however, The Rock would live forever, because when all these guys are old men, they will tell these same stories to their grandchildren. And anytime, a group of old jocks get together for a beer and storytelling, at some point in the evening, they will hold their glasses high to **The Rock and The Kangaroos.**

Coach Jenkins and the guys left early the next morning and Mr. Burnett asked me to stop by his office on my way to Ethel's. It was Saturday morning and there was no one in the school building except Mr. Burnett when I went in. I sat down and Mr. Burnett said, "Jim, I know my timing is bad on what I want to talk to you about but I can't wait on this. We haven't had much of a basketball program since you and Rock graduated and we just had to fire our second coach in the last four years. I know you have a good job and are making a lot more money than we can pay, but I also know you love basketball and Ferguson High School. You know our situation here. I've checked with Coach Jenkins and I can get a temporary certificate for you to teach math and art. You would teach two classes of each and coach high school basketball. Pat told me she was a teacher and if you all decide to do something permanent, there will always be a job for her. You would have to go over to OSU in the summers to get a standard certificate and you probably would want to work on a Master's. I'm going to give you a couple of days to think about it and I'm not going to talk with another applicant until you tell me no…any questions?"

I was overwhelmed, but said, "I pretty well understand what the deal is. I need to think about it but I'll give you a decision tomorrow."

I went from Mr. Burnett's office to Ethel's. Carol, Pat and I helped her start writing thank-you notes for all the flowers, food and other things that were done in Rock's memory. The day was very sad as we wrote the notes, but was broken with conversation about the many friends we were writing to. Ethel didn't know most of the people from college, Carol didn't know many from Ferguson and Pat didn't know anyone. We even laughed at one point about Pat writing notes to all those people she didn't know.

During the middle of the afternoon, I told them about Mr. Burnett's offer and, of course, it got their attention. Ethel was excited about the prospect of me moving back to Ferguson. Pat and Carol didn't like the thought of me leaving Dallas. They all knew it was going to be an agonizing decision. They agreed I had to do what I thought was best for me and thought The Rock would tell me the same thing. I told them, at some point, I wanted to coach and teach but my life was going pretty good right now. I liked my job and I sure didn't want to leave Pat. I also told them they were wrong about what The Rock would tell me, but I knew I had to do this for me and not The Rock.

About six, we stopped writing to have dinner. After we fixed our plates and ate in silence, I told them, I thought I'd take a walk and try to sort things out a little bit. When I walked out, Pat followed me and said. "Whatever you decided to do Jim, will be okay."

As I walked down those streets I had walked a hundred times, I tried to think of the advantages and disadvantages of my current situation and the pros and cons of my prospective situation.

I wanted to be able to "give it back," but I liked buying dinner for the gang at the Cattleman's and giving Ethel a nice Christmas present. I wouldn't be able to do those things on a teacher's salary.

As I pondered my future, I couldn't help thinking about The Rock and I was thankful he and Pat met in December, because I wanted to marry her and I didn't know if I could marry a woman who'd never met The Rock. I wanted to sing "Ole Paint," but for some reason, I couldn't.

I walked by the First Christian Church and noticed a light coming from the gym in the basement. As I walked down the hill to the door of the tiny gymnasium I could hear the thump of a basketball. I followed the sound and went in. Two kids were shooting on the far end. They were probably about fourteen and I remembered them from a few years ago when they were trying to get in pick up games at the park. As I walked toward them, one of them said, "Hi, Big Jim."

The other said, "We're sorry about The Rock."

"Yeah, I know guys, I am too," I said.

They tossed me the ball. " Why don't you shoot a few?"

I stood at the top of the circle, shot and hit it. They tossed it back and I hit another and another.

One of them said, "Wow, how do you do that?"

I then took the ball and demonstrated, as I said," Square up every time, spread your hands on the ball, keep your elbows in, release from your forehead, let the ball roll off your finger tips and follow through with your arm straight as a string and your thumb pointing down through the basket." I hit three more shots, told them goodbye and walked back to the door. When I turned back around, they were shooting again but not doing any of the things I had shown them.

I walked back toward them and firmly said, "Give me the ball."

One of them quickly tossed it to me.

I said, "I'm going to show you guys one more time how to shoot a basketball right." And again I demonstrated, as I said, "Square up every time, spread your hands on the ball, keep your elbows in, release from your forehead, let the ball roll off your finger tips and follow through with your arm straight as a string and your thumb pointing down through the basket...And if you guys think you are ever going to play ball for me, you better learn to do it right."

Their eyes were as big as dollars as I turned to leave again, then I turned back and said, "And from now on you guys don't call me Big Jim…. You call me Coach Green."

When I walked back to the door and turned around they were trying to shoot the ball right and going over with each other, what I had told them. I smiled, as I watched the two boys and for the first time in my life had an inner-peace as I heard some old ghosts rattling around in the rafters.

"Did I hit it Big Jim?"

"No"

"You lying son of a bitch."

# Epilogue

My grandson, Steven, woke me as he tossed a baseball glove on my chest. "Let's play catch Granddad." I could hear Pat and Stephen's mom, Anna, talking in the kitchen as Anna told us we didn't have time to play ball because we had to get ready to go to the party. Anna is thirty-three years old and assistant principal at Ferguson High School. In fact I've worked for her the past three years. It is sort of humiliating, but gratifying, for an old teacher to have one of his kids beat him in the state finals and the other one be his boss.

Pat told me I needed to get dressed because Coach Jenkins, Carol, Chris and Alex were all coming by the house before the party. Anna and Steven went home to get ready and I put on my suit and the new tie Pat had picked out for me. Pat said, "A Mercedes just pulled up in the driveway."

"It must be Chris, Carol and Alex," I said.

We hadn't seen any of them in about five years and Pat was as close to them as I was. After all Carol had introduced us to each other. Carol and Chris Wright started dating about a year after The Rock died and before they went out the first time, both of them called Pat and me to see if it was okay. Carol taught in Dallas and retired about the same time as Pat. Chris, just as we expected, was very successful as a stockbroker in Dallas. The last time we saw them was when Chris's dad, Robert, died in 1996. Chris and Carol have grown children and a couple of grandkids and have stayed in touch with us by phone and letters over the years. Alex worked for several Texas newspapers before he became editor of a San Antonio paper in 1986. He has remained in that position but is also thinking about retirement.

Coach Jenkins arrived shortly and Chris, Carol and Alex hadn't seen him in about twenty years. Coach and I see each other on a regular basis. He moved to Tulsa in 1985 when he retired and probably saw more of my games than anyone except Pat.

We had a great visit before we went to the party at 7:30 PM. When we got there, most everyone had already arrived and it was totally overwhelming for me. There were about three hundred people and I wanted to talk with each one. There were all the teachers and friends from Ferguson, at least a hundred former players, my friends from around the state and, of course, Coach Jenkins, Chris, Carol, Alex, Suitcase, All-American, Peters, Billy Joe and Slugger. It was nine o'clock before they got us to sit down and eat, but everyone enjoyed old friends. My family, Pat, Jeff and his wife Shannon, their daughter Mary, Anna and her husband Bill, Steven and Ethel Riley all sat at the head table with me. Ethel has been a part of my family since The Rock and I were in the first grade and she shared every holiday and special occasion with us. She is now eighty-six years old and in great health, but Pat and I still check on her every day. There was a special surprise for Ethel tonight and Dr. Edwards, the superintendent of Ferguson Public Schools, the school board and I were the only ones who knew what it was.

About 9:30 Billy Joe stepped to the podium and started the program as master of ceremonies. Dr. Aaron Savage, my son Jeff, Bob Dunlap, a guy I coached with in the seventies and All-American, all did "testimonials" about me.

This turned out to be the most emotional part of the evening as Aaron spoke first.

"Most all of you know, if it hadn't been for Coach Green, I would probably either be dead or in the penitentiary right now. Coach Green means a lot to all of you. To me he means everything. We are honoring him tonight for being a great teacher and coach and we are proud for his many victories at Ferguson High School. However, I wasn't a ball player or great student, but when I was fourteen years old, he believed in me when no one else did. I thank God everyday for the many hours I spent with this man. He taught me, virtually everything I know that is important to living life. The most important thing he taught me was what some guy he called The Rock taught him. That something is "giving it back." I want Coach to know that what he gave back to me, I will give back my entire lifetime. I love you, Coach Green."

As Aaron sat down, I was overwhelmed by his sincere and generous comments. Pat and I could not hold back the tears when Jeff took the podium. Our emotions consumed us and we completely broke down, as did he. He paused for a moment to allow us to gain our composure then proceeded to make his old man feel like a million dollars.

Each speech was so heartfelt and compelling. It is impossible to describe the warmth and feelings I experienced. All-American and I had remained close friends throughout all the years as our coaching careers paralleled each other's. We visited two or three times a year and our families were as close as two families could be. We talked by phone at least once a week and if it was possible, I think our friendship was as close as that of Rock and me.

Bob Dunlap was the football coach in Ferguson during the Seventies. He left to become the head coach at Tulsa Central in 1979. From the moment we met in 1968 when he reported for his first day of work in the Ferguson Public Schools, I knew we were going to have a lifetime bond. I never missed a co-worker more than I did him when he moved to Tulsa.

The art students presented their video and I was so proud of the skilled job they did with the presentation. When I started teaching art at Ferguson, video didn't even exist and now I had taught these kids to do a production like this. They made me wonder again why in the hell I had to retire.

They did a chronological account of my career, starting with playing basketball for Ferguson in the Fifties. Some old game film from Baker College had that "slam dunk" when we beat Kirby in '61. There were pictures, film clips and video clips from high school, college and games I had coached, including all five state championships, plus the one I lost to Jeff. Also included were music clips from the '50s through the '90s as background. They even put that "Ole Paint" stuff in the part about my high school and college days. The presentation was an hour long and I'm sure the other guests were getting tired, but I could have watched all night as Pat and I laughed and cried and enjoyed every second of our party. Billy Joe turned the program over to Dr. Edwards for a few words and a special announcement.

Dr. Edwards began by saying, "When I was fourteen years old, a guy we called Big Jim walked into the basement gym of the First Christian Church and taught Tommy Plummer and me how to shoot a basketball. Before he left that night he was no longer 'Big Jim', he was 'Coach Green'. I first remember Coach Green when I was a little kid watching him play ball for Ferguson High School. He taught and coached me in high school and I have worked with him for twenty-one years as a fellow educator. All I have to say about Coach Jim Green, as a man and an educator, is 'he's the best there ever was'."

Dr. Edwards then said, "You all know Coach Green has worked for the past five or six years raising money and developing plans to build a new high school gymnasium for Ferguson High School. Many of you have helped in this effort and I want to take this opportunity to thank you. The new gym is, of course, under construction now and will be dedicated prior to next year's basketball season. I wish we could talk Coach into coaching a few years in the new facility, but he tells me Pat and the kids say he's had enough, so we'll respect that. The school board did, however, ask Coach Green to name the new facility."

He then asked Ethel Riley to come to the podium and he read. "Be it resolved that on May 28, 2001, the Board of Trustees of the Ferguson Public Schools does here by name the Sports

Complex located at 411 West Penn, Ferguson, Oklahoma, **The Rock**, in memory of our greatest student, athlete and friend -- Rockford William Riley -- Class of 1959.

Tears ran down Ethel's face as she smiled and clutched the resolution.

Billy Joe helped Ethel back to her seat and then asked me to come forward and make my closing remarks.

The hour was late and everything that needed to be said probably had been taken care of. I did introduce my family and acknowledged Mr. Burnett's widow, Alice. Mr. Burnett, my principal the first twenty years I taught, had died in 1990. I expressed gratitude to Dr. Edwards and the school board for the opportunity they had given me. I complimented the students from my art classes regarding the video and thanked all the students I had taught and coached. I closed by saying; " The last few days I have struggled trying to come to grips with this retirement thing, thinking my life was over. After Aaron's speech a while ago, I realized, even though I won't be coaching, I'll be doing something and Rock, if you're listening, you were right and I hope you know... I'm not through...'giving it back'."

**A note from Zone Press:**

The Rock and The Kangaroos was originally published by Writer's Showcase in 2002. This second edition contains some minor revisions. The work is a collection of "old jock" stories combined into a sometimes funny, sometimes sad but always compelling adventure. The story is loosely fitted around author Jim Rogers' experiences at Austin College in Sherman, Texas from 1959 through 1963.

Characters in the Rock and Kangaroos, for the most part, are fictional. Two individuals that deserve special recognition, however, inspired the character of **Rock Riley.**

**Ron Elsheimer** - Ron grew up with Jim Rogers, played basketball with him, drove a "Ford" to Texas with him in 1959, really buried a Kangaroo and cut his head open on the rim in a basketball game. Ron is now a retired Teacher/Coach in Drumright, Oklahoma after 33 years of "giving it back."

**Tommy Puckett** – Tommy attended Austin College one year and finished his degree at The United States Navel Academy. Tommy was a tremendous leader and outstanding student/athlete. He died when his Navy trainer plane crashed near Pensacola, Florida in 1963.

# OTHER NOVELS FROM ZONE PRESS

*Taking the Dream to Prairie Point*
By Jim O. Rogers

*The Weaving of a Woman*
By Linda Walker Wickersham

*Drift to Paradise*
By Doyle Keeton

*Mortal Sin, Mattress Tag and Government Butter*
By Walter Trough

*Vice Grip*
By Michael J.V. Thomas

*Red River Dust*
By Shirley Phillips Porter

**www.ZonePress.com**

Printed in the United States
132297LV00002BA/17/A